About the Author

Aidan James Williams is a Canadian author born in Kitchener, Ontario. He studied business and English at McMaster University in Hamilton, Ontario. He continues to work and live in Ontario.

Edward Sting and the Five Realms

Aidan Williams

Edward Sting and the Five Realms

Olympia Publishers
London

www.olympiapublishers.com
OLYMPIA PAPERBACK EDITION

Copyright © Aidan Williams 2024

The right of Aidan Williams to be identified as author of
this work has been asserted in accordance with sections 77 and 78 of
the Copyright, Designs and Patents Act 1988.

All Rights Reserved

No reproduction, copy or transmission of this publication
may be made without written permission.
No paragraph of this publication may be reproduced,
copied or transmitted save with the written permission of the publisher,
or in accordance with the provisions
of the Copyright Act 1956 (as amended).

Any person who commits any unauthorised act in relation to
this publication may be liable to criminal
prosecution and civil claims for damage.

A CIP catalogue record for this title is
available from the British Library.

ISBN: 978-1-80439-676-6

This is a work of fiction.
Names, characters, places and incidents originate from the writer's
imagination. Any resemblance to actual persons, living or dead, is
purely coincidental.

First Published in 2024

Olympia Publishers
Tallis House
2 Tallis Street
London
EC4Y 0AB

Printed in Great Britain

Dedication

To Nana, who always loved my stories, and to Grandma, here's a new one.

Acknowledgements

First and foremost, I want to thank my family who supported me for years, even when I'm sure it seemed I would never finish this project, let alone publish it. Also, a big thank you to everyone at Friesen Press; Christopher for reaching out to me and, of course, Janet, my wonderful editor. Your suggestions helped me improve this book immensely. I would be remiss if I didn't also mention John Aclelland, who was the first person to read about Edward's adventures. I had the most fun on this project when discussing it with you, so thanks for suffering through those early drafts with me! Of course, thank you to James and everyone at Olympia for taking me on as an author and allowing me to share this story with the world. I also want to mention Gwen Bradley. It's true that this book was already in its early stages while I was still sitting in your classroom and you were a big part of why I decided to give writing 'the old college try'. Finally, thank you to everyone who read the book and stuck with Edward to the bitter end, I hope you enjoyed reading it as much as I enjoyed writing it.

Prologue

A bittersweet feeling came over Simon Sting when the clock struck midnight and there still had not been a knock at the door. It wasn't as though he was waiting for a knock necessarily, or even expecting one. In fact, if all went according to plan tonight, there would be no need for his son, Jack, to come home at all. Besides, Simon knew that the act of waiting—of idly watching the passage of time—was itself harmful to any undertaking. Still, he worried. He worried because he knew in his heart that even if Jack were successful, things would never be the same.

He drummed his fingers on the table and listened to the storm outside. Rain rattled against the house so loudly that it was as though it were inside his head. He glanced at the clock again. Its ticking hands skipped around restlessly, completely indifferent to his growing impatience.

Simon shuddered and lit a candle, suddenly conscious of the darkness. The dim light turned the creaky, old house into a cave, with him at the centre. *How poetic,* he thought, *that I should be here, presiding over an empty house while events that will decide my fate take place elsewhere.*

He gazed down at his hands, worn from years of hard work. Simon was an old man, but he'd sooner die than let anybody tell him that. He'd lived on the edge ever since he was a boy, and that's the way he liked it, thank you very much. He had never bothered much with the gossip of the village… or the kingdom for that matter.

It was all a distraction as far as he was concerned.

What was really important lay beyond, in the dark corners of the land, which they were told not to worry about. And it was in those corners that he had learned the lessons that guided him. He had seen things that had shaken him to his very core—things that he would never forget—that was for sure. But all of it had left him wiser.

That's what people didn't understand about Simon, and that's why he had a duty to protect them. And for years, he *had* protected them—or at least, he liked to think of it that way—which was why he thought it more than a little unfair that, after a lifetime of working in the shadows, he was surely to be remembered solely for his actions over the past few weeks.

Thunder cracked overhead, and in the next room, Edward began to stir. The old man hobbled out of his seat and rushed to the boy's bedside.

He knelt down beside the sleeping form. "Shhh…" he whispered, drawing a lock of blond hair away from the boy's forehead.

Edward shivered in the dark. "Papa?" he mumbled. It was a distant question, spoken not to Simon but rather to some version of him that existed only in the boy's dreams. Simon smiled and took the sleeping boy in his arms, wrapping him tightly in a blanket.

"Sleep well, little one. It will all be over soon." He dared a glance at the clock on the wall.

Quarter past the hour.

Simon smiled and felt calmed. He had known Edward was different from the day he was born. Jack had called it the preening of a proud grandfather, but Simon knew the truth. As the months went by, Edward's abilities grew enormously. At just the age of one, he was dashing through the meadows surrounding their house. A year later, and he could climb every tree in the forest with ease. Much to his mother's astonishment, he had the appetite and attitude of a wild animal.

So it was that Edward was allowed to roam freely through the countryside, so long as he didn't stray into Nodington Valley, where eyebrows could be raised at even the slightest irregularity. But Simon was okay with this arrangement, for it was not where the boy went that worried him but rather what he brought back with him.

Often Edward's escapades would end with him dragging home some ancient relic through the front garden, wandering out of the forest with strange artifacts long believed lost. Items grown men spent their whole lives searching for and never found. Simon always smiled and congratulated his grandson, but he never dared return the items or let news of them get out—no matter how valuable they were to Teradowa. The last thing he wanted was word to spread around the kingdom about Edward's unique gift.

He would show all of Edward's discoveries to Jack, but his son would brush him aside. Of course, it wasn't Jack's fault. Simon had never taken him along on any of his journeys outside the realm. At the time, Simon hadn't deemed it safe for children. He still didn't. As a result, even as an adult, his son did not fully understand the danger they faced.

But Simon had seen too much not to fear the supernatural forces that were at play. So, he'd continued to press the issue, until just a few weeks ago when, one hot summer afternoon, the fate of Teradowa had been changed. Perhaps forever.

On that afternoon, Edward, now a ripe three years old, had skipped away down into the meadow as he did most days. But when he'd failed to return for dinner, Simon had waited and grown concerned. By the time the boy had finally come bouncing up the hill, soaking wet and grinning from ear to ear, the sun was sinking low on the horizon.

When he'd reached Simon, Edward had scrambled up onto his grandfather's lap, ignoring the fretting of his mother, and held out his hands. In his palm had sat a glowing red stone, so beautiful in colour and so perfect in shape that Simon had been left with no doubt of its identity or significance. He'd quickly placed the stone back in the boy's palm and closed his tiny fingers around it. Carefully, he'd then explained that it was of the utmost importance that nobody finds out about this discovery and that it should be their little secret. Then he'd determined that Edward ought to go and put his little prize back where he had found it and tell nobody—including his grandpa—where it was. What he hadn't shared with his grandson were the possibly catastrophic consequences of his discovery.

Edward had trusted his grandfather, on that warm summer evening, and so while he didn't understand, he did as he was told and trudged back into the forest.

He returned sometime later, empty-handed.

That night, Simon had sprung into action. Calling in a lifetime of favours and connections, he'd managed to pull together a considerable number of allies. Jack could no longer ignore the warnings of his father. Now that the stone had been discovered, they knew it would only be a matter of time before *he* came looking for it. Together, they had come up with a plan.

Over the past few weeks, Simon had had his doubts about their plan, but they'd decided that this was the best way to protect the boy. After all, who would suspect a child could have found such a treasure? A grown man was much more likely.

Simon placed Edward back on his bed and glanced again at

the clock. Twelve thirty. The silence from the front hall was reassuring, but he had one more duty to perform tonight. He was about to start gathering his and Edward's things when there came a knock at the front door. His heart sank.

He rushed into the hall and threw open the door. The wind whistled in, bringing heavy rain with it. Two figures stumbled in from the night.

"Jack! Ally!" Edward's mother and father looked pale and beaten. "What's happened?"

Jack bent over, panting. "We have to hurry."

Ally was already sifting through the closet, packing a bag. Simon looked between them with earnest.

"Well? Is it good news or bad?"

Jack turned to him, and Simon could see the answer on his son's crestfallen face.

"We were ambushed on our way to see the king. It seems Gorlak's gotten to him first, and they've struck a deal." His eyes darted to Ally, then back to Simon. "They'll be here soon."

Simon gasped. "My God, do they know?" he asked, daring a glance into Edward's room.

Jack shook his head. "Not everything."

Simon felt relief wash over him. "Does the king have any idea what he's done? Getting Teradowa mixed up with *him*?"

Jack looked down, his expression dark. "I don't think anyone knows what he's really capable of. Not even the king."

Ally emerged from the kitchen carrying two bags which she dropped at Simon's feet. Jack rummaged in the closet and tossed two jackets on top, one big and one small.

Simon eyed the pair of bags.

"Where's Eddy?" Ally asked.

"Sleeping," Simon said, distractedly. "Aren't you two

coming with us?"

Jack frowned. "No, Dad."

"But everything's changed," he said, reaching for his son's burly shoulder, but Jack had moved away, shuttering the windows and locking the door.

Ally gasped. "They're coming." Down the hill, the flicker of torches burned in the rain. Lightning cracked across the sky, illuminating the dark outline of men racing up the path together like a pack of dogs.

Simon turned away from the window and faced Jack. "You can't stay here."

"This is the only chance we have, Dad."

Simon searched his son's face despairingly; he was strong, sure of himself. For a moment, he wondered if he would have had the same courage in his position. He wasn't sure… but he could see that it was selfish of him to ask them to come.

The old man nodded and embraced his son, holding him as tight as the grief that gripped his heart and wondered how things had come to this. Ally appeared then, holding Edward in her arms.

"You'd better take him," she said. Simon took the sleeping boy in his arms, feeling as though nothing would ever be fair in the world again. Ally rummaged in her pocket then and placed an emerald-green pendant in the folds of her son's blanket. "It was the first thing he ever found," she said, her eyes welling with tears.

Suddenly, there was a loud thud on the front door. Ally hugged Simon tight and then tenderly kissed her son's cheek. Another thud rocked the door, and it crashed inward. Six men in black armour flooded into the house, then stepped to the side, and a tall man with a grey beard ducked through the doorway. He wore lavish red robes and inspected Simon and the others through a pair of beady, black eyes.

Jack cleared his throat. "My lord, what is the meaning of this?"

The king strode inside. "We both know why I'm here, Jack."

"My lord?"

The king snarled. "The *stone*. I know you've found it. Where is it?"

Jack's face hardened. "You're too late. I destroyed it."

He laughed. "You wouldn't dare."

Jack glared at him.

The king's smirk vanished. He spat on the floor and took a step forward. "There's someone who will pay Teradowa very well for delivering the stone. Think of the kingdom, Jack! Don't be selfish." Another step and he was now mere inches from Jack's face.

Ally stepped between them, her eyes pleading. "Please, King Glasgow, you have no idea what you're dealing with."

The king chuckled. "And who do we have here, Jack?" he asked, his beady eyes fixating on Ally. He sneered as he grabbed her by the chin. She twisted away from his pale fingers.

Simon cleared his throat. "My lord, you must listen to us."

King Glasgow raised his eyebrows as if only just noticing the old man. "Simon? So, the old hermit lives! It's been too long, my friend. Perhaps you can deliver the stone to me, as I assume you're familiar with the legend." Glasgow grinned at the uneasy look on the old man's face. "Don't take me for a fool. I turn a blind eye to your escapades because you keep your mouth shut, but that will all change if you disobey me."

The king tucked his hands neatly behind his back; then his gaze shifted to Edward, nuzzled in his grandfather's arms.

"You've had a child, Jack?" Simon could see the muscles in his son's neck tighten as the king stroked Edward's pale head. "May I?" he asked, extending his arms.

Jack's fingers gripped the hilt of his sword. "You keep your hands off my son!" The king's men stepped forward, but Glasgow waved them away.

"I'll make this easy for you, Jack. Give up the stone or your son belongs to the kingdom." The king had Simon pressed in the corner now, his hands hovering over Edward.

"I'm warning you, my lord."

Simon could now clearly see what the night had been building towards—the undeniable certainty of it. For better or for worse, the powers of hate and greed and all manner of terrible things had conspired to bring them to this moment. His destiny was sealed. The king took one more fateful step towards the precious bundle in Simon's arms, but he never reached it.

Jack drew his sword, and in a flash, plunged it into the king's side who withered in agony and collapsed to his knees. At once, the king's men surged forward, and the world became a tangle of violence.

Simon staggered away as Jack blocked the men's path, and the ear-splitting screech of metal striking metal filled the room. Jack swung and jabbed like a madman, but he was hopelessly outnumbered.

"Run!" he yelled.

Simon rushed across the room, his head spinning as Ally leapt in the way of the faceless warriors. Simon gazed back and saw the colour fading from her face. He found her eyes and a nearly soundless whisper reached his ears—her last request:

"Protect him."

He felt the weight of her words, far heavier than the child in his arms, and he slipped away. Moving quickly through the house, he dashed past the candle on the table, now extinguished, and threw open the back door. Stumbling out into the rain, he found his horse and took off at a trot into the night. His path was covered in darkness, but he found his way by memory, as sharp as ever even in his old age. Until the dust settled and a new king was crowned, he would need to remain invisible. He would hide away and play the hermit. Simon Sting, the odd old man. Whatever he needed to do, he would do it.

He gazed down at his new charge, wrapped snugly in blankets. Edward's starry blue eyes were staring back at him now—he'd been awoken by the commotion. They were oddly calm, and Simon finally understood. It was a gift, or perhaps some curse of fate, that this child had been chosen to be his grandson. It was a realization that was too much to bear, and for the first time in many years, the old man began to weep.

He wept for the many things that had been lost. He wept for his family and for the unknown future. He wept for the past and for the secrets that had been buried—in particular, the secrets of that brilliant red stone. So beautiful in colour and so perfect in shape that Simon had instantly understood its significance. He closed his eyes. *And now, nobody else ever would.*

Fifteen Years Later

Chapter 1

Nodington Valley

A sharp knock jolted Edward from his sleep. He sat up fast, grimacing at the streaks of daylight peeking through his bedroom drapes. Had the knock been real, or had he dreamed it? He didn't get many visitors and even fewer so early in the morning. Most likely, it was that wretched garden gnome again. He had bought it to tend his gardens, but all it did was annoy him.

A second knock came, too loud to be the gnome. He slipped out of bed and stretched his legs. Then he threw on a shirt and shuffled down the stairs. He rolled his eyes as the third knock rang through the house. Only one person he knew knocked three times.

When he opened the door, a stout young man stood in the entrance. He had thick brown hair that matched his bushy eyebrows and was dressed in a dark green suit that didn't do his pear shape any favours.

Edward laughed. "Cliff, what are you wearing?"

The boy smiled. "You like it? It's my Life Day suit."

Edward groaned. "So, that's why you're here."

Cliff brushed past him into the house. "Don't act like you didn't know I'd be here." Of course, he did know. Cliff was the one person who—despite Edward's best efforts—hadn't given up on him yet.

"Why do you even want to go?"

Cliff's face darkened. "We have to. You know that. And you especially can't miss the Assembly."

Edward hated the Assembly. He always had. As a kid, his reason had been simple: It was boring. The whole valley—thousands of people—were expected to assemble in the village square to hear the king's speech, but now he hated it on a much more fundamental level. His grandpa had usually found a way to get them out of it, but this year, he was going to have to attend.

"Everyone's been asking about you," Cliff said, reading his thoughts. "You haven't been to work in weeks. The king could take your land... if he wants it."

Edward scoffed. "I'd like to see him try."

Cliff frowned. "Well, I wouldn't."

Edward sighed. He didn't want Cliff to get upset; nothing good ever happened when Cliff got upset.

"All right, we'll go."

His friend smiled. "Good. Now, go get dressed."

Edward shot him a look and sprinted upstairs. He threw on a blue waistcoat and his best pair of boots. They had belonged to his father and still shone like they were brand new. His grandpa had given them to him a couple of years ago, on his sixteenth birthday, and Edward loved them so much that he almost never took them off. He skipped back downstairs and found Cliff in the kitchen.

"You look great," Cliff said, through a mouthful of bread. It had been a running joke throughout Edward's childhood that Cliff could outeat anything with six legs or less.

Edward opened the door and they stepped into the morning sun.

Cliff took a deep breath. "I think you'll have fun today, Ed. I really do."

Edward supposed he was being genuine; his friend couldn't see what he saw: that Life Day, and all the celebrations, were designed specifically to distract them from all the lies the king told. Together, Edward and Cliff trotted down the stone path to Nodington Valley as the morning dew evaporated in the beating sun and thickened the gentle breeze. Soon, they reached the fork in the path where a beaten dirt trail led to the front steps of Bill Hurnet's farmhouse.

"Was he out when you came by?" Edward whispered.

"I tried not to look. Thought he might invite me in."

Bill Hurnet was nearly a hundred years old, and he'd lived next door for Edward's entire life. He was well known in Nodington Valley but not for anything good. Mostly people kept their distance. He was, after all, a hermit, and so mustn't be trusted. To those few who knew him personally, he was just called Scruff, due to the curly grey beard that hung from his chin.

"Think he'll be mad about you missing work?" Cliff whispered.

Edward shrugged.

Scruff's rickety house loomed ahead of them, casting a shadow over the path. The old man was on his front porch, gazing out at the hills.

"Morning, Scruff," Edward said.

"Mornin', boys," he said, without breaking his stare.

Edward hesitated. "I'm sorry I haven't been to work lately. I've just not been feeling myself."

Scruff turned his wrinkled face and peered at Edward. "That's all right, son. Crop ain't going anywhere." Typical Scruff. You could probably burn his whole house down, and afterwards, he'd just shake your hand and say there were no hard feelings. Edward felt guilty. Maybe he had taken advantage of

Scruff's kindness.

"I'll be back tomorrow. I promise."

Scuff merely nodded, like it was inconsequential. He had a way of being... a manner that made him seem always on the verge of saying something very profound.

Edward and Cliff exchanged looks and turned to go, but then the old farmer cleared his throat. "You just take care of yourself, Eddy," he said, his gaze fixed on Edward's clear blue eyes. The boy nodded, and then the pair continued over the hill and into the valley. Edward was glad to be away from the house. There was something about Scruff that always depressed him. It was as if life had passed him by a long time ago, and he'd never really got over it. Still, it was a feeling more familiar to him than he cared to admit.

The sun was hot now, and he pushed his wavey blond hair aside to keep the sweat from his eyes.

"Are you really gonna come back tomorrow?" Cliff asked.

Edward shrugged. The truth was he didn't feel like going back at all. "Sure."

His friend slapped him on the back. "That's great news, Ed! The lads will be glad to see you."

Edward tried to look excited, but all he could muster was a weak smile. Maybe it was the way Cliff had been raised. He could work at Scruff's farm for the rest of his life and be perfectly happy. Edward, on the other hand, found that idea dreadful, and he knew his grandfather did too.

Even if he'd never said so.

It wasn't that Edward didn't have fun on the farm. He'd had plenty of fun. There was a lot more freedom in the country than in the valley, where everyone was watched by someone.

Edward and his friends used to sneak out at night and race

bandoros in the fields. Twice the size of a horse, a bandoro used its thick, muscular legs, and brawny, clawed feet to run and jump enormous distances. They were favoured by farmers for their brute strength, though the nobles considered them rough, uncivilised creatures and preferred the more elegant horse for travel.

Edward knew very little about horses, only that they were rare in Teradowa and highly coveted by the nobles. He remembered the first time he had seen one. He'd been about ten years old, playing in the village, when a nobleman from Akmenia—a nearby city—had come to visit. He'd ridden through the town on a slender white horse, scowling at Edward and the other boys, as though the mere sight of them had given him a sour taste in his mouth.

Edward was no nobleman, and it was perhaps for the same reason the nobles hated bandoros that he loved them. There was no feeling more freeing than dashing through the hills atop their golden-coated backs, the landscape blurring around him, and crying out with joy. It was those kinds of moments that Edward longed for—moments of escape—and over the years, he'd found them more often on the farm and fields than he would have in the valley, though nowhere near often enough.

Of course, there were plenty of downsides to the farm as well. One season, a few years ago when they'd been planting seeds, a keble had nested in one of Scruff's fields. The slimy, little rodent had started digging up crops to lay its eggs. So, they had chased it across the field, and the next one, and the next… until they had left Scruff's land far behind.

None of them had realised how far they had gone until they'd been ambushed by soldiers. Edward could still remember the cold muzzle of a musket jabbing him in the back.

The men had told them they were too close to the border. Edward had tried to explain, but they wouldn't hear it. He, Cliff, and the others were marched into Nodington Valley and locked in the dungeons.

Cliff had been so scared that he'd vomited in the cell. Edward could still recall the stink. It wasn't until his grandfather had found out that they were released. Boy had his grandfather torn a strip off the soldiers when he'd gotten down to the dungeons. He'd even written a letter to the Porter of Nodington Valley, asking him how the kingdom expected to be fed if the farmers weren't allowed to do their jobs.

They'd been released the next day with a stern warning not to stray near the border again.

But all that was in the past now, and Edward wasn't sure how he would face a problem like that now that his grandpa was gone.

It had been six months since he'd vanished. Well... 'vanished' wasn't quite the right word for it since everyone knew where he'd gone, even if nobody said. 'Run away' was more like it. Packed his bags and left. And not just Nodington Valley. He had left Teradowa. Left the safety of their God-given, God-protected realm. In all respects, it was suicide.

Of course, it wasn't as if he'd announced to everyone one day that he would be leaving. Doing so would have gotten him arrested. Instead, he'd just quietly slipped away. Everyone knew he had gone though. Simon Sting was a well-known rule breaker, not to mention a hermit, and whatever his reasons, if he'd wanted to leave, he could have done so at any time.

Edward just wished he knew *why* he'd left. It had kept him up at night ever since that day when he had come home from the farm to find the house empty. No note. No sign of a struggle.

Nothing. What was even more odd though was the attention that King Sento had given Edward afterwards. Checkups from the bishops of Nodington Valley became routine. Sometimes, they came with soldiers, though sometimes not. In either case, they would knock on the door—acting very concerned of course—then search the entire house and leave. It rattled Edward every time.

"Would you look at this…" Cliff said, breaking him from his thoughts.

As they came over the last hill, Nodington Valley appeared. It spanned the horizon, from the piers along the Great River, to the Village Square, and all the way to King Sento's castle, which loomed over everything. People bustled in the streets, setting up shops and putting out banners. Children dashed in the alleys, flying kites and chatting feverishly.

Music drifted through the air, and Edward smiled. Perhaps this *was* better than lying in bed. Life Day was the only day of the year where everyone was allowed to roam freely, without a curfew. Everything was paid for by the king, and everyone was expected to participate. The festival went all day, followed by the Assembly in the afternoon. There were games and competitions, including a swizzleberry-juice-drinking competition, which Cliff claimed he would win every year (he had yet to make good on that promise).

"Come on. I know where the boys are this morning," Cliff said. They bounded down the hill and turned down the first cobblestone street.

Cliff stopped in front of a small tavern with a wooden sign hanging above the door: 'The Empty Bucket'. Edward grinned. He couldn't remember the last time he'd been to 'The Empty Bucket'. It used to be their favourite bar in town. The little bronze bell over the door chimed as they entered. He blinked as his eyes adjusted to the dim light, and took a deep breath, savouring the smell of musty sawdust and candlewax. A few figures glanced up from the shadowy corners of the pub, but the place was mostly deserted.

A man with thinning black hair was behind the bar, and his face lit up when he saw them. His belly jiggled as he came around the counter. "Eddy, my boy!"

Edward laughed. "How are you, Mr Lynus?"

"I thought I'd never see you again."

"I'm sorry to have scared you."

Mr Lynus squeezed him so hard that Edward gasped for air. "I was sorry to hear about your grandpa. But you know how he is. I'm sure he'll turn up."

Edward nodded. "I'm sure he will," he said, feeling the back of his neck burning. He didn't like the pity in the man's eyes.

"How's business?" Cliff asked.

Mr Lynus shrugged. "We're getting by, or so Nancy keeps telling me." Mr Lynus's wife, Nancy, kept The Empty Bucket in business, in addition to being a sympathetic ear to just about every down-on-his-luck man in Nodington Valley.

"The rest of the lads are in the back, Cliff," Mr Lynus said, wiping down the bar.

They waved goodbye and sauntered around to the rear of the bar. Three young men huddled around a table glanced up as they approached.

"I told you he was coming," said the first one, who was younger than the others at around seventeen.

"It was Dale who said he wasn't coming," said the second, accusingly. Then their eyes landed on Edward.

"Is that Edward Sting or am I seeing things?" asked the first boy.

"Hey, Sam," Edward said to his younger friend. Sam had just started on the farm last season; he was scrawny but tough.

The second boy was Louie. He was the oldest, at twenty-one, and had been working for Scruff for nearly ten years. Whenever anyone had a problem, they went to Louie. He got up and offered a chair. Cliff and Edward pulled up two more, and they all sat down.

"Happy Life Day," said Sam. "May we praise God, our one true creator." With that, he bowed his head in mock theatre.

Dale punched him in the arm. "You want somebody to see you doing that?" he snapped. He was tall and lean like Edward but had thick, dark hair.

Sam rolled his eyes. Mr Lynus came over and placed two glasses of swizzleberry juice on the table for Cliff and Edward.

Edward turned to Louie. "How's work?"

He shrugged. "Goin' all right. Rumour is we're getting horses next week. We sure could use an extra hand."

Edward nodded. "I'll be back tomorrow."

"That's good news," Louie said.

Edward didn't like how his friends were looking at him, the same way Mr Lynus had, as though they were walking on eggshells around him.

"Where's Kirk?"

Louie's expression darkened.

"You didn't hear?" Sam asked.

Edward shook his head.

"He was caught sneaking around the border," Louie said. Edward's jaw dropped. "They thought he was out to cause trouble."

Sam grunted. "He was fooling around. You know how he

is."

Dale took a long sip of his juice and slammed his mug on the table. "Well, he outta know better."

Edward felt a knot form in the pit of his stomach. "Where is he now?"

The others shrugged.

"That was two days ago. Nobody's seen him since," Louie said, fiddling with his glass.

Dale gulped down the rest of his juice. "We'd better get going." He jumped to his feet. "See you later?"

Edward nodded and waved goodbye.

Louie slapped him on the shoulder. "Good to see you, Eddy."

When they had gone, Edward leaned back in his chair and rubbed his chin. Blond stubble was growing in, making his skin scratchy.

Kirk was a hothead. He'd probably wound up in the dungeons. A week from now, he'd turn up, bitter and dishevelled, and whine about the whole thing. Dale was right. He should know better. Still, a week in the dungeons… That was harsh. Of course, everything was harsh nowadays. He could step on an ant, and the king would say, *'Never again!'* and watch him, every day, with his beady little eyes. One day, he would bring his boot down and crush a thousand ants just to spite him. That was the problem. Sooner or later, people couldn't take any more… and when they reached that point, they all ended up like Kirk.

"What are you thinking?" Cliff asked.

Edward gulped down his drink. "Nothing. Let's go."

They paid their bill and slipped out the door, waving goodbye to Mr Lynus. Back on the street, Cliff gazed up at the clock tower.

"The race will be starting soon."

Edward groaned, his memory returning. Every year, the king put on a sailing contest in the Great River. It was Cliff's favourite part of Life Day. Edward hated the contest. Mostly, he hated it because the same person won every year: whomever Shanley Brooks picked to represent him. The Duke of Teradowa was the king's right-hand-man and he was a slick, smooth-talking creep who always found a way to win.

The shore of the sandy riverbank was packed by the time they arrived, and riders were already testing the water. Wooden boats danced in the choppy waves like kernels on a stove. In order to enter, one had to build a boat that could handle the fast flow of the river. Each vessel was steered by a kite that was controlled by its rider.

There was no age limit, but the boats had to be small, so most entrants would sponsor a child to do the actual racing for them. Children from all over Teradowa came to compete.

Edward had raced when he was a kid. It was fun, and his grandpa had coached him. They would spend weeks together, building a boat and testing it in the river. However, as Edward got older, he realised that the race was rigged, and the king *always* had the winning boat. That was the year he'd stopped racing.

Cliff tapped him on the arm.

"Look," he said, pointing to the opposite shore. A man was kneeling before a child, barking commands in the pale boy's ear.

Edward felt his face contort in disgust. Shanley Brooks was clad in his usual black cloak and had his jet-black hair greased back over his ears, making his sallow features appear ghostly. His sharp, grey eyes ran up and down the boy's boat, inspecting every inch.

Cliff chuckled. "Poor kid probably hasn't been allowed to sleep in weeks. Did you hear Brooks is the new Porter, by the way?"

Edward jerked around. "What?"

"It's true. He's in charge of the border all the way across Nodington Valley."

Edward gritted his teeth, watching Brooks stroll over to the stands, his pale features looking like they were made of stone. "Who would put him in charge?"

Cliff shrugged. "You know how close he is to the king. He practically runs Teradowa."

Life would be much more difficult with Shanley Brooks as Porter, especially for Edward. There had always been rumours about Edward's family—odd rumours, mostly thanks to his grandpa—but Edward always suspected Brooks of spreading stories. He even had a hunch that it was Brooks who had tipped off those soldiers who'd taken them to the dungeons a few years back.

A wiry little man standing on the shore raised a bow and called for the racers to take their places. All the children lining the shore shuffled into their boats, and a lull fell over the crowd. On the count of ten, the man let fly his arrow, which struck a gong, sending a chime echoing out around the river.

Instantly, scores of boats splashed down into the water like a herd of wild beasts. Skysails shot upward. Just a trickle at first, but then countless colourful kites filled the clear afternoon air. One after the next, the sails snagged updrafts and dragged their boats out into open water, cutting through the choppy surface. Edward soon spotted Brooks' boat. The skysail was decorated with the green and white royal flag of Teradowa. The boy commanded his ship like a true captain. He weaved between the other boats, cutting off dozens at a time and slipping into first place.

"Look at him go!" Cliff said.

The boy zoomed past them, spraying the shore with mist. Behind him, a cohort of boats was in close pursuit.

Edward rolled his eyes. "And here come the blockers."

Their sails cleverly disguised with private flags, the blockers worked for the king and ensured that he always won. They banged and smashed into one another, and any potential challenger, but never made any real effort to overtake the leader. What bothered Edward most though was that nobody seemed to care. Everyone was content to watch. Perhaps it was a lack of options that made them flock to the riverbank, or maybe—and this was what Edward feared above all—they were actually rooting for the king.

Several crafts were gunning up behind the blockers now, trying to find an opening. This was perhaps the one interesting part of the race: Nobody ever got through the blockers, but it was still exciting to see them try. One boat slipped up into a narrow lane between two blockers and looked poised to overtake them, but at the last second, he was spotted. One blocker nosed his craft sharply to the left, striking the would-be challenger. The boat veered off and crashed into a rock that was protruding from the water, disintegrating it and sending the boy overboard.

Another boat suddenly sprang from the pack, and taking advantage of the new opening, burst through the blockers' barricade. The crowd, including Edward, gasped. This was altogether unheard of.

"Woah!" Cliff cried. The challenger sliced through the choppy water, hot on the leader's heels.

The racers were approaching a bend in the river now, and the crowd was shuffling down the shore to catch up.

"Come on!"

Edward followed Cliff down the coast, craning his neck to get a glimpse of the two boats in the lead, which were almost even now. He wished it were him out there, slicing through the waves and slamming into the king's prized leader. He couldn't help envying the children out there. Their innocence gave them some semblance of freedom. The boats were approaching the bend in the river known as the hardest part of the race, and it would be particularly difficult this year. Once every ten years, like clockwork, the racers would have to battle the Vortex.

Navigating the Vortex was something even the most experienced racers dreaded. It was, in essence, a giant whirlpool that formed on the sharpest bend in the river and was powerful enough to swallow a man whole. No one knew why or how, but the Vortex had been appearing once a decade for as long as anyone could remember.

The only way around it was to shoot across the river and catch the cross current to get back on course. But if you were caught by the Vortex first, it was a one-way ticket to the bottom of the river. The ferocious young captain in the lead was streaking towards the bend in a straight line.

Edward squinted. "What's he doing?"

Cliff went pale. "I think he's gonna try and cut the corner."

A murmur spread through the crowd, and Edward realised with a dreadful feeling that his friend was right. The boy was skimming the nearside of the riverbank, racing towards the Vortex's grasp. Behind him, the underdog contender bailed out and careened across the river.

Edward stared open-mouthed as the leader's tiny vessel raced along, just out of reach of the whirlpool's spinning arms.

Suddenly, the boat struck a wave, and the boy soared over the stern, splashing into the water as the crowd roared with excitement. He managed to catch a hold of his vessel's edge with one hand, and with the other, struggled to control his sail, which whipped about freely overhead.

Edward and Cliff sprinted further up the riverbank as the boy sped towards certain doom. In a moment, the Vortex would swallow him up. Edward held his breath and gazed across the river to where Brooks watched the scene with indifference.

"He's not even gonna do anything!"

The cries from the shore reached a peak as the boy was sucked nearer to the eye of the whirlpool. In a last ditch effort, he tugged his sail down nearly to the surface of the water.

"He's going to ground himself!" Cliff said. But the boy then released the kite, and it soared upward, searching for a gust of wind. Suddenly, it caught one, and the boy shot out of the water, swinging himself back into the boat and fanning the sail out across the sky. The boat obeyed its master once again and skimmed just outside the clutches of the Vortex, and beyond.

The crowd cheered and hooted. And just like that, the race was won. Nobody else would come close. Nobody else would dare the shortcut. On the far side of the river, Brooks applauded his success.

*

Edward trudged up the dirt path to his house, in a bitter mood and panting in the afternoon heat. The image of Brooks, grinning smugly as his boat crossed the finish line, kept replaying in his mind. A gust of wind blew across the hillside and kicked dust in his face. He clawed at his eyes and grumbled.

Cliff glanced at his friend. "What's the matter?"

Edward shrugged. He just wanted to forget about the whole thing. They rounded the last hill, bringing Edward's house into view, and he stopped dead in his tracks. His front door was open, and soldiers were carrying his belongings outside and loading them into a nearby wagon.

Edward clenched his fists and broke into a sprint. The solider in charge—a stout, grey-haired man—saw him coming and flashed his musket.

Edward stopped short, seething. "What do you think you're doing?"

The man smiled, with what looked like great effort. "This land belongs to the king now."

"You can't take his house," Cliff said, finally arriving behind Edward and bending over, heaving as he tried to catch his breath.

"The homeowner no longer lives here, so yes, we can."

"I *am* the homeowner!" Edward shouted.

"Not according to the king, you're not. That would be your grandfather: a Mr Simon Sting." The sergeant gave him a sly look. "You wouldn't happen to know where he is, would you?"

Edward's muscles tensed. "No, I don't."

The man clasped his hands and sighed. "Well then, there's just nothing I can do, I'm afraid."

"But I live here!"

The man put on a fake smile, and spoke slowly, as though Edward were child. "You must *work* in order to own land, Mr Sting."

Edward stuttered. "I-I have a job." The other soldiers had stopped what they were doing and were leaning on the wagon, watching with amusement.

"Oh?" the sergeant said, pulling out a sheet of paper. "Not

according to your employer. Mr Hurnet, is it?"

"Let me see that." Edward snatched the paper out of the man's hand. It was a notice of termination with Scruff's signature on it.

"How did you get this?" he demanded.

The sergeant huffed. "That's none of your business. The fact is that you don't have a job, and thus, you can't own this house."

"But I'm going back to work!"

The man sighed. "I'm afraid the decision has already been made. You'll be moved into the valley and given a new job."

Edward laughed. The whole thing was so obviously contrived, yet the little sergeant held himself with such an air of legitimacy that you would have thought he was the king himself. He felt his fists tighten again, and he pictured himself swinging at the man. The soldiers eyed him gleefully, as if daring him to do it. Edward suspected that they'd enjoy roughing him up; anyone foul enough to work for the king had to have a certain sickness to them.

He turned to the sergeant. "Fine. I'll gather my things then." The man stepped aside, a bemused look on his face, and Edward stormed past him.

The front hall was empty. His grandfather's coffee table had been taken, and they had even ripped the pictures from the walls. He rushed upstairs, and relief washed over him when he saw that they hadn't gotten to his room yet. He swept across the creaky floor and fetched a few items from his cabinet. There wasn't much to take, just an old hunting knife, some matches, and his pocket watch. The rest, he surrendered to its fate.

He doubted he'd ever see it again.

Back downstairs, Cliff was sulking in the kitchen. "I'm sorry, Ed."

Edward shrugged. "You tried to warn me." Depressed, he stared at the empty kitchen shelves. A stack of unopened mail lay spilled on the counter. He hadn't touched it in weeks. He picked up the top envelop: a notice of eviction from the Porter's office. Suddenly, a fresh wave of anger surged inside him as he realised exactly who was behind this. He sifted through the rest of the pile. Notice after notice of eviction. He gritted his teeth. How had he let them do this to him? He got to the bottom of the stack and stopped.

The last envelop was unmarked. The wrapping was faded and sealed by a thick drop of red wax.

Cliff peered over his shoulder. "What is it?"

"I'm not sure."

Edward tore at the seam, and the wax broke apart into brittle pieces. Inside was a single sheet of paper. He scanned the page, and all the colour drained from his face.

"My grandpa," he said. "He's in trouble."

Chapter 2

Scruff's Tale

"Let me see." Cliff inclined his head, eager to get a peek at the letter.

Edward grumbled, "Here." He held out the paper so they could both see it.

Edward,
It is crucial that you share this letter only with the most trusted of eyes. I have travelled far from Teradowa to a realm very different from our own. It exists beyond the Sea of Tydor, and those who know of its existence call it Regnum. I cannot share my reasons for leaving, but I have made a powerful enemy here, and I fear I may not make it back. If this note finds you before I return, then I have surely fallen into danger. There's someone in Teradowa who can make sense of my words. Find them. They will help you. Please, for both our sakes, you must come to my rescue.

"Where's the rest? That can't be it," Cliff said, flipping the page.

"I don't know," Edward said, unable to suppress a smile. His grandfather was alive, and he needed his help.

Cliff narrowed his eyes. "You don't actually think this is real, do you, Ed?"

Edward frowned. "Of course, it's real!"

Cliff put his hands up. "It's just that some people thought your grandpa was a bit... odd."

Edward furrowed his brow. "So?"

Cliff sighed. "What if this is some kind of joke?"

Edward scoffed. This was his chance to do something exceptional, and Cliff didn't have the courage to believe in it. "Who would do that?"

He shrugged. "I don't know, but you have to admit, it sounds strange. I mean... the *Sea of Tydor*?" He raised his eyebrows.

Edward grabbed his friend by the shoulders. "That's exactly why we must go. Haven't you ever wondered what's really out there?" he asked, excitement rising in his throat.

Cliff fidgeted. "There's nothing out there but wastelands. It's dangerous. That's why the gods created Teradowa in the first place."

Edward rolled his eyes. "That's what they *want* you to think. Why would my grandpa leave if there was nothing out there?"

Cliff twisted away from his grip. "You know I don't like it when you talk like this."

He did know, but he didn't care. This time, he had proof.

"And anyway, we're going to be late," Cliff said, glancing at his watch. "The Assembly starts soon." He dashed into the hallway, eager now to get away from his friend. Edward tucked the letter into his waistcoat and ambled after him, excitement swirling in his stomach.

A part of him had been waiting for a letter like this for a long time.

They rushed across the front path and past the soldiers who were still lounging outside. The stout sergeant waved them goodbye, but Edward no longer cared. Let him have his fun. They sprinted down the hill into the valley.

As they approached the first street, a man leaning on a porch stool strolled down into the road. Edward groaned; he was none too happy to see Shanley Brooks for the second time that day.

"Afternoon, gentleman," Brooks said, running a hand through his slick black hair. Edward set his jaw as a swarm of knights, the king's elite soldiers, appeared behind Brooks, clad in black armour.

Edward spat. "You're not gonna get away with taking my house, Brooks."

The duke sneered. "Haven't you heard? I'm the new Porter. I can do as I please. Besides, it's for the best. We would hate it if something were to happen to you, what with your grandfather away and all."

Edward shifted on the balls of his feet at the mention of his grandfather and glanced at Cliff, who was staring at the ground.

Brooks narrowed his eyes. "Something on your mind, boys?"

"Nope," Cliff said. "Nothing at all."

Brooks' eyes darted between them, his expression dark. "You better hurry," he said, "or you'll miss the Assembly."

They bounded down the street, and Edward could feel Brooks' beady eyes digging into the back of his skull the whole way.

Cliff grumbled. "He gives me the creeps."

Town square was packed to the brim when they arrived. Wooden buildings stood like giant guards on all sides of the courtyard, caging them in. Edward and Cliff stood shoulder to shoulder, shuffling forward with the crowd, mere inches at a time. A wooden stage decorated with red banners stood at the front of the square.

As they approached, the unmistakable creak of the dam reached Edward's ears. Builders had diverted the Great River around the village many years ago, but the ancient structure was weak and in need of repair. King Sento had demanded a new, ultra-modern dam be built. It had been a labour-intensive process, but it was nearly complete, and there was talk that, today, Sento would officially reveal the superstructure. It was almost comical, how much stock the king put in all the wrong things. Sure enough, beside the stage, a giant red tarp towered over everything, and behind it, three hundred metric tons of water. Edward jerked around as men began rolling twelve-pound guns out onto the stage.

"That's new," Cliff said. One of the men produced a linstock and lit the fuse at the end of the barrel. Edward counted to three and covered his ears. A plume of smoke erupted from the gun and rose into the clear sky. The crowd hushed at once.

The faint sound of boots on wood echoed around the square, and as the king marched on stage, Edward dropped to one knee with the thousands of other onlookers, hating every second of it.

"Rise." The word boomed around the square.

Edward got to his feet and dusted himself off as the king took the podium. Despite the heat, Sento wore a dark green fur coat and a golden crown. His bushy black beard was neatly trimmed, and he smiled down at the crowd with carefully honed showmanship.

"Welcome, my friends. Today we celebrate our Giver of Life." Looking around, Edward could already see the sweat dripping from those around him. The king extended his arms towards the sky. "We thank the gods for their creation of Teradowa and their eternal protection of our realm from the terrors of the unknowable."

Edward scoffed, drawing dirty looks from the crowd.

King Sento closed his eyes. "Praise the gods!" he shouted.

"Praise the gods!" the crowd repeated.

The king's lips curled into a wicked smile. "Now," he said, crossing his arms, "we must remember to stay vigilant in our prayers. We must remember what happens when we insult the gods by taking their protection for granted." Edward and Cliff exchanged looks. Heavy footsteps sounded on the stairs leading to the stage.

Edward craned his neck to get a better look and saw something that made his heart stop. Beside him, Cliff gasped. Two knights had arrived on the stage, Kirk hung between them, shackled in chains. Their friend was barely recognizable. His dark brown hair and pale skin were covered in dirt and dried blood, and his face was beaten and puffy.

The crowd shuffled anxiously.

"Let this be a warning," the king said. "This is what happens to those who insult the gods."

Edward's mind went into a spiral, and suddenly, he was pushing his way through the crowd.

"Ed!" Cliff whispered harshly, trying to yank him back. But he was too late, his protests vanishing behind Edward as he pressed forward, unaware of anything but the knight standing over Kirk, drawing a sword and shoving his friend to his knees. Kirk's head lolled uselessly, and Edward wondered if he was even aware of what was happening.

"Stop!" he shouted, breaking into a sprint. He streaked towards the stage like a madman. People dove out of the way as he stormed forward. Reaching the front of the crowd, he leapt onto the stage and right past the stunned king.

Without thinking, he charged at the knight and slammed

right into him. Taken by surprise, the man crumpled. Edward wrenched the sword from his grip and tossed it aside, but then someone grabbed him around the waist, and he fell to the ground. The second knight was on top of him then, pinning him to the stage. Edward clawed at his armour until his hands slipped between the thick sheets of metal on the man's chest, his hands searching frantically for some advantage. He could feel the force of the man's grip threatening to squeeze the air from his body.

Finally, forcing his hands upwards, they found the knight's throat, and he closed his fingers around it. The man gasped and released his grip. Edward scrambled to his feet and was shocked to see that, while most of the crowd watched in horror, a few had actually joined him.

Several wide-eyed young people were swarming the stage, but the king's men were now pouring into the square like bees to a hive. A few feet away, the young soldier manning the cannon locked eyes with Edward. A renewed energy washed over him, and he sprang at the man and tackled him. Snatching the linstock out of his hands, he rushed over to the cannon and spun it around, heaving under its weight, until the barrel faced the king. He stood then, gasping for air, his heart pounding in his chest.

The king, being sheltered by his knights, was shouting over the uprising, trying to be heard. "Stop!" he shouted, then glared at Edward. *"You..."* he hissed. His eyes roamed over the cannon to the linstock in his hands. "Drop it!"

Edward gestured to Kirk, laying helplessly on the stage. "Let him go."

Sento pressed his lips together and gazed out at the crowd who were frozen in place by Edward's threat. When he turned back towards him, the king wore a wicked smirk on his face.

"I've got a better idea. Why don't you take his place, boy?"

Edward's heart sank. Humiliation was the king's only aim now. He would make Edward look small and pathetic in the eyes of crowd and then kill them both. Edward had never been surer of anything. He glanced at the crowd. He knew that, somewhere out there, Cliff was staring back at him, begging him to put down the linstock, but his friend still didn't understand. They were so far past that. In one rapid motion, he lit the fuse.

Sento's cries of protest were drowned out by the shouts of the crowd. The king's men leapt forward as the spark shot down the line, and Edward dove to block them. The nearest man slammed into him, sending him crashing into the cannon, which slid across the stage. Edward covered his ears just in time to see the spark hit the base of the barrel.

The explosion shook the stage and deafened him for a moment. In the smoky blur, men dove for cover as the acrid smell of gunpowder filled the air and stung their eyes.

Edward staggered to his feet, coughing, and then the groan of wood under pressure nearby let him know that his hearing had returned. He looked up, and to his horror, realised that the shot had missed its target and struck the dam instead. The crowd stood motionless. Even the king stared up at the enormous barrier in silence.

For a terrible instant, everything was still.

Then came a sharp crack, and the tarp split open as water shot through a pressurised crack in the dam. Then the wood buckled, and the full force of the river surged into the square. Cries erupted from the crowd as the river poured in like a tsunami, scooping people up and washing them away. In an instant, the street became a lake. Wagons and barrels floated and spun aimlessly, like lost souls. People splashed in the water and clung onto whatever floated by. Edward felt the stage shudder, and then suddenly, it too was sailing across the square. He whirled around at the sound of shouting behind him. The king was still on the stage, wobbling towards him with a deadly look in his eye.

Edward tried to dodge him but lost his footing and plunged into the cold water. It bit at his skin and soaked his heavy waistcoat, making it feel like he was made of stone. Wave after wave washed over him and carried him farther across the square. The stone front of the blacksmith loomed ahead. In a moment, he would be crushed against it.He thrashed desperately, looking for something to grab onto to delay the inevitable.

Then a hand reached out and grabbed him. Leaning over a high porch railing, Cliff tugged his friend to safety. Both boys dropped to their knees, wheezing.

Edward shivered. "Th-Thanks."

"That was some trick," Cliff said, eyeing him. They spun around then at the sound of soldiers from the stage loading into a rowboat that had been carried past and shouting orders to each other.

A few moments later, the overloaded boat pushed off and out into the melee, but by the time it reached the porch, Edward and Cliff were already gone.

*

Edward couldn't take another step. He and Cliff had just slogged up the last hill outside of town, sweat dripping off them, and now collapsed into the grass. Edward ran a hand through his thick blond hair and wiped it on his shirt. Cliff lay beside him, face buried in his hands.

"What have you done?"

"They were going to kill Kirk!"

"And now they're going to kill *us!*" Cliff shouted. "*Why* couldn't you just trust the will of the—"

"Don't you get it yet?" Edward snapped. He sat up. "They're lying to us, Cliff! They make up stories about gods and monsters and shove them down our throats because they *want* you to be afraid, so that they can control you!"

Cliff scowled. "So what if they are? I don't care! Things were fine the way they were."

By the look in Cliff's eyes, Edward could see that he wasn't going to understand. Or didn't want to. That was the difference between them.

"So, you would have just let Kirk die?"

Cliff slumped back onto the grass and looked away.

"That's what I thought."

His friend blew out a huff of hot air. "So, now what?"

Edward looked at him, downcast.

Cliff's expression softened. "You're really leaving, aren't you?"

Edward nodded.

Cliff tore at the dirt. "You know I don't want any part of this," he said, tossing a handful of grass at his feet. Then he shook his head and sighed. "But... if I stay here, I'm dead anyway. So, congratulations, you win." Edward slapped him on the back and they stood and brushed themselves off. "So... where to?" Cliff asked.

Edward smiled. He knew just the place to start.

*

The silhouette of Scruff's farmhouse glowed golden brown in the evening light. The wooden structure, worn with age, looked ready to collapse, and the cracks in the stone foundation threatened to do the trick any moment. Edward had long suspected that a strong gust of wind would be enough to bring the whole house down. He leapt up the creaky steps two at a time and stopped in front of the door.

"What is it?" Cliff asked.

Edward shook his head. If Scruff wasn't who he thought he was, they were in big trouble. But he didn't believe that. Scruff was old, he knew his grandfather, and he had even specifically asked for Edward to come and work for him. That had to count for something. He rapped on the door. After a moment, footsteps sounded inside, and the door squeaked open. Scruff poked his head out the crack and stared at them with his watery eyes.

"Hullo, boys," he said, scratching his ruffled beard. Edward was about to ask if they could come in, but to his surprise, Scruff turned and walked back into the house, leaving the door open for them. Edward and Cliff exchanged looks and stepped through the door, following the old man, who wore a pair of brown overalls and nothing else.

Thin streaks of light broke the darkness of the single room inside. Edward strode towards the nearest window and drew back the curtain. As he turned back around, he smacked his head off a dangling object, then blinked and rubbed his temple.

Scruff grunted. "Watch your step."

"What are all these Scruff?" Cliff asked, inspecting one of the metal trinkets that hung from the ceiling like pendulums. He'd seen them before, of course, but had never bothered to ask about them.

"Just something I've been working on." Edward had been to Scruff's enough times to know that this was as far as that conversation would go. The old farmer shuffled across the room and sank into his brown armchair. "I'm sorry 'bout your home, son. The king came to see me—came right into my home. Uninvited. Can you believe that? Anyway, they threatened to take the farm and everything I had if I didn't sign those letters. I should have warned you."

Edward dropped into the chair opposite him.

"That's all right, Scruff. We've got bigger problems. Cliff and I trashed the Assembly today, and Sento's gonna kill us. We need to get out of Teradowa and something tells me you might be able to help us with that. I... I have something I want you to see."

Scruff's face darkened, and he studied Edward for a long moment. Finally, he dug into his pocket and produced a pair of glasses.

"I thought this day might be coming. What do you have for me, son?"

Edward glanced at Cliff, who shrugged. Rummaging in his waistcoat, Edward produced his grandpa's letter. The old man took it in his gnarled fingers, his eyes scanning the page and growing wearier with each line. When he was done, he set his glasses on the coffee table and sighed.

"You boys have gotten yourself mixed up in something indeed. I knew when your grandfather left that he would find nothing but trouble."

Edward sat up in his chair. "So, it's true then?"

Scruff nodded solemnly. "Oh yes. He came to me before he left. I should have told you, but he made me promise not to. He said that he had something very important to do."

Edward's mind was racing. "What was it?"

Scruff stared at the clock. "He wouldn't say, but he was in

an awful hurry."

Edward shuffled in his seat. The cushions were old and threatened to swallow him up.

"What did you two talk about?"

Scruff rubbed his temples. "I told him he was mad. See, it was like your grandpa to… exaggerate, but this time, he seemed determined. He just kept going on about something big happening. A problem that had been growing for a long time now." He chuckled, but there was a hint of sadness in his eyes. "He tried to get me to go with him, but I'm afraid I'm not what I used to be. See, years ago, before you were born, I would sometimes go with your grandpa into the unknown regions— course, it was a lot safer back then." He crossed his legs and smiled, as if fondly recalling a time long lost.

"Safer?" Cliff said, leaning his elbows on the counter.

Scruff's smile vanished. "It doesn't matter. You cannot go. I'm sorry I couldn't stop your grandfather, but I will not allow *you* to go too." He shot out of his chair and began pacing and shaking his head. "Your father always knew the danger. That's why he never went along with us."

Edward furrowed his brow. "What danger? Is it true what they say? Is it really a wasteland beyond Teradowa?"

Scruff sighed. "Not exactly." He hobbled across the room to a chest in the corner and returned holding a stack of yellowing papers. "When we were young, Simon had a theory. He believed that there were other realms, like Teradowa, beyond our own."

"Like in the letter," Cliff said, fiddling with a trinket from the counter.

"Right." Scruff took his seat, fanned the papers out on the coffee table, and snatched one from the pile. It was an old map. "We soon discovered that your grandpa was right."

Edward and Cliff exchanged looks.

"Right beyond our border," Scruff continued, "Candosia begins, the *second* realm. Full of people with no knowledge of our existence!"

Edward's jaw dropped. He had been right after all, but he had to admit that it felt unbelievable all the same. He scooped up the stack of papers then, flipping absently through them, his head suddenly ablaze with questions. Why didn't everyone know? How could the king keep everyone so completely in the dark?

"But why?" he asked. "Why keep it a secret?"

Scruff frowned. "The kings know that fear has a way of keeping them rich. They make you believe in the gods because they need them to be real so that you'll listen to them. So that you'll fear the unknown rather than seek it out. It's the same story in Candosia. The world is a desolate, rotten place, save for their own little slice of paradise, generously created by the gods."

Edward shook his head. "Why haven't you told them the truth, Scruff? I mean, there have to be people who would listen."

Scruff smiled sadly. "There was a time when I believed that. Now I'm not so sure. Besides, the king keeps a close eye on men like me and your grandpa. We were sworn to secrecy years ago and banished to the countryside. We are tolerated, I suppose, because we are occasionally useful, but if any of us were to speak out, we'd vanish for good."

Scruff's words hung in the air for a moment; then Cliff cleared his throat.

"What about the rest of this letter?"

Scruff nodded. "In Candosia, we learned of even more realms beyond *their* borders: Decius, the desert; Tydor, the water world, and..." His face became grim. "And Regnum... the fifth realm. Nobody could ever tell us much about Regnum. Nothing good anyway."

Edward was confused. There was something missing from Scruff's story.

"Why did you stop? Exploring, I mean."

Scruff pursed his lips. "After your parents' accident, Simon focused on raising you, and I decided it was wiser just to keep myself busy with the farm." He spoke with no emotion, as though he were reciting lines from a script. Edward wasn't sure if he believed it was that simple.

"Well, we're going after him."

Scruff shook his head. "Simon never should have left, and neither should you."

"We have no choice. If we stay here, we're dead."

The old farmer stared at Edward until his wrinkled face softened. Finally, he sighed and lumbered out of his chair. "Come with me."

He led them across the room to a rusty hatch in the floor. He pried it open, the old hinges screeching like a spirit being awakened from the dead. As they shimmied one at a time down the narrow ladder, Edward felt the air thicken and cool. He landed with a thud on a sandy floor just as Scruff lit a lantern, illuminating an old cellar with yellow light.

Along both walls hung racks of swords and muskets.

"Holy…" Cliff said, picking up a bayonet and eyeing the old man. "Scruff!"

"Still have them papers?" the old man said, looking at Edward, who handed over the pages from the coffee table. Scruff took them and shuffled to a cabinet against the far wall. Blowing a thick layer of dust off the handle, he opened the top drawer and pulled out a single large paper, inspecting it for a moment before looking back at the stack of drawings. Satisfied, he laid the stack in the cabinet and studied the sheet he had chosen. "This," he said, as he returned to them, "is the most complete map we have." He handed it to Edward. "It's based on your grandpa's memory though, so it's not the best."

"It's perfect," Edward said.

"Here is where you should head." He pointed to a mark on the map. "Dobson's Canyon. We used to travel there frequently. It's a big city. You'll be able to blend in and find passage out of Candosia. After that," Scruff said, looking at the boys uncertainly, "you're on your own."

"How will we know who to talk to?" Cliff asked.

"The realms are full of hermits like me and your grandpa, drifters, we call 'em—people who are on the inside of information but the outside of society. Those people will be your friends."

Edward tucked the map away and turned his attention to the wall of weaponry. Countless swords shimmered in the yellow light. He pressed his palm against the cold steel of the nearest blade and ran his finger tentatively over its sharp edge. A rush of excitement shot through his body. He gripped the hilt and unracked the sword. It was heavier than he expected. He swung it slowly from side to side then, conjuring up horrifying monsters that crumbled before his wrath. Then he was standing over them, triumphant. People everywhere praised him. His name was whispered in the dark corners of pubs. *'Haven't you heard of Edward Sting? He's only the most formidable swordsman in all the realms.'* He turned to Scruff, a smile burning on his face.

"I'll take this one."

*

The sun was sinking over the horizon by the time they were ready to go. Edward tightened the last strap on his bandoro's back and stroked its long, golden fur. The mighty beast stood solemnly on its four powerful legs. Nearby, Cliff was struggling to calm his own steed. He had never been a talented rider.

"It won't sit still."

"Relax. He can tell you're anxious."

Scruff hobbled off the back porch.

"You sure 'bout this son?" he asked, his voice quivering. "I hate to see you go."

Edward set his jaw. "It's the only way… I'll come back. I promise."

Cliff trotted up next to him, hunched over on his bandoro.

He groaned. "Let's go before I change my mind."

Edward looked down at Scruff. "Thank you for everything." He hesitated a moment, and then asked, "Is there anyone else who knows about all this?"

Scruff paused. "Years ago, Simon spoke 'bout taking on an apprentice. Don't know if he ever did." Edward nodded and turned to go.

"Eddy," Scruff said, stopping him, "whatever happens out there… just remember who you are."

*

The hills rolled by as night spread across the sky. Fields of wheat turned into forests dotted with pogui. Half the size of regular trees and scattered among them like buoys in a sea of foliage, a pogus grew in the shape of a cone, its hard shell changing colour with the seasons. This time of year, they were a brilliant red and gold pattern.

"We're nearly there," Cliff said as they rode through the bush. Scuff had explained that they needed to cross the border to the far north, where a steep embankment had made building a wall impossible and a regular guard inconvenient. Ahead of them, the rocky ground sloped upwards. The rise was blanketed in darkness. Edward's eyes scanned the trees and suddenly stopped on a small orange flame that was burning high on the hillside.

"What's that?"

Cliff grunted with dismay. "I don't believe this. They're waiting for us, Ed. We're cooked!"

"Keep your voice down. They haven't seen us yet."

They rode quietly up to the base of the steep hill, and Edward squinted up at the campfire, rubbing his chin.

Several deep voices drifted down the hill.

The two steered their rides up the rocky incline until the bandoros wedged into the slope and refused to continue on.

Cliff groaned. "I thought these things were supposed to be fearless?" he whispered.

"Just make him calm down, like this," Edward said, stroking the beast atop its golden head. Cliff scrunched up his face and attempted to emulate the motion, his thick fingers moving awkwardly. Eventually, they inched up almost level with the fire and stopped behind a thin line of bush.

"Get it to crouch down," Edward whispered.

Cliff pushed on the back of his bandoro. "He won't."

"We don't want to be seen."

Cliff shot him a look. "Show me how it's done then."

Edward scowled in the dark. He did not want Cliff to get the best of him.

"It's easy," he said. He twisted sideways and leaned on the hind quarters of the animal. Startled, the bandoro let out an ear-piercing whine and bucked him off, shooting him straight through the bushes, now in plain sight of whoever was awaiting them.

Chapter 3

Borders and Bounty Hunters

Edward lay frozen on the ground, hidden only by the darkness. The light from the fire flickered mere inches from his face, yet the four burly men remained hunched over the fire, shovelling roasted meat into their mouths. The aroma wafted through the air, making his stomach growl; he held his breath and hoped they didn't hear.

Something was strange about the scene. The men wore tattered clothes, and their thick necks were hidden behind mountains of bushy hair. They chortled and laughed as they ate, and Edward wondered if they were intoxicated. *They must be if they didn't hear me hit the ground,* he thought.

He certainly was not going to hang around to find out. He began to crawl towards the bushes, careful to avoid the firelight. He was almost there when a voice called out from behind him.

"Oie!"

Panic washed over him. A man rose from the fire, his gut sagging below his belt, and staggered over to Edward. "Who er you?"

Edward stared up at the man's pudgy face, half masked by darkness.

"What's wring, Enzo?" called a voice from the fire.

"There's someone over here."

Enzo's companions shuffled over and peered curiously

down at Edward.

"Y'all right, mate?"

Edward nodded dumbly, eyeing the axe in the man's hand.

"Well, what er you doin' on the ground?" a voice from the back demanded.

"What if he's one of them boys they're lookin' for?"

Edward's stomach churned, and he saw Enzo's eyes turn to slits. Then an idea struck him.

"Have you seen them?" he asked.

Enzo scratched his beard. "Well... er... no."

Edward got to his feet and brushed himself off. "Hm... that's interesting. We haven't seen anything ourselves."

The men exchanged looks. "Who are you?"

"I'm Lieutenant... Lynus," Edward said. "I'm part of a covert mission to find the fugitives that terrorised the Assembly today." He brushed past them and strode towards the fire.

"You don't look very covert."

Edward rolled his eyes. "That's the point, isn't it?"

He picked up a jug of dark liquid and pretended to inspect it.

"You know, I'd hate to have to tell the king that, instead of doing your job, you're drinking the night away."

The men grumbled incoherently.

"This is your fault, Enzo!" one of them said angrily.

Enzo put up his hands. "Neil told us to watch the camp!" he said, sweat breaking out on his brow.

So, there's more of them, he thought. Perhaps Neil was the leader.

"Now we won't get paid!" one of the younger men complained fiercely.

With a chill on the back of his neck, Edward felt the curtains being lifted in his mind, the men's tattered clothes and lack of discipline suddenly making perfect sense. These men were not soldiers, they were bounty hunters. He supposed that this was his first encounter with the type of men Scruff had deemed 'occasionally useful' to the king. These men almost certainly knew all about the secrets and the lies, but they didn't care—in fact, they probably preferred it this way.

"Well," he said, trying to sound casual, "I suppose there's no real need to report you... Perhaps, I'll just leave you to it." He turned to go, but Enzo grabbed his arm.

"Please stay. I'm sure Neil will want to clear things up himself."

Edward hesitated; he was beginning to feel like he didn't want to meet Neil. "Very well."

Enzo pointed at the two younger men. "Cal, Derek, go start lookin' for them boys." The two nodded and chugged off down the hill without another word. "This is Truss," Enzo said, gesturing to the remaining man and heading back to the fire. Edward noticed that he walked with a limp. In the firelight, it was clear that Truss and Enzo were both quite old, with grizzled grey hair on their heads and the beards to match. Years spent in their line of work probably took quite a toll on a man. Edward begrudgingly took a seat between the two of them at the fire. Not a moment passed after they sat down before there was a rustle in the bushes and a plump young man appeared, looking pale as a ghost.

Cliff cleared his throat. "My liege," he said, bowing at the waist, "I have searched the area and found nothing."

Edward looked between Cliff and the bounty hunters.

"This is my... servant," he said.

Cliff dipped his chin in an awkward acknowledgement and squatted across from them on a small rock. Enzo pulled out his axe and started sharpening it.

"So, Lynus, you ever been outside the border?" Truss asked.

"No."

Truss gave him a toothy smile. "We have. All the best gigs are out there."

Enzo shot his friend a look. "Neil says we ain't supposed to talk to the nobles about outside."

"Ah, these ain't nobles, thems' workin' men like us."

Before Edward could ask for details, there was yet another commotion in the bushes, and a man in a dark waistcoat stepped into the clearing.

"Neil," Enzo said, getting to his feet. "You were gone a long time."

Neil gripped a lantern in one hand, and in the dim light, Edward could see an eyepatch covering one eye. A scar ran down the right side of his face and intersected the eyepatch at an angle.

He strode into the firelight, and the orange glow illuminated his athletic build. He glared at Edward.

"This is Lieutenant Lynus and his servant," Enzo said. "They work for King Sento."

"The king?" Neil asked, a note of surprise in his voice.

Enzo nodded. "They're looking for the fugitives."

Neil's good eye darted between Edward and Cliff. "Well, I hope everything here is to your liking, *Lieutenant.*"

Edward nodded, avoiding Neil's gaze. The bounty hunter set the lantern down with a heavy clank and slumped against a log, then propped one arm up on his knee and rummaged in his coat, pulling out a metal flask.

The others stared at the fire while Neil took a long drink, the crackle of the flames roaring and popping in Edward's ears like musket shots.

Neil put down the flask. "So," he said, "how long have you been in the service, Lynus?"

Edward shrugged. His mouth had gone dry.

Before he could answer, Truss cleared his throat. "See anything on the outside, boss?"

Neil's gaze turned up sharply. He stared at Truss for a moment, as though trying to say something; then his eyes darted around at the forest. "Dogs," he whispered.

Truss shivered. "I pity the man who comes across them." Edward swallowed. Attack dogs were one thing he could not outrun. Across the fire, Cliff chewed his lip.

Enzo chuckled. "Relax, kid. They're not for us."

Edward drummed his fingers, feeling Neil's eye burning a hole into his skull. "We should probably be going."

"No," Neil said. "Stay. I insist. I wasn't expecting company tonight, and I'm sure the king would appreciate… a full report."

"We'll fill him in."

Neil took another long swig from his flask. "How exactly did you find our camp anyway?"

"He was over there on the ground," Truss said.

Neil raised his eyebrows. "On the ground?"

"Mhm."

"We really should be going," Edward said, feeling his heartbeat quicken as he climbed to his feet. "We're expected."

Now Neil sprang forward like a wild animal ready to strike. "I doubt that," he said, flashing his sword under Edward's chin. Truss and Enzo stumbled backwards, wide eyed.

"What you doin', boss?"

"You fools!" Neil roared. "These *are* the boys we're looking for!"

Edward dashed around the fire, twisting away from Neil's

blade. "Now hold on!" His heart was racing so hard he thought it might explode.

Neil skipped over the fire in a fit of rage, his sword poised to strike.

"That's far enough!" a voice boomed from behind them. They all whirled around and peered into the darkness. A tall figure emerged from the trees, and a moment later, the haughty face of Shanley Brooks flashed in the firelight.

Edward let out a dry laugh. He wasn't sure if he was relieved or devastated to see the duke. Soldiers were filing out of the woods and soon had the fire surrounded.

Neil pointed his finger at Brooks. "You!"

Brooks sauntered up to them and extended his hand to Neil. The bounty hunter looked at it in disgust.

"Good to see you, Neil," Brooks said, his tone thick with aristocratic snobbery.

Even in the low light, Edward could see that Neil's face was flushed red. He spat at Brooks' feet. "What are *you* doing here?"

Brooks nodded to his men, and Edward felt a hand grab him and cold iron clamp down on his wrists. "We'll take it from here."

Neil shook his head and pointed a finger at the duke. "You can't do this! I found them and I am going to get paid!"

Brooks frowned. "Looks more like they found you, from where I'm standing."

Neil's mouth hung open. "You can't be serious!" His whole body was shaking. "You're up to your games again. I know you are!" He stepped back like he was going to hit Brooks, then thought better of it.

"I'm sorry you're upset," Brooks said, not sounding sorry at all, "but there's nothing more you can do." He then slipped him a folded piece of paper. "Perhaps this will make up for it."

Neil glanced at it. "You think you can buy me with another job?"

"I think you'd be well advised to take that job."

Neil tore up the paper and tossed it in the fire. Then he grunted harshly—the sort of noise a wounded animal makes just before it's eaten.

"Very well," Brooks said. He turned, and his shadowy figure strode back into the forest, quickly melting into the darkness. Edward felt the butt of a musket press into his back, and suddenly, he too was being led into the woods. Edward looked straight on as he walked past Neil, whose face was contorted in silent rage.

After a few moments away from the fire, Edward's eyes adjusted, and he could make out soldiers all around him, at least a dozen and all clearly from Brooks personal staff, judging from their uniforms. They marched him for a long time along the wooded hillside until he was sure that he was lost; then they came to a stop. The sound of twigs snapping grew louder, and then Brooks re-emerged before them, scowling.

"Well, you found us," Cliff said with a sneer. "What now? You gonna take us to your master?"

Brooks' scowl remained fixed, only his eyes roamed between them. Finally, he sighed and strode away, taking one of the older soldiers aside. The rest waited where they were as the two men talked in hushed voices. Finally, the soldier nodded, and Brooks gestured in understanding.

Then they shook hands.

Edward furrowed his brow as Brooks broke away and approached them again with the same scowl on his face. Pointing uphill, he said, "You'll find your bandoros on the far side. The border is just beyond. March through the night. Do *not* stop." With that, he stepped forward and removed their cuffs. Then he turned to leave.

Edward blinked, still stunned by the strange turn of events. "You're letting us go?"

"Why?" Cliff asked, his voice dripping with disbelief.

Brooks grinned. "You think you're the only ones who want to see the king on his knees?"

Chapter 4

Hikoo

The grassy trail came in and out of focus as though a shade were being waved in front of his face. When he heard his named called, he slumped his head sideways to look at Cliff, who was riding a few feet away.

"It's been a few hours," his friend said. "Maybe we should think about stopping to rest."

Edward nodded. Brooks had told them not to, but what did his word mean anyway? Edward didn't believe that Brooks would betray the king so easily unless, perhaps, he wanted to sabotage Sento and take the throne for himself, which at least sounded like the Brooks he knew—the Brooks who didn't have a shred of honour—not this unforeseen ally they had just encountered.

They found a grassy burrow in the earth near the edge of the forest, opposite the trees there was only darkness cascading over open grassland.

"Why is it so dark?" Edward asked, curling up in his sleeping sack.

Cliff shrugged. "We're not in the valley anymore; there's no light but the moon, I guess."

Edward stared up at the sky. "I don't see the moon."

"No… you're right. It's already set maybe?" *Strange,* he thought briefly, but then dismissed the notion, running his thumb over the hilt of his sword, lying on the grass beside him. He liked the coolness of it; it felt reassuring.

A breeze rustled through the trees. He listened carefully until it faded and wondered if this forest ever ended. It had looked so big when they'd first come over the escarpment. He sighed. It was a question for the morning.

"Good night, Cliff," he said, but the other boy was already fast asleep.

*

Edward pointed to a spot on the map. "As far as I can tell, we're right here."

"That far? We only rode three hours last night." Cliff was munching on fresh bread, and the two were hunched over Scruff's map. The sun—just peeking through the trees—cast shadows over their camp, and a strong wind was sweeping the dew off the plains like a shopkeeper opening his store for the day.

"Dobson's Canyon is right here," Edward said. "So, all we need to do is keep going straight," He disliked the way that had come out, sounding as though it were a question. Cliff mumbled something about going in circles, and the pair climbed on their bandoros.

They rode all day along the edge of the woods. Although the terrain was flat, there seemed to be no pattern to the weather. For some stretches, the wind was so cold and powerful that it seemed as though a tornado were forming, churning up thick clouds of dust that turned Edward's blond hair a dusty brown. For other stretches, the complete lack of wind made the heat almost unbearable.

Stranger yet was that when the boys moved under the shade

of the trees, the temperatures became immediately frigid, so much so that ice would form on the soles of their boots. And so, they would move between the sun and shade, heat and cold, never able to get comfortable.

They rode until there was no shade left, and the only light in the sky were the stars. It was then that they found another grassy burrow to camp in. This cycle continued for several days.

About a week into the journey, while riding along the same line of trees under the same merciless sun, Edward suddenly stopped.

"What is it?" Cliff asked.

"We missed a turn."

Cliff frowned. "I thought you said all we had to do was go straight?"

"I know but look." On the horizon, their path was blocked by another forest.

Cliff blew out hot air. "Well, we can't turn around now; we just have to go through it."

Edward stared at him. "You want to go through it?"

"Why not?"

"I don't know. I just have a bad feeling."

"I have a bad feeling."

Edward gave his friend a sideways glance. "That's what I said."

Cliff scratched his head. "I heard you."

Suddenly, something caught Edward's eye, and he veered around.

A small creature was dangling off a tree branch nearby. It was covered in bright-blue fur and had pointy ears that lay flat against its head. Whiskers protruded from around its nose, and it peered at them with big brown eyes.

"Hello," the animal said.

Cliff gasped.

Edward blinked. "You—you can *talk?*"

"Sure can," it said, puffing out its fluffy chest. "'I have a bad feeling'... See?"

Cliff was as white as a sheet. "W-what are you?"

"My name is Hikoo, and I live in this forest," the creature said.

"Nice to meet you, Hikoo," Edward said, saddling up next to him. "I am Edward Sting, and this is my friend Clifford Milly."

Hikoo wagged his bushy tail and leapt off the tree branch, landing smoothly on Edward's shoulder. "A pleasure it is for Hikoo to meet you, Master Sting." He scampered down Edward's front and shoved his tiny hands into his pockets.

"Hey! Cut that out!" he said, yanking the little creature off him. Hikoo landed on the bandoro's back and quivered. "Forgive me, Master Sting, for Hikoo is very hungry." Edward looked at Cliff, who was now more than a stone's throw away and shaking almost as bad as Hikoo.

Edward sighed. "All right." He dug into his ration bag and tossed Hikoo a stick of dried meat. The animal sniffed it with his stubby nose, and then nibbled it down like a rabbit.

"Better?" Edward asked. Hikoo looked back at him, beaming, then sat up on his hind legs, the fur on his pale belly fluttering in the wind. Then he tilted his head to the side, and for a moment, Edward thought he might run back into the forest, but instead, he looked back at Edward.

"What does Master Sting have a bad feeling about?" Hikoo asked.

Edward hesitated. "Do you know a place called Dobson's Canyon?"

Hikoo's ears perked up. "Oh, yes. I do know this place."

"You do?"

"No kidding?" Cliff asked, moving closer now.

"Oh, yes. Very busy place. Hikoo doesn't like it very much."

"You see," Edward said, "we're not from around here, Hikoo, and we're a bit lost."

The creature became giddy. "I know a way! I can take you! Hikoo will take you through the forest!"

"Is it safe?"

"Yes, very safe... Master Sting will be very safe as long as he stays on the path."

Edward and Cliff exchanged looks as Hikoo bounced up and down like a child awaiting a present.

"Okay, Hikoo," Edward said. "Show us the way."

"Of course, Master Sting! For this will be such fun for Hikoo!" He scurried up the bandoro's back, perched on its head like a captain at the prow of his ship, and they quickly got underway once more.

The afternoon sun was hot but not scorching, and Edward found himself enjoying the warmth. Cliff rode beside them, having gotten over his shock at meeting Hikoo (although his eyes kept darting back towards him) and after some time became curious.

"So, Hikoo, what *are* you?"

"I am Hikoo," the creature said.

Cliff pursed his lips. "Right. But what *are* you?"

Hikoo scrunched up his nose, clearly not understanding the question.

Cliff sighed. "If Ed and I are humans, then what do we call your people?"

"Humans..." Hikoo said, rolling the word over his tongue.

Cliff shook his head and resigned himself to riding in silence.

Edward had other ideas. "So, how come you're all alone? Don't you have a family?"

Hikoo sat back on his hind legs again and fondled the bandoro's back with his clawed fingers. "Hikoo has many brothers and sisters, but he has outgrown his nest and now must live alone for one whole forest-year before returning to his tribe, see."

Edward grinned. "Like a rite of passage!" He liked the idea.

Cliff smirked. "Isn't this kinda cheating then? Since you're not technically alone?"

The animal shuddered. "It is good that Hikoo found friends. Many brothers and sisters do not return home…"

Edward peered into the forest and wondered what else might be lurking in its shadows.

*

The moon was glowing brightly by the time they reached the convergence of the two forests, and the pale light made the trees appear ghostly. The bush stretched out for miles in front of them. Tall, thick trunks blocked their way like wooden bars, beyond which lay nothing but darkness and eerie silence.

Hikoo fidgeted. "We shouldn't enter in the dark."

Edward narrowed his eyes. "Is there something we should know about, Hikoo?"

Hikoo trembled. "Only that Master Sting must be cautious around this forest."

"What's different about it?" Cliff asked.

Hikoo looked between them, nose twitching. His little mind seemed to be racing. "There is no difference, only that we must always be cautious."

"All right," Edward said, but he didn't like Hikoo's nerves; they were compounding his own misgivings about the forest. "I'll take the first watch." The two boys and their guide dismounted and set up camp. Soon, Cliff slipped into his sleeping sack, and much to the plump young man's annoyance, Hikoo curled up on top of him and fell fast asleep.

Edward, meanwhile, dropped onto a nearby log with some sticks and leaves he had gathered, and to keep himself awake, attempted to start a fire the old-fashioned way, as his grandfather had taught him when he was small. After half an hour, all he had to show for it were a few stinging blisters.

He sighed and threw the sticks down, rubbing his hands and feeling a little drowsy. He thought about waking Cliff up as cold air bit at his ears, and he pulled up the collar of his waistcoat to cover them. The warmth felt better.

Soon, he forgot all about Cliff and began to fall into a drowsy slumber. He could feel himself fading but was powerless to stop it. Then there was nothing. Suddenly, Edward's eyes shot open as he became aware of something creeping around in the darkness nearby. He sat up, following the faint sound of footsteps, his heartbeat quickening. He knew that he couldn't have been asleep for long; Cliff was still snoring loudly, and Hikoo hadn't moved. Something crunched on the earth behind him then. He jerked his head around, but there was nothing but his breath fogging up the air, and the sound of his pulse pounding in his neck.

Gripping his sword with one hand, he got to his feet and crept around a small mound in the earth and towards the forest's edge, until he was so close that he could reach out and touch the nearest branches. The trees stared back at him like faceless warriors guarding some hidden secret. A hollow echo was emanating from the woods like music, and suddenly, Edward felt perfectly calm, like someone had draped a warm blanket over his shoulders. The music grew until it was ringing in his ears, and then it faded. He rubbed his eyes and blinked in the darkness, but the forest was still. He let out a dry laugh then. He was imagining things.

"I wouldn't go in there if I were you."

Edward whirled around, sword raised, and his jaw dropped. Shanley Brooks was staring back at him, and he had never looked so pleased.

Chapter 5

A Walk in the Woods

"Would you like to join me?" Brooks was hunched over a small fire.

Edward stumbled towards him. Surely, he must be hallucinating.

"You won't need that," Brooks said casually, nodding towards his side.

Edward glanced down and realised that he was still gripping his sword. He dropped it in the grass. The move was meant to be dramatic, but Brooks paid no attention.

Edward rolled his eyes. "What do you want me to say?"

Brooks threw some wood on the flames. "You could start with 'thank you'."

"I could," Edward said as he slumped on the ground near the fire. The heat felt good on his numb hands. "You've been following us?"

Brooks nodded. "Your escape has proven rather embarrassing for the king." He paused. "People are starting to ask questions they're not supposed to ask."

"We know all about the realms," Edward blurted. He'd expected Brooks to be taken by surprise, but the duke didn't even raise an eyebrow. Instead, he leaned back and laughed.

"Actually, the king wanted me to kill you. Your execution would be the easiest solution, and one he will no doubt enact upon your return."

Edward swallowed. He was beginning to regret making a fool of King Sento. His grandpa had been right to slip away quietly.

"So, why aren't I dead yet?"

Brooks smiled. "Good question." Edward scowled at the condescension in his voice, like a teacher congratulating a child. "You're not dead because I'm not here to kill you. I'm here to help you."

Now it was Edward's turn to laugh. "You're kidding."

Brooks' small, dark eyes dug into him. "You won't last a week without me."

"Why do you even want to help?"

He gazed past him, across the hills. "Your grandfather didn't deserve what happened to him."

Edward sat up in the firelight. "You knew my grandpa?" Then it hit him: the apprentice Scruff had mentioned.

"Simon was a good friend. When you were young, too young to remember, he showed me the secrets of Teradowa and the realms. I wouldn't have become a duke without him." Edward's head was spinning. All this time, he'd had no idea. "If I can, I'd like to save him."

"But until we left," Edward said, the pieces starting to fall together, "you couldn't go after him without Sento becoming suspicious."

"As far as he knows, I am pursuing you."

For a moment, Edward almost admired Brooks, realizing that it must have been exhausting, playing a role like his for years. Then a thought struck him.

"Why did my grandpa go to Regnum?"

Brooks shook his head. "He never talked about it; he was

very secretive about such things."

Another shape crept out of the darkness then, and Cliff plopped down by the fire, his thick brown hair ruffled from sleep. He stared at Brooks for a moment, and then looked pointedly at Edward, as though to ask for an explanation, but all that came out was a dry laugh.

*

"I don't buy it," Cliff said, a few minutes later.

"Buy what you want. I wouldn't be here if it wasn't true."

"You've never once been on our side. Why start now?"

"This is important," Brooks said, tossing more sticks on the fire.

Edward put up his hands. "He has a point. And we need him."

Cliff's face twisted with rage in the orange glow of the flames. "You've already decided without me!"

Edward sighed, and with a gentle voice said, "He wants to help." He didn't want Cliff to get upset. Nothing good ever happened when Cliff got upset.

"Just because he says he knew your grandpa, suddenly he's all right?"

Brooks' eyes were looking back and forth between them, following the conversation with seeming indifference.

"Yes, he is!"

Cliff grunted, his lip curling somewhat in anger.

Brooks turned to Cliff. "You should listen to Sting."

Cliff growled. "We don't need you."

"Really?" The duke laughed. "You have no idea where you are, and you've allowed this skulposis to lead you into a dead end."

"This *what?*" Edward asked.

"This creature." Brooks pointed at Hikoo, curled up on the grass. "He's a skulposis. They're attention seekers, notorious for playing tricks on strangers."

Upon hearing this, Edward blushed, and Cliff looked likely to kick the sleeping creature... or perhaps Brooks. *Yep,* Edward thought. *He's upset.*

Brooks continued. "It seems obvious to me that you do need my help." With that, he crossed his arms and fell silent.

Cliff blew out a gust of hot air and jumped to his feet.

"Where are you going?" Edward asked.

Cliff shot Brooks a look. "Away from him!"

Edward hesitated, unsure what to say as he watched Cliff storm away into the darkness.

"Let him go," Brooks said.

Edward slumped back in the grass, already exhausted by everything that had happened. He wished it could be morning already. He was anxious to get to Dobson's Canyon. Being in a new realm had so far turned out to be much less exciting than he'd imagined.

*

Sunlight seeped through the trees and pierced Edward's eyes. He yawned and stretched his long legs. The blazing fire was now a pile of smouldering embers, and the air smelled sweet.

Across the fire from him, Brooks was sprawled on his back, his chest rising and falling with deep relaxed breaths. Edward looked around, but Cliff was nowhere to be found. Suddenly, he jumped up, remembering his friend's anger from the night before, and his breath caught in his throat.

"Brooks!" Edward dashed over to the sleeping man, wincing and gritting his teeth, having inadvertently stepped on burning red coal. "Brooks!" He shook the nobleman.

One eye cracked open, then the other. "What?" he asked, annoyed.

"Have you seen Cliff this morning?"

Brooks sat up and rubbed his eyes. "Well, I've only just woken up, Sting."

"Maybe he went to find some food?" Edward suggested, unable to keep the desperation from his voice.

"No. I didn't hear anything."

"You don't think he got lost, do you?"

Brooks stroked his chin. "Well, whatever happened, he couldn't have gone far."

"You don't think so?"

He shook his head. "He'd be killed long before that. There're things in this forest that ought to be left alone."

"What! Why'd you let him go then?" Edward cried.

Brooks rummaged around the fire, gathering his things.

"I thought he would come back last night. He probably ran into trouble and decided to wait until morning, that's all."

That's all? This was ridiculous. He wanted to punch Brooks right in his stupid face.

"What if he's hurt?"

"Relax," Brooks said, slinging his bag over the back of his bandoro. "Now come on," he said. "We'd better find Mr Milly before something else does."

*

The first thing Edward noticed about the forest was how cold it was. As they rode through the dense woods, he felt like he was trapped in an ice box. Hikoo was agitated as well, but not because of the weather. The little skulposis was pressed up against Edward's stomach, his blue fur standing on end, and his eyes kept darting into the bushes at every tiny rustle. Despite his effort not to let Brooks see him shiver, Edward couldn't help but chatter his teeth and rub his arms as they trotted down the beaten dirt path.

"W-why is it so cold?"

"The forest doesn't want us here," Brooks said. "It's trying to drive us out."

Edward's head was swimming. Was that why the weather had been so strange?

"But how can a forest have—"

"You might find that the farther you get from Teradowa, the less you understand."

Edward rolled his eyes; he'd had enough of Brooks' condescension for one day. The man seemed to despise him for no reason. Was he jealous of Edward's relationship with his grandfather? He couldn't imagine Shanley Brooks being jealous of anyone, but maybe he didn't like the attention Edward got from his grandpa. Maybe he wished Simon had spent more time teaching him and less time with Edward.

As they trudged along, the brown tree trunks started to blend until Edward could have sworn that they were going in circles. The trail wound up and down, cut corners, and crossed rivers like a snake that trampled over everything. It was so naturally carved that he wondered who had made it, and suddenly found himself peering nervously into the woods along with Hikoo. The idea of unseen creatures lurking about—or people for that matter—didn't appeal to him.

Brooks tugged on the reins of his bandoro, and the beast came to a stop.

"What is it?" Edward whispered. The older man put up his hand for silence. Up ahead, the bushes rustled, and a dull rattle filled the air. Hikoo sprang from Edward's lap and darted for cover. The rattle came again, and Edward swallowed a lump in his throat.

"Move," Brooks hissed, leaping to the ground and dragging his bag with him. Edward quickly followed suit, dismounting, and dashing across the path before diving into a hollow behind some trees. He pressed up against one of the trunks, gritting his teeth, and dared a glance back.

A monster was striding out of the woods on two legs. Red eyes peered out from its skull and scanned the path. Its tall, muscular body was covered in dark orange fur and two horns looped up from either side of its head, forming a sort of crown. It looked like something out of a nightmare. The thing teetered forward, mere inches at a time, and Edward realised suddenly that its tiny red eyes could barely see. The creature stopped, scrunching up its snout for a moment, and then sprang forward with a snarl, following the pungent odour of the bandoros.

The beast's tongue lolled from its open mouth as it dashed down the path—showing no signs of its previous uncertainty—revealing razor-sharp teeth. The three bandoros formed a wall, and the earth shook as the four bodies came together. The first bandoro dodged a blow, and with amazing agility for such a powerful creature, slid between the beast's legs.

The monster swung low after it and roared as a set of jaws clamped down on its arm. Then it lashed out with its claws, and the bandoro slammed into a tree. The other two leapt onto the creature then and sunk their teeth into its back. It growled as fur and flesh were ripped away. The first bandoro returned to the fight, latching onto one of the monster's legs. The other two were shaken off but not deterred and quickly took hold of its other one.

The beast slipped then and crashed to the earth, but the bandoros did not relent, shaking it between them like an enormous ragdoll. Orange and golden fur flashed in a tangle of limbs, and Edward's ears were filled with the most horrific sounds he had ever heard.

In a last-ditch effort, the monster jabbed the first bandoro with his horns. The other two charged but not before the beast rammed the first again, which squealed in agony and collapsed. The monster then shoved past the two remaining steeds, and suddenly, it was streaking towards Edward and Brooks.

"Run!" Brooks shouted.

Edward didn't need to be told. He was already charging through the bush with Brooks hot on his heels, but it was useless, and within a few strides, the wounded beast had caught up to them. Brooks dove behind a tree just as its claws came down. Missing him by a hair, they struck the trunk and sank deep into the wood. The tree crashed to the ground. The monster roared with rage, and Edward felt his whole body vibrate.

Brooks tried to shimmy away, but this time, he wasn't as lucky. The beast grazed his left leg with its claws, and he crumpled to the ground. Edward watched in horror as the monster raised its arm for a final blow. But before it could strike, an arrow whizzed through the air and struck the giant between the eyes. It fell to the ground dead.

Chapter 6

The Drifter in Exile

Edward scanned the trees. The forest was completely still. It was as if nothing had happened. His pulse pounded in his neck and his breath came out in short bursts. A loud groan pierced the air then, bringing him back to the present. He scrambled through the bush to where Brooks was lying with his back up against a tree, gripping his wounded leg. Edward knelt beside him and looked at the bloody gash, then looked away, gagging.

"Oh gee. You're cut pretty bad."

"A brilliant observation."

"W-what should I do?"

"If you would be so kind…" Brooks gestured to his bag. "Bandages…"

"Oh, okay." Edward fumbled with the bag for a moment, and finally pulled out a set of wrappings.

"Pretty lucky, that arrow, huh?" he said, getting to work on Brooks leg, his eyes darting around the forest all the while. "Where'd you think it came from?"

"Ow!" Brooks wheezed, clenching his fists.

"Sorry."

Edward was nearly done. Suddenly a shout arose from behind him: "Hands in the air!"

He spun around. A young woman, no older than himself, stood several yards away. Her black hair was tied in a tight bun, and she wore a brown tunic that was tied at the waist and made her blend into the trees. She stared at Edward with bright-green eyes.

So startled was he that it took him a moment to notice the drawn arrow aimed directly at his forehead. He threw his hands in the air.

"Who are you?" she demanded.

Edward glanced at Brooks. "Um... My name is Edward Sting, and this," he gestured to the fallen duke with a slight nudge of his head, "is Shanley Brooks."

She glared at them. "You almost ruined that kill for me."

"What?"

"That noguchi," she said. "I've been hunting it for weeks."

"Oh," Edward said, wondering what on earth she was talking about.

She stormed past them and knelt down over the carcass; a thin streak of green blood oozed from its wound and trickled down its orange fur. She yanked the arrow out of its skull and wiped it on a bush.

"I guess it's lucky for you that I was," she said, returning the arrow to her quiver.

"Thanks for that, by the way," Edward said, letting his hands fall to his sides as he gazed into the noguchi's face; its permanent snarl stared back at him. He felt nauseous.

Brooks spat. "You couldn't have killed that thing *before* it attacked us?"

The girl glared at him then turned to Edward. "What are you doing way out here?"

He hesitated but only for a moment. He wasn't sure who this girl was, but he didn't think lying would help them. "We're looking for somebody."

Brooks grunted. "Our business doesn't concern her."

She raised an eyebrow. "You're in my forest, so I think it does."

Edward raised his hands in appeasement. "We don't mean to intrude. A member of our group went missing last night."

"Is that right?"

"Look," he said, "you seem to know your way around here; we could really use your help."

She eyed him for a moment, and suddenly, Edward felt completely naked, as though all his shortcomings were on full display. Then she stuck out her hand. "I'm Willow."

Edward smiled. "Nice to meet you." He took her hand and shook it. It was warm and soft.

"I think you and your friend better come with me," Willow said; then she turned and began weaving back through the bush.

Edward looked at Brook's injured leg and then back towards the path, hoping to spot the bandoros, but they were nowhere to be seen. Finally, resigning himself to the effort, he helped Brooks' up, slung his arm over his shoulder, and headed after her. She took them deeper into the bush, crossing creeks and streams, hobbling up rocky ridges and down steep ravines until Edward was certain that he would never be able to find his way back to the path. All the while, Brooks leaned heavily on him, making the journey feel more impossible with every step.

When Willow finally signalled for them to stop in a dense area of the forest with no shelter in sight, he was dripping with sweat and ready to pass out.

Her eyes were darting through the trees.

"What's wrong?" Edward whispered.

"Is it possible someone is following you?"

Brooks scoffed. "Most certainly not."

There came a rustle in the bushes then, and Willow raised her bow.

"Don't shoot! Please!" a small voice squeaked.

She pushed the leaves aside, and Hikoo dashed into the clearing, his blue fur shining like a beacon amidst the greenery.

"There you are," Edward said. Hikoo bounced around at his feet like an excited child. "This is Hikoo." Edward looked at Willow. "He's—"

"A skulposis," she said, smirking. "They don't usually wander into this part of the forest. I think I scare them."

"Master Sting... Hikoo followed your scent, see? And I brought the creatures too!"

Edward gasped. By this time, he had forgotten all about the bandoros. Hikoo shot Willow a nervous glance and then darted past them through the bush. They followed him into a small clearing where the two surviving bandoros were grazing, their golden fur matted from battle. Edward's heart leapt, and he gaped at the little trickster.

"You did this?"

Hikoo's blue fur glowed deep purple for a moment at the admiration.

Willow laughed. "He's a smart little guy. He knew exactly where we were going."

Edward furrowed his brow. "What do you mean?"

She pointed to an enormous tree at the edge of the clearing. "We're here."

Edward crept over to the tree with Brooks limping behind him. When he was only a few feet away, he noticed that rungs had been carved out of the trunk and darkened with soot to match the colour of the bark. *Cleverly disguised.* Craning his neck upwards, he saw that the rungs disappeared into the high foliage of the tree.

He gaped at her. "You live up there?" He had never seen something so incredible.

"Yup." She brushed past him and started up the ladder. Edward followed her. They climbed until he could see the sky poking through the very highest branches, where they reached a platform made from old, dry logs that had been sanded down and tied together.

Half the platform was covered by a straw roof that brushed against the treetop, and on the other side, a makeshift pavilion stood in the shade of another branch. The deck perched between three thick limbs as if a giant had reached up from the forest floor and was holding them in its palm.

Edward peered over the side of the deck to where they had left the bandoros tethered to the base of the tree. Willow appeared by his side. "Are you sure they'll be okay down there?"

She nodded. "Noguchis are very territorial; you won't find another one for miles. Besides, not much can challenge those beasts you've got."

"I see," Edward said, feeling more unsure by the minute. A young woman living alone in the forest, hunting monsters? It all seemed very strange to him. "How did you build all this?"

She shrugged. "I have a lot of spare time."

There was a loud crash behind them, and they turned. Brooks had attempted to lower himself into a mesh hammock and slipped, slamming into a wooden table and spilling glass vials across the deck.

Edward raced over and scooped up the vials, setting them carefully back down where they belonged.

"You better let me look at your leg," Willow said.

Brooks scoffed. "I'm fine."

"You don't look fine."

She snatched up one of the bottles. A dark green fluid swished around inside. "Here," she said.

Brooks gritted his teeth as she pulled back his bandages. The gash was deep and ran the length of his shin. She poured out some of the liquid over the cut, and Brooks' sallow face contorted for a moment. Then the broken skin tightened, and the wound closed. Edward's eyebrows shot up.

"You'll have a nasty bruise for a few days," she said, tossing the bandage aside, "but it beats wearing this thing."

Brooks grunted.

"How did you do that?" Edward asked.

Willow folded her arms. "I've got some questions of my own first."

He swallowed nervously as she plucked the bottles off the table and strolled over to a shelf under the roof, where she set them next to a row of sealed jars full of a gooey substance. Edward strained his neck to get a look at the sheltered area. Yellowing papers hung on the wall behind her—rough sketches of maps and charts.

"So," she said, returning, "this missing friend of yours, does he have a name?"

"Cliff."

Willow's green eyes searched his face. Her fair skin made her cheeks seem to glow, and when she stared at him, Edward felt like he had nowhere to hide.

After a moment, she laughed.

"What's so funny?"

She crossed her arms. "You're from Teradowa, aren't you?"

Edward stuttered. "How did you—"

She waved her hand dismissively. "Because I've already

found your Teradowian friend."

"*What?* Where is he?"

She inclined her head, and Edward followed her gaze across the deck. A curtain made of dried flora hung in the corner. He crept over and drew it back. Another hammock—this one sagging heavily—hung just a foot off the ground, and the faint sound of snoring drifted from it. He put his hands on the bottom of the hammock and tipped it.

Cliff dropped onto the deck and was jolted awake. "Ow!"

Edward cheered. "Cliff!"

His friend blinked a few times; then his face lit up. "Ed?"

Edward slapped his friend on the back.

"So, you two do know each other," Willow said.

Edward nodded. "You could say that."

Brooks growled. "Why didn't you say something before?"

She shrugged. "I thought maybe there was a reason he ran away from you two. He was pretty hard to get answers out of last night."

Cliff scoffed. "This place is a nightmare, Ed."

"Tell me about it. Brooks and I got attacked by this huge monster, and Willow saved us."

Willow dropped into a chair. "Seems like all I've been doing lately."

Cliff chuckled. "She try to kill you too?"

She glared at him. "Maybe Edward would like to know how I found you: curled up in a ball, looking like you might cry."

Cliff blushed; then Hikoo dashed over and leapt onto his shoulder.

"Hullo, Hikoo," he grumbled.

The skulposis licked his ear. "Hikoo is so happy to see Master Milly is okay."

"I told you not to call me that."

By this time, the sun had melted away and been replaced by the moon, which cast a pale light through the tops of the trees. Willow yawned and nodded to a stone firepit near the centre of the deck. "If you two would like to make yourselves useful, you could build us a little fire."

Edward and Cliff busied themselves while Brooks brooded in the corner. Edward elected to use matches this time rather than repeat his pitiful failure from the night before, and soon they had a sizzling fire.

"So, what are four Teradowians doing sneaking around Candosia?" Willow asked when they were all seated around the flames.

Edward glanced at Cliff, who was watching him expectantly. Brooks had resigned himself to observing the scene, his will to control it tempered by irritation and the lingering ache of his injury.

Edward leaned forward. "We're going to Dobson's Canyon."

Willow raised an eyebrow.

"Do you know it?" he asked.

She gazed at the fire; her eyes filled with gloom. "Sure, I know it. I used to live there."

Cliff frowned. "And now you live in a forest?"

"Things change." She sighed and shook her head. "I used to love my kingdom. We all did. Believing everything that was taught in the stories read to us as children. That the gods protect us. That the king speaks for them and thus must be worshipped. That our realm is the gods' gift to us… and that we are the last pocket of civilization in an otherwise barren world. But it's all a lie. The gods aren't real. The nobles brainwash us so that they can control us. Once I learned that, I decided that nobody could be free until the borders separating our realms, the kings, and the whole rotten ruling class was gone."

"You're a drifter then?" Edward said.

She frowned. "I do not know this name, but I have no love for the king, if that is what you mean."

"How did you find out the truth?" Cliff said.

Willow shifted in her seat. "I trusted some people I shouldn't have. But I wasn't going to keep quiet once I knew, so King Pentheus gave me a new home." She gestured to the forest. "Somewhere I couldn't cause any more trouble."

Edward nodded. Something was off about her response, and he got the feeling she wasn't telling them the whole story.

"Why not just kill you?" he asked, feeling uncomfortable discussing such a weighty issue, but Willow didn't seem to notice or care.

"He wouldn't dare. King Pentheus's rule isn't as strong as he makes it look. If he steps too far out of line, there are people who would be more than happy to see him go."

Brooks narrowed his eyes. "And those people are your friends?"

Willow shot him a look. "Some of them."

Edward put his elbows on his knees and leaned forward. "Do you think you could get us passage through Dobson's Canyon?"

She stared at him again, this time with obvious suspicion. "Why? Where are you heading?"

"Regnum."

Willow laughed. "Are you crazy? Have you not heard the stories?"

"What stories?" Edward asked.

Willow shook her head. "All I've heard is that the king there is some kind of real-life wizard, and not the good kind. Not exactly a pleasant place to visit."

Edward's stomach churned, and for the first time since this adventure had begun, he thought about what might be waiting for them at the end of all this.

"We have a good reason for going," he explained to her about his grandfather and his sudden departure, about the letter he had received, the chaos of Life Day, and how they had also discovered the truth about the realms, from Scruff, before escaping Teradowa to rescue Simon.

"I'm sorry," she said when he was finished, "but it's not like you can just walk through the city and out the other side. If I go back there, Pentheus will kill me, and I'm guessing you as well."

Edward thought about that for a moment, then with a confident nod, sprang to his feet. "So, we get rid of him."

"What?" Cliff said in disbelief.

Willow laughed. "It's not going to be that easy."

Edward shrugged. "Look what we did in Teradowa. And you said it yourself: there are people here that can help us."

She gazed at him, and he saw something else in her green eyes for the first time, something intense. "Maybe… and maybe not. But either way, you two are going to have to get in better shape if you expect to have any sort of chance of coming out of this alive."

Cliff swallowed hard, and Edward patted his friend on the back. He could feel his energy returning to him, like a jolt of lightning. He soaked it in.

"And what about you?" Willow said, turning to Brooks. "Are you in?"

Brooks grunted. "Whatever gets us out of this tree."

*

Over the next week, the group stayed with Willow, training and planning. Edward was reluctant to hang around at first. Having found Cliff and gotten Brooks back on his feet, he was anxious to reach Dobson's Canyon. But Willow had insisted that they were not ready, and within a few days, Edward found that he was enjoying the lessons she was giving them.

She taught Edward how to track prey and shoot a bow. They spent hours practising together in the forest; however, by the fifth morning, he was still struggling to hit his targets. Willow watched with her hands on her hips.

"Aim a little higher. You're starting to fall flat again."

Edward let another arrow fly. It sailed through the bush and wedged into the tree bark a foot and a half below the orange marker.

"Remember what I said about the wind."

He set his jaw and drew back another arrow. It whizzed through the air and landed nearly as low as its predecessor. He sighed and swallowed his frustration. Almost a week, and he still couldn't get it right.

Willow yanked the arrows out of the tree. "Better, but remember… at this distance, the wind will have more effect than you think."

Edward nodded. "All right. Again?"

"No, that's good for now. Let's go eat."

Edward gathered his things and caught up to Willow. He could hear his stomach growling; he hadn't eaten all morning.

When they got back to the treehouse, they found Cliff deep in an argument with Hikoo while Brooks sat nearby, sharpening his dagger, and frowning at the squabbling duo.

"All I'm saying is that, if you're gonna sleep on me, at least wash yourself first."

Hikoo's dark pupils ballooned. "Master Milly does not like Hikoo's company?"

"That's not what I said."

They glanced up as Edward and Willow appeared.

"Where have you two been on this fine morning?" Cliff asked. Seeing the quiver around Edward's shoulder, he added, "Any improvement today, Ed?" Having gotten the handle of the bow much quicker than Edward, he was enjoying having a leg up on his friend.

Edward fidgeted. "A little."

"He's doing fine," Willow said. "Haven't you had enough of that?" she asked, as Cliff stuffed another hunk of bread into his mouth. "It doesn't grow on trees you know."

Cliff blushed.

Brooks rose from his work and made his way to the table. "Perhaps we should talk about our plans?"

Willow dropped into a chair. "I'm beat."

The duke made a dull huffing noise and stormed back to the corner.

Willow watched him go. "What's his problem?"

Both boys laughed. "We have a number of theories," Cliff said.

*

After they ate, Edward and Willow, along with Cliff, gathered their gear and prepared to head out for the day. Hikoo, as always, tagged along. The sun was shining through the trees, casting a green glow around the woods.

"Sure you don't want to come, Brooks?" Edward asked.

The older man nodded. "I am. Someone should watch the camp."

Willow reluctantly allowed him to stay. She hadn't taken her suspicious eyes off him since they'd met. Edward supposed it was because Brooks was a duke. Willow seemed to hold a grudge against the nobles, even more than most.

"How do we know he isn't going to run off with my things?" she asked, on the way down the ladder.

"Brooks may be a grump, but trust me, he wouldn't do that," Edward said, giving his bandoro a pat as they passed.

As they made their way along a nearby ridge, he pushed a few locks of blond hair out of his eyes. There was something about the forest that fascinated him. He didn't know what it was, but he thrived on it. Like there was a rope tied around him, tethering him to some unknown source of comfort. The cold that he had felt upon entering the forest had long since gone, and now it felt as though he had been reunited with an old friend.

Willow put out her hand, and they stopped. Cliff, Edward, and Hikoo crawled up beside her and poked their heads out of the bush.

"I think we've got a live one," Willow said.

"I'll shoot it," Edward said, excited for the chance to prove himself.

Willow grinned. "All right, hotshot," she said and pushed aside. Edward felt his heartbeat quicken. Willow was right. He could hear an animal rustling in the bushes up ahead. Propping his arm up on a fallen tree, he drew back the bow until the string was taut. A moment later, about thirty yards away, the animal appeared: a large, grey dog, which began prowling in their direction. Edward closed one eye, trying to centre his shoot.

"Let's go," Willow whispered tensely.

"It's all right. I've almost got him."

More dogs appeared then and started creeping towards them, but he nearly had the shot.

"Come on!" Cliff hissed, already on his feet, a hysterical Hikoo scooped under his arm.

He could do it. He was so close. *Just hold still,* he thought. The air was ringing with canine snarls.

"Edward!" Willow tugged at his arm, and he finally looked up. She was white as a ghost. Suddenly realizing the danger, he sprang to his feet, staggering backward, his pack slipping from his shoulder.

"Leave it!"

They rushed through the bush as the dogs barked and growled and nipped at their heels, so close that Edward could smell their feral odour.

"They're getting closer!" he shouted.

To his amazement, Willow stopped dead and turned to face them. Fumbling with a little bottle, she twisted off the lid and released an arc of clear liquid that fell in waves on the ground all around her. Then she lit a match and dropped it. Instantly, Edward's vision was engulfed in orange flames.

"Hurry!" she shouted. They dashed through the forest away from the flames as the dogs whimpered on the other side of the growing inferno.

They reached the treehouse nearly thirty minutes later and stopped to catch their breath.

Cliff panted. "What *were* those things?"

"Attack dogs," Willow said. "Bred to hunt."

"But why are they out here? Unless…" His voice trailed off, and he glanced at Edward.

"Unless Pentheus knows you're here," Willow finished for them.

They climbed the ladder.

"You're back early," Brooks said.

Edward quickly recounted what happened… to Brooks' dismay. "Sento must have notified Candosia about your escape," he said. "They'll be looking for us now."

Willow gazed out over the forest.

"It won't be long before they find us." Edward could feel dread hanging in the air.

"We go tonight then."

Brooks scoffed. "We should have left a week ago."

"That doesn't matter now. We need to get ready." They spent the afternoon packing supplies and piling it on the bandoros until the two beasts were weighed down with blankets, canteens, pans, and what seemed like all the food in the world. It was dusk by the time they finished, and an orange glow hung over the woods.

Edward had found a rucksack and was using it to store his belongings: a knife, some matches, and a few odds and ends. He slung the bag over his shoulder just as Cliff came huffing and puffing down the ladder. He wore a satchel that was shaking violently. Edward frowned at it for a moment, and then Hikoo's furry blue head popped out.

"Master Sting, we are leaving?"

"I already told you we are," Cliff said, dropping his bag to the ground. Hikoo wiggled out of it and climbed quickly up onto Cliff's head.

"Yes, yes, yes," he said, dragging his fingers across Cliff's face. Cliff shook him off and one look from the red-faced boy sent the little skulposis scurrying back up the ladder.

Cliff eyed the bandoros. "How are we doing?"

"Ready to go," said Edward. "What's the matter?"

"I don't know," Cliff said. "This place gives me the creeps."

Edward didn't understand that; he thought the forest was beautiful. "Listen, I'm sorry about Brooks. I know you don't want him here."

Cliff shrugged. "You were right though. I think we need him."

Edward grinned. "He should be so lucky."

They climbed back to the treehouse to ensure they hadn't forgotten anything vital just as the stars were beginning to peek through the trees.

Willow appeared by Edward's side, her black hair hanging smoothly down over her shoulders like a waterfall. It was much longer than Edward had thought.

"You okay?" she asked.

He shrugged.

She bit her lip. "It's just that earlier, with the dogs... it was like you weren't there."

He had almost forgotten about the incident with the dogs. Embarrassed, he shook his head. He'd heard all his life about what a wonder he had been as a child, his grandfather always eager to regale him with tales of the remarkable acuity and physical competence he'd displayed practically from the womb. Sadly, it seemed he had grown out of it. Part of him wanted to tell Willow the truth: that he still wished he could have just taken the shot and at least shown *himself* that he could do it.

He cleared his throat. "Sorry about that. And thanks for bailing us out again."

She laughed. "Don't worry. I'm getting used to it."

Her green eyes danced over him, and he suddenly felt

lightheaded. "Here," she said, and he glanced down at her hands. She was holding a long canvas wrapping. "It's for you."

He unfolded the package, and inside, he found a polished, wooden bow. She looked back and forth between him and the bow. "I know it's a bit old, but what's the use of learning to shoot if you don't have a bow of your own."

"Willow… it's beautiful."

She smiled. "Just don't go and break it on me."

Edward held the bow up to his shoulder and aimed it over the deck rail. Its weight felt good in his grip. He wished he were a better shot though, it seemed phony of him to have a bow of his own when he couldn't really shoot. He closed one eye and pretended to scan the woods. Then something made him stop.

"What's that?"

Willow peered over the rail, and her face grew dark. "Oh no. They're here."

A hooded figure was zigzagging through the trees towards them. Then more emerged, one by one, until a swarm of men was circling the tree (careful to stay out of reach of the bandoros). Then, from the heights of the surrounding trees, cloaked figures swung outward and onto the deck. Two landed on either side of Edward and Willow and ushered them with the tips of their cutlasses away from the edge of the deck and into its centre.

"Hey! Watch where you point that thing!"

Edward glanced up at the sound of Cliff's voice and found that his friend and Brooks were facing a similar fate.

Soon they were surrounded by men covered from head to toe in green robes. One held a torch and was lighting the torches of the others in turn. Finally, there came the sound of footfalls on the ladder, and a man appeared.

He was in his mid-thirties with dark hair, and he wore a

smart green waistcoat. When he saw Willow, he smiled, exposing a row of perfect teeth.

"Willow, darling, it's been too long."

Willow sighed. "Hello, Kincaid."

The man strode into the circle of light, where Edward could see him clearly. He had handsome features, but there was something devilish in his dark eyes that made his good looks almost eerie.

Kincaid took Willow's chin between his fingers. "Look at you. You're all grown up," he said, his gaze lingering.

She twisted away from his grip. "I'm a little insulted... You only brought twelve men."

Kincaid paced around the circle. "There are thirteen of us, sweetheart."

"*You* don't count."

His smile faded. "I'd forgotten how charming you are. I think it was that attitude that got you banished. If only you'd been a bit more... open minded... things could have worked out better."

Willow shifted uncomfortably beside Edward, who got the idea that Kincaid had struck a nerve.

"Maybe we can work something out," Edward said before he could stop himself.

Kincaid stopped pacing and turned towards him. "Ah, you must be Mr Sting. You see, Willow, it's your new friends here that you have to thank for my little visit. As you know, King Pentheus likes to keep in touch with our Teradowian friends." He glanced back at Edward. "And it sounds like this one's been making a little trouble."

"I think you'll find we can make trouble very easily."

Kincaid laughed. "King Sento called you a coward, Mr

Sting, but perhaps he had you wrong."

Brooks stepped forward. "We don't want to cause trouble for Candosia. If you let us go, nothing will come of it."

"I wish I could believe you, but then... I'd have to ask myself what you're doing with her," he pointed to Willow, "a known danger to Candosia."

Edward glanced at Willow, but her eyes were locked on Kincaid.

"Besides," he continued, eyeing Brooks, "I was told I'd find two fugitives, and here I am with three, which begs the question of who *you* are?"

Brooks glared at the man.

Kincaid smirked. "Perhaps we don't need to find out. It doesn't really matter." He strolled over to the shelter. "This is a nice little place you have, Willow," he said, squinting at a jar of some dark, slimy paste. "It's a shame this will be our last visit."

"Then you'd better kill me. Cause if you don't, and I see you again, you'll wish you had."

Kincaid stopped by the ladder and a flicker of something crossed his face—so quick that Edward wasn't sure he'd really seen it. Unfortunately, he was far too familiar with the look of pity in a man's eyes to mistake it.

"I'm sorry," Kincaid said then, and gave a shrill whistle. The men in robes began ransacking the treehouse. They toppled shelfs and smashed tables until the deck looked like a battlefield. Then, one by one, they dropped their torches and set the tree ablaze. Shouts drifted up from the ground, and Edward knew the same thing was happening below.

He looked back at the ladder then, but Kincaid was gone. Immediately, the cloaked figures pounced on them, their swords slicing the air with ferocity. Just as fast, Willow drew her bow, her arrow catching the first man just above the armpit. Edward felt his heartbeat quicken as the man sank to his knees.

He unsheathed his own sword for the first time. The crackle of fire boomed in his ears as flames crept around the deck. Another man, following quickly behind the first, charged at Willow. She let another arrow fly, but he smacked it aside. She ducked as he swung his blade at her throat.

Edward found himself staring in amazement until something struck him on the side, and he crashed to the deck. A man crouched above him; his sword raised above his head. Panicked, Edward slid out of the way just as the blade came down. A surge of adrenaline shot through him, and he pounced on his attacker, taking the man by both wrists and wrestling the sword from his grasp. It fell to the deck with a thud.

The man wrenched his clenched hand free and thrust it into Edward's gut. Edward felt all the air escape him then, and he collapsed to the deck. The wood was hot against his skin. The man reached for his sword, but Edward kicked his feet out and slammed him into the rail. Undeterred, the man staggered back towards Edward and swung at him, missing by a mile before losing his balance and flipping over the rail, plummeting to the flames below.

Edward wiped the sweat from his forehead. The fire was eating the treehouse alive. It roared like an angry predator, gobbling up everything in its path. Flames licked every branch and were reducing the leaves to ash. The roof of the shelter suddenly collapsed in a burning heap, crushing a warrior who was fighting Brooks.

Edward spun around, shielding himself from the heat. Through the haze of smoke, he could see Willow, struggling against her attacker. She narrowly avoided the man's cutlass and kicked his feet out from under him, but he was up before she could pin him. Edward lunged forward, catching the man off guard, and tackled him.

"Look out!"

Behind him, Willow had lifted a wooden barrel to her shoulders. He rolled out of the way just as she brought it down on the man's head, leaving him unconscious on the deck. She glanced at Edward, panting.

"Thanks." The air was filled with another crack as one of the tree branches above them snapped.

"Jump!" Edward shouted as it came sailing towards them. They leapt aside as it smashed through the deck, splitting the treehouse in two.

For a moment, the large branch teetered between the two halves of the deck, then it lurched forward and slid through the opening. It disappeared into the flames below, and a moment later, it slammed into the forest floor. The broken deck faltered then, tossing Edward and Willow towards the gap. Edward clutched frantically at the wood as they rolled towards certain doom.

Finally, he managed to wedge his fingers into a crack, and with his other hand, he grabbed Willow's arm and pulled them to level ground. From his knees, he squinted through the smoke and saw Brooks by the ladder. He watched as the man jabbed the last remaining warrior in the chin and pitched him over the rail. Beside him stood Cliff. The gap that separated them was too great, and there was no way to get across.

He tried to call over to them, but his voice was lost to the roar of the flames. Below his knees, the wood was beginning to weaken; it was only a matter of minutes, possibly seconds, before it gave way.

"What now?"

Willow coughed. "Come with me." She waved for Brooks and Cliff to start down the ladder, then taking Edward's hand, she led him around the corner of the pavilion—now a smouldering wreck—and onto a narrow stretch of wood. After a few paces, the wood ended abruptly and gave way to the open night air. It looked as though Willow had been building an extension, but it was not yet complete.

Edward furrowed his brow. "How do we get down?" Then he saw Willow grip a thin rope that was hanging from the tree, and a terrible feeling washed over him. "You've got to be kidding me."

He looked down at the forest floor, barely visible in the darkness, and felt his head spin.

"Put your arms around me," she said.

"What?"

"Grab me around the waist!"

"Oh... okay..." He wrapped his arms around her and was thankful that she couldn't see him blush in the dark.

"Ready?"

"Oh, God."

"On three." She tightened her grip. "One..." Behind them, the wood cracked and broke apart. "Two..." Edward swallowed hard. "Three!"

The deck fell away, and cold air rushed past his face, stinging his eyes. His stomach dropped, and he squeezed Willow hard. Below, the dark forest floor grew larger.

"Hold on!" she yelled.

The earth was mere feet away when he found himself soaring upwards again in an arc... and then down they swung once more, though more slowly. Willow let go of the rope, and they dropped to the ground. Edward stared up at the sky, his eyes wide.

He chuckled. "Incredible,"

He turned to Willow then, and his smiled faded. She was staring up at the flames with a very different expression on her face.

"My whole life…" she started. "My whole life was in that tree."

Edward put a hand on her shoulder. "I'm sorry."

They stood in the darkness and watched the treehouse crumble to the ground in a ball of orange flames. "Will it spread?"

"No, not here. The forest will make sure of that."

Edward shuffled his feet. "What does that mean for us?"

Willow peered at him. "What do you mean?"

"You know… Is it mad at us? The forest?"

"Oh." She considered for a moment, and then shrugged. "I don't know."

Cliff and Brooks emerged from the undergrowth then, covered in dirt and soot.

Cliff chuckled. "Boy, that's what I call a campfire gone wrong." Edward shot his friend a look, but the plump boy only took it as encouragement. He nudged Edward on the arm. "We really burned those guys, eh?"

Willow smacked him on the head.

"Ow!"

"That's my *home* you're talking about."

"Geez! Maybe you shouldn't have built your house in a tree then. Think of that?"

Edward had to step between them to avoid a scrap.

Brooks grunted impatiently. "We need to move. We're not

safe sitting here."

"He's right," Edward said.

Behind them, the bandoros came sauntering out of the charred wreckage, completely indifferent to the commotion around them. Edward dashed over to his ride and climbed on. In front of him, Brooks mounted the second creature, and Edward looked down at Willow.

"You can come with me. I mean… if you want."

She shrugged. "Sure." She mounted behind him and rested her hands at his sides. Cliff begrudgingly joined Brooks on the lead bandoro and sat as far back as possible without tumbling off. Hikoo, as always, tagged along with him.

With no moonlight able to penetrate the thick canopy of trees, the only lights were small lanterns hung from the bandoros' harnesses. It was all he could do not to lose track of his friends in the dark. After nearly an hour spent battling fatigue and poor conditions, it was decided that they would stop for the night.

A short time later, as Edward lay in his sleeping sack gazing up at the trees, the events of the day flashed through his mind. After being nearly eaten by dogs and then burned alive, he found himself extremely intent on finding out what tomorrow would bring.

Chapter 7

Dobson's Canyon

Edward awoke to the sound of bickering voices. He sat up and rubbed his neck, fondly recalling the softness of his bed back home. The night before, they had stopped in a small clearing amongst shrubs and fruit trees. All around him, berry bushes swayed in the breeze and waved their blue leaves at him as if to say good morning. It was a pleasant picture. Naturally, Edward found the sight of Brooks and Cliff shouting over one another, and doing a fair bit of finger pointing, an unwelcome addition.

"I just don't understand why you need two?"

Cliff waved a jar of beans in the duke's face. "I told you! This one is from my private stash."

"We're trying to ration!" Brooks argued. Edward approached the fire, over which bread and bacon were toasting in a pan.

"Good morning," he said, not meaning it at all. Cliff and Brooks jumped. "Are you two done? I'd like to enjoy my breakfast."

Brooks grumbled. "I'd say mine has been sufficiently spoiled." He marched away to pack his things as Edward dropped down onto a stump and plucked a piece of crisp bacon from the pan.

"Where's Willow?" he asked. Cliff pointed to a tall tree near the edge of the clearing. "What's she doing up there?"

"Dunno. Been there since I got up."

Edward munched down some food and strolled over to the tree, careful not to crush any berries as he did. Willow was perched on a thick branch, looking through a spyglass. When she heard Edward's approach, she shimmied down the tree and jumped to the ground.

"Nice of you to join us," she said.

"See anything interesting?" Edward asked.

"Actually, yes. I found the ravine."

"What ravine?"

Willow reached into her belt and pulled out a map, which Edward recognised as having come from the treehouse.

"See these lines?" she asked. He nodded. "Dobson's Canyon sits at the bottom of a ravine, or *canyon*. Hence the name."

Edward pulled out his own wrinkled map which he kept in his breast pocket. The markings that his grandfather had sketched matched Willow's. He couldn't believe it. Here was proof that he wasn't chasing a fairy tale.

"Your grandpa must have come this way too," Willow said, looking at his map.

Edward smiled, feeling his heart leap. "So, Scruff was right. They did visit the city."

"It's possible."

He turned and rushed back towards the camp. "Come on!" he called to Willow.

They hastily packed their things and were on the trail to Dobson's Canyon before the sun had risen fully above the trees. Edward basked in the fresh air, listening to the chirping and singing of the birds.

"So, Willow," Cliff said, as they rode along, "how will we know who to trust when we get into the city?"

"I'll know."

"But you haven't been there in over a year."

"Just let me do the talking."

Cliff narrowed his eyes. "Why?"

She smirked. "Because if *you* do the talking, you'll probably end up dead."

Cliff's eyes did a full reverse and nearly popped out of his skull.

As the morning passed, the sky grew darker, and by midafternoon, a storm was gathering. Wind whipped around them like a possessed spirit, throwing debris in their faces.

"What's going on?" Cliff yelled. Edward had no answer. Willow's hands pressed tighter against his stomach as the earth began to rumble. He turned to Brooks and Cliff, but they were gone. Lost behind a wall of dust and rock.

"Hold on!" he shouted and sent his bandoro into a mad dash. Ahead of them, cracks erupted in the forest floor, spraying mud and rock into the air. Dirt stung Edward's eyes and he fought to keep them open as the bandoro leapt from one chunk of earth to the next. Edward glanced down as they sailed over another crack and felt his stomach roll as he lost sight of the bottom. He couldn't even tell whether Willow was still behind him. The massive beast streaked on, careening from side to side as rock and debris crashed down around them.

Then, in an instant, the world imploded.

Mud and rock reversed direction, dropping back into the ground, dragging Edward free from his mount and down along with them, spiralling down, deeper and deeper into the abyss until nothing but blackness remained.

*

Edward's eyelids cracked open, and he sat up, letting his vision adjust to the dark. Throbbing pain shot through him, and he groaned. He felt as though he had been clubbed in the head by a giant. The air was thick, and his breath condensed into a misty cloud when he exhaled. He staggered to his feet and gripped the cold, rock wall. He must have somehow fallen underground. There was wet sand underfoot, which made his footing uneven as he shuffled along the wall. Moving down what seemed to be a tunnel, he thought he could see some light shining in from above at its end.

Then suddenly he thought of Willow. She had been with him when the earth had erupted, hadn't she? Or had she fallen off their bandoro before he'd been swallowed up?

"Willow?" he shouted. The sound boomed off the walls and came back to him. He was all alone.

He crept along the tunnel, keeping one hand on the wall, but then stopped dead. The light at the end had vanished. Instead, there was a wide pool of water up ahead. He strolled up to the edge and peered out over a shallow pond... or perhaps even a lake. He couldn't tell. A deep, grey mist hung over the surface, hiding its far shore.

The surface was as smooth as glass, and he grimaced at his bloody reflection. He was about to turn away when something made him stop. He glanced back at the water and out into the mist.

A hollow, singing voice was drifting wordlessly across to him.

Edward frowned. "Hello?" Perching on the water's edge, all his senses alert, he waited, but the song seemed to have ended. Silence roared in his ears. This was foolish. His mind was playing tricks on him. He grunted and turned to go but had barely gone a step when the melody returned. It echoed around the chamber as clear as day, like an angel was calling to him.

This was no trick of the mind. Edward ripped off his waistcoat and shirt, unbelted his sword, and dove into the pool. The water was cool and tasted salty on his lips. His feet grazed the bottom, and he stood, wading out into the mist with his eyes closed, just following the music. It was as if the cavern itself was speaking to him. When his foot hit a rock, he opened his eyes. A small island was protruding from the water up ahead. Wading quickly onto its shore, he listened for the music, but it had vanished again.

He began to panic. What was this place? Then a terrible thought struck him. Had he died? Was this some kind of interim space in which his soul would be made to wait before judgment was passed? He turned then and slipped, falling flat on his face and knocking the breath out of himself. He groaned.

It sure felt like he was still alive.

Beneath a layer of moss, he realised that the ground was soft. A revelation hit him then, like a curtain had been lifted in his mind.

He crawled over to the middle of the island and started clawing at the moss, stripping back years of untouched earth below. He gritted his teeth, thinking himself mad. But he wasn't. There was some yearning deep inside him, telling him to dig. Chunk after chunk of mud and grime fell away before he ripped off the final layer of sediment, and the darkness was pierced by a beam of light. He peered into the hole.

A bright red stone shimmered in a pool of water. Streaks of dazzling red light emanated from it, illuminating the walls of the cavern. Edward had never seen anything so odd; the stone was so perfectly shaped and brightly red that it didn't look real.

He picked it up and rolled it over in his hands. A warm sensation ran through his body at its touch. Then it started to pulse, glowing brightly and then fading, over and over. It slipped through his fingers then, and as it dropped to the ground below, a booming thud echoed around the entire chamber, shaking the earth on which he knelt.

Edward stared wide-eyed at the little stone. Without thinking, he picked it back up and shoved it into his pocket. Whatever it was, it wasn't doing anyone any good buried in some damp cave. He stood up, dusting himself off, and headed back the way he had come. He was about halfway back to the shore when the sound of rushing water reached his ears. He whirled around and saw something that made his stomach clench. The dark mist had dissipated now, and an enormous wave was rushing towards him from the far end of the cavern, sweeping up everything in its path.

Water was flowing down the walls now, being drawn into the wave, adding to the surge. Edward broke into a sprint, splashing back through the shallowing wake. He reached the shore and grabbed his things, throwing his waistcoat back on, behind him, the wave decimated his little island before continuing towards him. He dashed down the tunnel but tripped and slammed into the rock. Behind him, carnage filled the tunnel. Edward put up his hands as he was swept up in the current. Water washed down his throat and filled his eyes and ears as he went shooting down the tunnel like a lava flow spewing forth from a volcanic eruption, only it was clear, cool water that whisked him along. It was as if the water was on a journey, and he had just been scooped up and taken along for the ride.

Suddenly, blue sky filled his vision, fresh air filled his lungs, and he found himself bobbing along in the surf, his heart racing. After taking a few deep breaths and trying to calm himself, he realised that something felt odd—or odder, he supposed. His kicking feet didn't seem to feel any resistance, moving as freely as they would in the air. Wondering once again if he were either dead or dreaming, he dropped his head under the surface and swam towards the bottom. Sure enough, his head broke another surface, beyond which he was met once more with fresh air. He watched in stunned silence, as the land rolled by far below. Forest and fields checkered the landscape like patches of a quilt, as the current continued carrying him along.

He didn't know how much time passed in this way, but eventually, the current seemed to slow, the trees growing clearer and larger as the water carried him earthward. Then, finally, the wind and current stopped entirely, releasing him just high enough for him to right himself in the air.

His boots hit the ground with a soft thud, followed by a splash as the remaining water seeped quickly back into the earth as if it had never been there at all.

Disoriented, he dropped down onto a fallen log to catch his breath and closed his eyes, trying to shake off the lingering strangeness of what must have been a dream.

Sometime later, starting to feel like himself again, Edward opened his eyes and reached into his pocket, wrapping his hand around the little red stone. *It can't all have been a dream,* he thought. The stone seemed to almost bounce around in his hand, as though to thank him for rescuing it. As he drew it out into the light—dismissing the idea as pure fancy—he scanned it carefully, looking for any detail he might have missed. It was still perfectly smooth and perfectly red but not much else stood out to him.

Finally, he put the stone away and looked around the woods, in which a flock of birds had gathered, gawking at him. One hopped down onto a tree branch, practically right beside him. Edward smiled at the little bird. It was bright yellow and had a long orange beak. Then he did a double take. The bird was wearing some sort of contraption on its head. He blinked a few times, but he wasn't mistaken. There was some kind of strange headgear, with a *spyglass* attached to it, strapped to the bird's head.

Edward jumped off the log, his eyes darting around. None of the other birds seemed at all concerned with their friend's unusual hardware.

The bird continued to squint at Edward—if a bird could do such a thing—through its spyglass until it was apparently startled by something and abruptly flew away. Edward turned to see what had sprung the little spy from its perch and spotted somebody dashing towards him through the bush.

"Edward!" Willow cried. "There you are!"

He stared at her as though she were a complete stranger. She flung her arms around him and then suddenly let go.

"What happened to you? Why are you soaking wet?"

"I…" He didn't know how to explain what happened. He wasn't even sure himself. His thoughts kept jumping from the stone to the rushing wave, and finally to the bird.

"Didn't you see?" he said, pointing to the branch where the bird had been, then to the sky, and then started to helplessly spin in place, as though searching for something that wasn't there and had never been.

She frowned. "Come on. I think you should rest."

Together, they trudged through the bush until they arrived in a small grassy knoll. Brooks and Cliff sat huddled around a fire.

"Ed!" Cliff cried when the two emerged. His friend had a few small cuts but looked to be okay.

"Nice of you to join us, Sting," Brooks said.

"What happened, Ed?"

He shrugged. "Nothing really," he lied. He was too tired to even try to explain what had happened.

"Nothing?" Brooks said, eyeing his wet cloths.

"Well... I fell into a lake," Edward said, avoiding their gaze.

"A lake?"

He nodded. "So, where are we anyway?" he said, eager to change the subject.

"See for yourself," Willow said, motioning towards a row of nearby bushes. Edward strolled over, poked his head through and gasped. On the other side, an embankment sloped steeply down into a valley, on the far side of which a sheer rock face climbed back towards the sky.

Edward gazed down into the valley, where a sprawling city was glowing in the deepening shadows of the evening. A smile spread across his face. They had made it to Dobson's Canyon.

*

When Edward had first heard of Dobson's Canyon, he had pictured a bleak, lifeless city. But as they made their way through it, he realised that he could not have been more wrong. The heart of Candosia, named after the king who had founded it, Dobson's Canyon was a maze of sweeping streets, carving through the city like artwork. Cobblestone walls, cracked with age, separated and sculpted the varying elevations of the city, while also separating the rich and powerful from those who inhabited the slums.

And the people! Edward had never seen so many. They all

seemed to be dressed in robes, from pristine and elegant to shabby and dishevelled—the latter more and more obvious the lower into the city they descended. People utterly filled the streets, all walking or riding to and from. Horses galloped along the roads, as did some other creatures that were similar in general shape but smaller and strongly muscled. Upon inquiring with Willow, he discovered it to be an unusual breed of bandoro called a hople that was common in Candosia.

In the centre of the ravine was the city's main attraction: 'The Line', a boulevard that stretched the length of the city and sliced it roughly in half.

It had been no small feat getting into the city either. After night had fallen, Edward and the others had scrambled down the embankment, leaving Hikoo behind. There had been a lengthy debate about whether it was safer to bring the skulposis along, but in the end, it was decided that he would attract too much attention. Thus, deeply hurt, the little creature had been left to watch the camp and the bandoros and offered every reassurance that he would not be alone for long.

Once down the ravine, they'd slipped into a ditch on the edge of town, and Willow had lit a torch in order to signal her friends. But after an hour waiting, there'd been no sign of anyone.

*

"I don't understand," she said, as they crouched in the grass, the torch flickering on the road in front of them.

"Maybe you aren't as close with your friends as you thought," Cliff said. Willow shot him a look.

After another hour of waiting, she finally conceded that nobody was coming and instead led them to an abandoned building on the outskirts of the city, apparently the ramshackle, old mill was one of "her spots" as she put it. She took them through the building to a two-room apartment on the second floor. The walls were faded, and the floor was rotting, but a dusty chandelier hung from the ceiling and Edward suspected the place had once been a lavish apartment.

They all settled down to rest, but as there were no beds, forcing them to sleep on the wooden floor, Edward slept horribly, leaving him with a knot that he was trying to rub out of his neck the next morning. A few streaks of daylight were peeking through the roof.

"So, how do we find this secret society of yours, if they won't even answer us?" Cliff asked, throwing open the window. Edward joined him and peered down into the street.

Willow stretched out on the couch. "I know someone who will have answers for us," she said, fiddling with a vial of green liquid.

Cliff laughed. "Funny. It's almost like you've said that before." She put the bottle away and glared at him.

Brooks strode in from the other room and scowled at them both. "We need to get moving."

"Why?" Cliff asked sarcastically, "You got plans tonight?"

"We'll leave soon," Willow said.

Brooks whirled on her. "I would have thought *you* would be taking this more seriously."

She kicked her feet up on the sofa. "I am. But let's get one thing straight: We're doing it my way because I know this town, and you don't." Brooks scoffed.

Down in the dirt street, a group of soldiers was marching quickly towards the building. Edward pressed his hands up against the glass. The men were dressed in green button-down vests and had muskets slung neatly over their shoulders.

"You sure about that?" he said.

Willow dashed over to the window and looked out. "You know what? I think it is time to go."

Edward and Cliff shot across the room and snatched up their bags as heavy footsteps pounded up the stairs. They slipped out the back door where Brooks was already waiting, muttering under his breath something about telling them so. The narrow staircase was crumbling with age and rattled as they descended, but they made it down and quickly headed out, sprinting through the alley. At the entrance to the street, they turned left and slowed to a walk. The street was busy, and they soon blended into the crowd.

"What was that?" Edward asked.

"I don't know," Willow said, "but somebody saw our torch."

*

It was early evening by the time they made it across the city to a seedy district in a deep cleft of the ravine. Steam floated out of the alleys, and the air was thick with the stench of garbage. All around, young Candosians were trickling into shady pubs for a night of drinking. Their faces were caked with dirt, and they carried an invisible weight on their shoulders. Edward avoided their gaze as he sauntered down the street. For some reason, they made him feel guilty.

"There." Willow pointed to a narrow building across the road. It was squished between two larger buildings, and Edward would have missed it had she not said something.

Two men lounged on wooden crates outside the door and shot them a nasty look as they approached. "Keep moving," said the first one, who had bulging arms and a thick neck, and actually ducked under the doorway as he stood to block their path.

"We're here to see her," Willow said. The two men exchanged looks.

"Leave now," said the second man, who was equally as gigantic as the first and had a scar that ran the length of his face. Edward thought for a moment of Neil and his hot temper.

Willow frowned at the two giants. "I'm not going anywhere."

Edward felt his mouth go dry.

Brooks growled and stepped forward. "This is foolish—"

Before he could complete his thought, the first man threw back his meaty arm and jabbed him in the stomach. Brooks collapsed gasping to the ground. Willow had an arrow nocked and drawn before the other man could move. Slowly, the men raised their hands.

"Tell her it's Willow," she said. The two men looked at each other, then disappeared through the doorway. When they emerged a few moments later, they looked bitter.

"Just her," the first man said.

Willow hesitated, perhaps wondering how far she could push her luck, then pointed to Edward. "Him too."

The man eyed Edward for a moment, then nodded and held out his hands. Edward furrowed his brow briefly before realization dawned, and he unbelted his sword and handed it over. The man opened the door and stepped aside. Inside, the walls were dull and peeling, and the air was musty, as though they had stepped into an attic that had been closed up for years. The floor creaked as they were led to a narrow staircase. At the top, their guide led them to a closed door at the end of the hall, and then he left. Willow turned to Edward then, dusting off his waistcoat and parting and smoothing his blond hair.

He blushed. "What are you doing?"

"Just trust me," she said, inspecting him, then she knocked on the door.

Footsteps sounded inside, and the door cracked open. A middle-aged woman peered out. Short and plump with thin brown hair, when she saw Willow, she squealed and threw the door wide open.

"Oh dear!" she cried, embracing Willow. "We thought maybe—"

"I'm okay,"

The woman released her grip. "Come in," she said, then she spotted Edward.

"This is Edward Sting," Willow explained. "Edward, this is Patrice."

"Good to meet you," Edward said, and they shook hands. Hers reminded him of the kind of handshake King Sento would give to children on Life Day, carefully practiced.

"Any friend of Willow's is a friend of mine," she said, stepping aside and holding the door open for them. The room was large and well lit. Windows lined the wall, facing the back of the building, giving them a view of the scummy streets beyond.

A group of men sat hunched over a table at the back of the room. They were playing some sort of game with a set of rocks. Patrice quickly cleared her throat and pointed to the door like a mother scolding her children. The men got up from their game and shuffled out, eyeing Edward as they left.

Then Patrice gestured to a sofa near the window. "Please make yourselves comfortable." Edward and Willow took a seat, and Patrice perched on the chair opposite them. "Tea?"

Edward shrugged. Patrice glanced at the door, and a young

woman rushed over, carrying a tray with three cups of steaming liquid. Edward took a sip of his drink; it was bitter.

"So, Willow," Patrice said, crossing her legs, "how is it that you have come back to me?"

Willow recounted the events of her meeting with Edward and his fellows and their eventual arrival at her door, including the difficulties she'd faced in getting her attention.

When she was finished, Patrice sighed. "We don't use that road for messages anymore. It's not safe; the king has known about it for some time." Then she turned to Edward. "So, you're from Teradowa?"

"That's right," he said tentatively, quite relieved that Willow had kept the details of his own journey to herself.

She laughed. "Must be strange," she said, looking around. "All this." Edward nodded. "Of course, now you understand why we do what we do."

He hesitated for a moment, though it was apparent to him that she wanted him to ask what it was that they 'do'.

"And what is that exactly?" he said finally.

Patrice paused to take a sip of her drink before answering. "Anything and everything that might lead to the liberation of Candosia. We want to reunite the realms once and for all."

"And how do you know about the realms?"

She laughed as if the question was rather silly. "We were all like you at some point. Curious and open about such things. We just have a little more discretion now."

Edward drummed his fingers. So, she didn't trust him, that was fine by him, the feeling would be mutual then. He glanced at Willow, but she was somewhere else, the sharp edge in her eyes missing now.

"And you have a plan?"

Patrice nodded. "Yes. One we'd appreciate your help with. We have a spy working for Pentheus, and when the time is right, we're going to kill him."

Edward's jaw dropped. "You're going to kill the king?"

Patrice scowled. "The king is a threat to Candosia, my dear, and he must be dealt with."

"Believe me, I know all about that," he said. "But do you really think killing him is going to solve your problems?"

Willow put her hand on his leg. "Edward, the king is a terrible man. Trust me. Patrice is right. We're better off without him."

Edward shook his head. Did Willow really hate the king enough to murder him? An uneasy feeling was beginning to form in his gut. He gazed at Patrice, her plump face smiling at him with motherly warmth.

"So, you want me to help you assassinate the king and in return, you can get us into Decius?"

Patrice glanced at Willow. "If that's what you want then of course, we would love to help you."

We? Edward furrowed his brow. *Does she mean her and Willow?*

"How do I know you won't forget about us when our help is no longer needed?"

Willow gasped.

"It's all right, Willow dear," Patrice said, putting up her hands. "I like this boy. You will know, Mr Sting, because I give you my word—something that I think you and I can both agree is very important. Wouldn't you say?"

Edward studied her. There was something not quite right behind her motherly smile. "Yes, I would say so."

Patrice squeaked. "Excellent." With that, she rose from her

seat with the air of one who had achieved their goal. "Oh, just leave those, my dear," she said, waving Willow away from the empty cups. "I'll have Hugo set you and your friends up on the top floor. I think you'll find the rooms acceptable. We'll talk again tomorrow."

At the door, she gave Willow one more hug. "It's good to have you home, dear."

Willow smiled. "I'm glad to be back."

Patrice let her go and peered up at Edward, and for a moment, he thought she was going to hug him too. Instead, she reached into her pocket and pulled out a comb. Then she stood on her tiptoes and ran it through his hair.

"There," she said. "That's better."

*

'Hugo' turned out to be the giant who had socked Brooks in the gut, and his scar-faced friend was called Feelus. Together, the doormen brought their gear to the top floor of the narrow building, which to Edward's shock and Cliff's delight, was like a private palace. Four bedrooms sat at the corners of a lounge that shone with polished marble flooring and glass doors that led onto a stone balcony.

"Boy, would you look at this place!" Cliff said as he paced from room to room. "Willow, who did you say this woman is again?"

"Patrice's outfit runs this part of town, not to mention the entire resistance." Edward didn't like the admiration in her voice. He didn't have the same feeling after their meeting.

"And are the rest of us going to meet her?" Brooks asked, glancing around the room, his face twisted with disdain.

Willow glared at him. "Patrice prefers to operate through as few people as possible. It makes it harder for the resistance members to be identified. But I'm sure you'll get your chance."

Hugo delivered dinner, and they ate. Edward had to admit that the roast meat was far better than anything he'd had since leaving Teradowa. After dinner, Brooks threw on his cloak and made for the door.

"Where are you going?" Edward asked. Patrice had told them it was best to stay in their rooms as it was likely they were being pursued, especially after their close encounter earlier in the day.

"To see what's really going on around here."

Willow narrowed her eyes. "You shouldn't be so distrusting."

"You could get into trouble," Cliff said. "If this Pat lady says we outta lay low, then that's what I'm gonna do."

Brooks scoffed. "I'm not too concerned what Pat thinks."

"You should be," Willow said. "She knows what she's talking about."

"I'm coming with you," Edward said. He was feeling oddly trapped in the luxurious apartment.

Willow raised her eyebrows. "What?"

Edward shrugged. "Might be helpful."

Brooks grinned. Edward grabbed his coat and could feel Willow's eyes drilling into the back of his skull as he dashed out the door. Why was she so concerned with what Patrice thought anyway?

Out in the alley, the cool night air bit at his ears. They crept down the scummy street, listening to the drunken voices of men, mixing with the clatter of glassware drifting out of the taverns. Suddenly, a shadow swept low over the buildings like a giant blanket, blocking out the starry sky as it passed in the low light Edward could make out a pale underbelly.

"What was that?" he asked with wide, eyes.

Brooks peered up at the sky. "That was an arubbak. They're extremely rare. Sento and Pentheus use them to secretly move goods between Candosia and Teradowa." The duke scanned the sky. "There must be an airfield nearby."

Edward shuddered. He had never flown before—if one didn't count being carried along by floating water in an apparent dream, which he didn't—but it looked like something that would make his stomach churn.

Brooks sighed. "Let's get a drink." They crossed the street to a saloon on the corner. The wooden gate creaked as they entered.

Settling at a table in the corner with their drinks, Edward said, "I don't like this."

"What?"

"Not knowing what's going to happen." He rubbed his eyes. "How is killing the king going to help the resistance?"

Brooks shrugged. "Not everyone is willing to use words to change things. And sometimes words simply aren't enough."

Edward shook his head. Even though he knew Brooks was right, it still felt wrong. "I guess I just didn't expect Willow to be okay with it. But she seems to trust Patrice."

Brooks nodded. "For now, we may just need to have faith that Patrice knows what she's doing."

"You think she does?" Edward asked. He was glad to have Brooks to talk to. At least he seemed to have some sense.

The Duke of Teradowa pressed his lips together. "I think she knows what she's doing. But that doesn't mean that what she's doing is what she claims."

Edward felt the hairs stand up on the back of his neck. "What are you saying?"

Brooks frowned. "Don't forget that we were set up today."

Edward's mind raced as he pieced together Brooks' words. "You don't think Willow—"

"She's the only one who knew where we would be, and she is too close to that woman; we can't trust her." Edward's breath caught. Brooks was wrong. He had to be wrong. "Besides," the duke added, "she won't be with us much longer."

"What do you mean?"

He gave him a sideways glance. "You didn't really think she'd come with us to Regnum, did you?"

Edward leaned back in his seat and thought of the meeting earlier that day. Too many ideas were suddenly swimming around in his mind.

He noticed some of the denizens of the saloon shooting them nasty looks, as Brooks downed his drink and whispered, "Look at them. Why even bother freeing them? What would they do with freedom if they had it?"

Edward actually liked the scene. It reminded him of a Friday night at Mr Lynus's pub back home. He smiled at the memory. Then his smile faded. Had he been under the same spell then that these Candosians were now? Made a fool by some formula designed to keep him distracted? The thought made him sick.

"Let's go," he said.

Back on the street, Edward shivered in the cold. They searched the area for another hour but found nothing of interest. As they were making their way back, they passed by an alley, and Edward saw something flash in the shadows. He stopped dead in his tracks.

"What is it?"

"I'm not sure. I thought I saw something."

Brooks squinted into the alley; it was hopelessly dark. "Come on," he said. "Let's go."

They returned to Patrice's building a few minutes later to find Willow and Cliff fast asleep. Edward was about to turn in, but a sudden thought struck him, and he paused at the door.

"Brooks," he said, "when you worked for the king, you travelled to Candosia and Decius, right?"

Brooks hesitated. "Occasionally."

Edward pressed his lips together. "Did you ever find any strange… artifacts?"

The duke frowned. "No, I didn't."

Edward nodded.

Brooks eyed him. "Is there something else?"

"No. Nothing at all."

Chapter 8

The Game is Over

The cellar was where the resistance held their most clandestine meetings. The air was stale, and Edward guessed the whole room had been dug out beneath the building after the fact. The room itself was empty except for the long wooden table they sat around.

The late afternoon sun crept in through metal slits near the ceiling, casting beams of light across the dirt floor. After his night out with Brooks, Edward had decided to trust Patrice for now. After all, Brooks was right. There was no way to prove she was anything other than what she claimed to be.

He leaned back in his seat and scanned the table. Across from him, Cliff yawned and rubbed his eyes; he had slept till noon. To his left was Brooks, who kept glancing at the door impatiently, and beside him was Willow's friend Jade, a pale girl who had been homeless when Patrice had recruited her. Beside Jade was a young man named Melix, who had jet-black hair just like Willow and didn't seem to trust Edward. Several times already the Teradowian had caught Melix glaring at him from across the table.

The one person not at the table was Willow. Edward hadn't seen her all day. Hugo had told them that when he'd knocked on Patrice's door that morning, she'd been with her going over plans. Edward wished he could be more involved. Hadn't Willow said that this was a big operation and Patrice needed everyone to do their part?

Feelus stood stoically by the door, like a sleeping giant. Edward was about to get up and stretch when the door opened, and Patrice flounced in with Willow by her side. They were giggling about something, but when they took their seats, Patrice's face returned to its normal tender yet firm demeanour. She put her hands on the table.

"I'd like to thank you all for coming. Jade and Melix, the time has come for you to gather your forces."

Edward cleared his throat. "What forces?"

Patrice glared at him, then raised her nose in the air and said, "I suppose that, to you, this is just a means to an end, Mr Sting, but to some of us, it is important. So, please be patient, and all will be revealed soon enough."

Edward rolled his eyes. If she thought that all he wanted was to get out of Dobson's Canyon, then she didn't know him at all.

Melix glanced between Patrice and Edward. "I got a question," he said. "How do we know these Teradowians are on our side?"

"Edward and Cliff are here to help," Willow said. "They hate the kings as much as we do."

Edward scowled. Did Willow feel she needed to speak for him when they were around Patrice?

Melix slouched in his chair and stared at Edward. Then there was a knock at the door, and Feelus peered into the hall before opening it.

Patrice squeaked. "It seems our spy has arrived."

A tall man in his early thirties strolled into the room. He wore a green vest and smiled, revealing a row of perfect teeth.

Edward's heart jumped when he recognised Kincaid.

Instantly, Willow sprang from the table, rushed forward like a wild animal and slammed Kincaid in the jaw. He reeled over and touched his cheek, drawing away bloody fingertips.

Willow whirled on Patrice then. "What is *he* doing here?"

"We need him."

"He works for the king!"

Kincaid straightened up. "Actually, I work for *her*," he said. "I'm sorry about your treehouse, Willow, but those were the king's orders. I couldn't blow my cover."

"You tried to kill us!" Cliff shouted across the table.

Willow frowned at Patrice. "Why didn't you tell me?"

The rebel leader sighed. "I didn't want to upset you. You'd only just come back."

Willow stood glued to the spot for a long moment, as if making up her mind. Finally, she dropped back into her chair. "Well, let's hear what his highness has to say then."

Kincaid shuffled to the head of the table, giving Willow a wide berth. "A week from tomorrow," he said, "the king will be leaving his palace and travelling by carriage to dine with the Lord of Promelic who is in town."

"So, we're gonna knock him while he's on the road?" Melix asked.

"Exactly. You and Jade will need all your people. We can't miss this chance. Cavalry and royal guard will be everywhere."

Edward raised his hand. "And what do you need from us?"

Kincaid stared curiously at Edward and the others, as if noticing them for the first time, then smirked. "Well, kid, if you're up for it, you and your friends can come with me undercover." Edward perked up at this. "Can you ride a horse?"

"Sure," he answered automatically.

Across from him, Cliff went pale. "A horse?"

Kincaid looked excited, and Edward got the idea that this was part of his plan.

After the details were hashed out, Patrice dismissed everyone. As they funnelled out the door, Kincaid took Edward aside.

"So, you're the runaway I've been hearing all about?"

"Yep."

"I'm afraid the last time we met, I made a rather bad impression."

Edward shrugged. "You did what you had to do."

"Well, I'd be careful if I were you because the king knows you're alive. He's been obsessing over the 'wretched Teradowians' running lose in Candosia." Edward didn't like the sound of that.

Kincaid rubbed his jaw. "I'm going to visit with another group tonight. I think you should come with me."

Edward thought for a moment. A terrifying image of him accidentally impaling a fellow rebel with his sword crossed his mind. He shivered. Perhaps it was a good idea to meet the other members of the resistance.

"Okay."

*

Half an hour later, they descended a set of stone steps into a dingy, dimly lit pub below street level. Edward had to suppress a gag. The stench was so pungent that it seemed to cling to the air.

"Fiddleberry beer," Kincaid said, seeing Edward's disgust. "They brew it down here." At the back of the room, a row of large wooden barrels was hidden behind a thick haze. Tubes ran from their tops and disappeared into the ceiling.

Edward stuttered, "But... we have fiddleberry beer in Teradowa!"

Kincaid chuckled. "Where do you think you get it from?" Edward furrowed his brow. "It's a big money maker for Pentheus," Kincaid said.

A slender, older man appeared out of the mist. He was balding and had a round face. "Hey, boss," he said, shaking Kincaid's hand.

"Edward, this is Bailo."

Bailo smiled. "You a new joiner, kid?"

"Something like that," Edward said.

The rebel smiled and patted Edward's arm proudly, then shuffled off on some clandestine mission. The room was deeply shadowed, and for the first time, Edward noticed dozens more men and women scurrying about. They were all dressed like Bailo—with tattered, dirty clothes dangling off their bodies like rags—and milled about carrying tools and weapons. One man walked by carrying an axe with a blade the size of a dinner plate, and Edward felt queasy at the thought of what it was for.

Kincaid led the way through the room, and they took a seat in the corner. "So, you must have had a hard time getting out of Teradowa."

"You have no idea."

"We're sure grateful for your help."

Edward nodded. Kincaid was apparently not aware of the conditions of their participation.

Kincaid sighed. "See these people?" Edward looked around. "These are some of the original members of the resistance. They toiled hard but fruitlessly until Pat came along. She really saved us."

"Is that how you were recruited?" Edward asked, eyeing

Kincaid.

"I was a street kid, like Willow. We were both taken in by Patrice." He smiled.

"Willow was raised by Patrice?"

Kincaid shook his head. "People like Willow don't need someone to raise them, but Patrice gave her a home." He sighed. "Of course, that was before we joined the royal guard."

Edward's jaw dropped. "Willow worked for the king?"

Kincaid furrowed his brow. "She didn't tell you?"

Edward shook his head.

"Well, I suppose it's not something she'd care to remember."

"But what about Patrice? What about the resistance?"

"Pat always wanted us to decide for ourselves what we thought of the king, that way she could trust you. She never even told us about the resistance until after we learned the truth about the realms for ourselves. It works better that way. Pat was able to flip me, and I've been spying for her ever since. But Willow took it worse than most. She let Pentheus know exactly what she thought of his little game."

"So, he sent her away," Edward said.

Kincaid nodded. "Pat was devastated."

Edward's mind was spinning. Why hadn't Willow told him?

"So, this Shanley Brooks... What's his story?"

Edward shrugged.

"He's a duke like you, and I guess... turned against the king." Kincaid seemed to mull that over. "What?" Edward said.

"He just doesn't seem like the type."

Edward laughed. "He's not the most chipper, I'll give you that, but he's got it where it counts. He had a good teacher."

Kincaid shrugged. "You would know better than me."

Edward drummed his fingers on the grimy table. Kincaid

wasn't the man he thought he was. He was... better somehow.

He opened his mouth to speak, but suddenly there was an explosion from the back of the pub. Edward was sent soaring across the room. He landed with a thud against the far wall and felt splintered wood dig into his back. He staggered to his feet, his ears ringing. The air was filled with dust and muted shouting. Then men in uniforms started pouring in from the back, where a chunk of the wall had been blasted away. The sound of musket fire filled the air and several rebels crumpled to the ground in front of him.

He dove behind a toppled table as bullets ricocheted off the wall behind him, and crawled towards the door. Then someone grabbed his ankle, and he whirled around. Kincaid was kneeling behind the table, moving his mouth, but no words were coming out. Edward ducked as a windowpane shattered behind them, sending shards of broken glass raining down on them.

Kincaid dug a pistol out of his jacket and fired into the murky air. In the haze, Edward felt himself get yanked to his feet, and all of a sudden, they were stumbling out the front door. Out on the street, he blinked the dust out of his eyes and dashed after Kincaid into the cool evening. They didn't stop running for several blocks, and when they finally did, Edward doubled over, gasping for breath.

"What happened?"

"We got raided," Kincaid said, his face grim.

Edward's stomach rolled. There was no avoiding danger anymore. "What now?"

"We have to move against the king tomorrow, before they can hit us again."

*

It was dark by the time Edward got back to the top floor of the narrow building. He opened the door and found Cliff, Willow, and Brooks in the midst of a deep argument.

"Ed, they're saying now that we have to kill the king tomorrow?"

"That's right. I was just with Kincaid, and we got ambushed."

Cliff paced the room. "What if we just leave tonight? Sneak out of the city?"

"That's impossible," Willow said. "Besides, we had a deal."

Cliff scoffed. "A deal to help you, not get ourselves killed!"

"Bickering is pointless," Brooks said. "We'll sort this out in the morning." With that, he blew out the candles, plunging the room into a darkness broken only by the moonlight that crept in through the terrace window.

Later that night, Edward lay in bed, tossing and turning. He was too anxious to sleep. His mind raced with thoughts of what might happen in the morning. Who had tipped off the king? It all seemed so sudden. He lit a match and looked at the clock: eleven thirty.

Suddenly, a noise caught his attention. He crept out of bed and into the lounge. He scanned the room; the glass doors to the balcony were ajar. He tiptoed across the room and slipped out. The night air was cool on his face. From the top floor, he could see clear across the city. Funnels of steam drifted from the slums and then faded as the streets curved upwards, and the lights from the higher levels shone down on them. It all seemed very far away.

"What are you doing?"

Edward almost jumped out of his skin at the sound of

Willow's voice as she swung off the roof and landed beside him.

He clutched his chest. "I was just clearing my head," he said, straightening up. "What are *you* doing?"

She shrugged. "Same thing, I guess." Her eyes were gloomy, and her black hair hung loose over her shoulders. For the first time since Edward had known her, she looked unsure.

"What's wrong?"

She eyed him. "I don't know what Patrice has planned for after the king is dead."

Edward pursed his lips. He suspected that he knew what was really bothering her. "What do you have planned?" He wanted her to say that she wanted to be with him. That she would come with them on their journey.

She glanced up at him, her figure hidden by the darkness. "What do you mean?"

Her eyes pierced his like daggers, all the vulnerability of the moment before completely gone now.

He sighed. "Kincaid told me about you. About Patrice raising you and... about the royal guard."

Willow's face darkened. "He shouldn't have told you that. He's trying to manipulate you. Kincaid chose the king when he found out about the realms. I chose Patrice."

Edward hesitated. "You know, you didn't have to keep your past from me. I would have trusted you all the same. Besides, don't you think it's odd that Patrice was keeping secrets from you at all? That she allowed you to work for the king, knowing it would hurt you?"

Willow glared at him. "First, if you knew I worked for the royal guard, and you still trusted me, that would have been a mistake, and anyway, that's not why I didn't tell you. I didn't tell you... because I was ashamed. As for Patrice, you don't know her like I do. She saved us."

Edward rolled his eyes in the dark. That was the second time he'd heard that today. "Still," he said, finding his voice, "I think Brooks and I were followed the other night."

Willow gave him a sheepish grin. "Well, I didn't want you to get into trouble."

He stared at her. "That was *you?*"

She smirked, and soon they were both laughing. Edward breathed in the crisp night air. Maybe Willow was right. Maybe he just couldn't get past the fact that she was getting pulled away from him. And maybe something else was clouding his judgment of her.

She pushed her hair back behind her ear and bit her lip, her smile fading.

Edward leaned on the rail and sighed. "So, after tomorrow, that's it? You're going to stay?"

She stared at the ground.

He nodded and turned for the door, then stopped. He couldn't help himself. He glanced back and locked eyes with her. "Whatever happens in the morning, just remember who you are."

She looked at him like she wanted to respond, then just nodded.

Edward tiptoed back to bed and didn't hear the glass door open again for a long time.

*

Edward gazed at his reflection in the slender mirror. Kincaid had arrived at their rooms before the sun was even up and brought them three uniforms and weapons. Edward adjusted the cuffs on the crisp green waistcoat and buttoned it up. Then he flipped on his black tricorne hat and slung his new musket over his shoulder.

Cliff thumped into the room, struggling to button up his vest. His friend had squeezed into the largest uniform, but Edward still thought his gut might burst out at any moment. He sighed. A sick feeling was starting to grow in his stomach, and he wished Willow were here. She had dashed out that morning; apparently Patrice had given her a special assignment.

Kincaid knocked on the open bedroom door. "Everyone ready?"

Edward nodded, while beside him, Cliff groaned.

"I think I'm going to be sick," he said, nervously fumbling with the last button on his vest, which kept popping out of its hole.

"Take a deep breath," Brooks said from behind them. He was as cool as if this were nothing more than a game. For once, he was playing the role he was used to.

Kincaid opened the door, and they followed him into the hall, bounding down the stairs and out into the morning sunshine.

As it turned out, King Pentheus travelled frequently in his carriage, and they'd had no trouble picking up his route for this morning. As they marched, the streets became busier, with people milling about everywhere. Edward noticed that practically no one would look at them, seemingly spotting them from far off and giving them a wide birth.

He adjusted the strap of his musket, the gun feeling uncomfortable on his shoulder. They soon crossed a shallow river on a cobblestone bridge which was connected to a market square. Beautiful gardens littered the front lawns of stone manors on either side of the square.

As they marched along, Edward's thoughts drifted to Willow. Was she watching them right now? Training her bow on them from atop one of these buildings? He wondered what it would be like to say goodbye to her.

A shot rang out, and ahead of him, Kincaid suddenly clutched his leg and rolled to the side of the bridge. Another shot came then, and chips of stone exploded from the bridge's surface beside him. Edward felt his heart pound in his chest as the air erupted with the crackle of gunfire. People screamed and dashed for cover as soldiers stormed the square. Edward rushed to the corner of the nearest building, where Kincaid was pinned down. Brooks and Cliff lay trapped in the ditch on the other side of the bridge.

"It's a trap!" Kincaid shouted over the high-pitch whine of bullets whizzing past. Edward fumbled with the safety on his musket, raised it to his shoulder, and pulled the trigger. The force was greater than he'd expected, and his shot sailed harmlessly into the sky. Beside him, Kincaid fired his musket, dropped it to the ground, and then pulled out a pistol from his belt and fired around him like a madman. Several soldiers collapsed in the street.

The shouts of men filled the square as the soldiers reloaded; then the hail of bullets came again. From open windows and alleys, more shots screamed at them. Edward watched in horror as the men across the street rolled out a field cannon and took aim at them. "Look out," Kincaid shouted. The blast hit the corner of the building and exploded, showering them with brick. Edward coughed up dust and scanned the street; men were rushing forward under the cover of the cannon's blast.

"Run!" Kincaid cried.

Edward staggered to his feet and followed him up the street, the smell of spent gunpowder filling his nostrils. Behind him, Brooks and Cliff were hobbling out of the ditch after them.

Edward flinched as the wall of a building exploded just behind them. They kept running, rounding the corner and sprinting uphill along a narrow, brick path as the sound of battle began to fade. At the top of the hill, Kincaid paused. Tall buildings loomed on either side of the street like giants looking down at them.

Cliff panted. "What happened?"

"I don't know," Kincaid said. Edward did not like the look on his face. "But this is where we were to come if something went wrong."

"You mean everyone knows about this spot?" Edward asked, a terrible feeling coming over him.

Just then, the door to the building beside them creaked open, and Patrice stepped into the road.

"Patrice," Kincaid sighed. "What's going on?"

She crossed her arms and smiled her warm, motherly smile, now exposed in all its ugliness. Behind her, soldiers stormed out of the building and encircled them.

Kincaid gasped. "What is this?"

The men raised their bayonets, and Edward stuck up his hands, feeling as though he had already been stabbed.

Patrice stepped into the circle. "Kincaid, by the order of the king, you and your fellows are under arrest."

Edward sighed and closed his eyes.

"Don't look so disappointed, Mr Sting. The way I see it, I'm doing you a favour." Patrice smirked. "You would have died horribly if you'd gone on to Regnum." Edward raised his eyebrows. She giggled. "Oh yes, I know all about your little adventure. King Sento sends his regards. He assumes you are going after your grandfather. That's a one-way trip if you ask me." She smiled knowingly.

Edward scowled. He hated that she had been given the

chance to gloat. And how did Sento know about his grandfather anyway?

"I'd rather take my chances than rot here," he said.

Patrice frowned with mock sympathy. "I'm afraid you won't be staying here. You'll be going home to Teradowa, my dear." Edward's heart sank. He knew what would happen if he went home now.

"People need to learn to stay put," she said, wagging her finger like a mother lecturing a child. Then she gestured to the guards. One man stepped forward, holding iron chains. He raised them to Edward's wrists, but before he could cuff him, there was a high-pitched screech from above. An arrow whizzed through the air and snagged the chains out of the man's hands before continuing on. It sank into the open door behind Patrice, the chains rattled against the wood before coming to a rest. Edward and the others followed the arrow's path back to the top of the nearest building.

Willow stood on the roof with her bow raised.

Edward couldn't help but grin at the look of shock on Patrice's face. "Willow? What are you doing here, my dear?"

Willow's bowstring was held taut once again, her arrow's point roaming over the street.

Patrice gave a nervous laugh. "We've just discovered that your friends have sided with the king! It's upsetting news, but they will have to be dealt with."

Finally, Willows arrow settled on Patrice.

"You've never been anything but a liar!" she called back.

Patrice chuckled humourlessly. "Willow, please... Don't let these fools drag you down with them."

For a second, Edward thought Willow was going to shoot Patrice right there, but the bowstring remained pinched between her fingers.

"Let them go."

Patrice's face hardened now.

"And how do you intend to make me?" she sneered. "If you shoot me, your friends will die."

Edward jumped as a bayonet poked him in the back. He turned to find himself looking down the barrel of its gun. Beside him, the others were facing the same fate.

Patrice glared back towards the roof. "It's your choice, my dear. Throw away your life with that arrow or save your friends."

Willow stood still as a statue. Then, for a fleeting moment, she met Edward's gaze, and even from three stories below, he could see a tear roll down her cheek.

Slowly, she lowered her bow.

Chapter 9

The Duel

Edward slouched against the wall and rubbed his swollen feet. After surrendering, they had been blindfolded and marched—for what seemed like hours—across the city before being thrown in a dungeon and abandoned. The room was cold and damp and smelled like it had never been cleaned. A thin streak of daylight peeking through a steel grate near the ceiling was their only connection to the world beyond. Edward leaned his head on the stone wall, playing back the events that had led them here. How had he been so stupid? Cliff sat cross-legged against the opposite wall, picking at a piece of straw, while Kincaid was walking slowly across the cell and back with his head in his hands.

Next to Edward, Melix and Jade were conversing in hushed voices. Melix's distrust for the Teradowians seemed to be gone—perhaps erased by the fact that they were all now in prison together—and the rebel had assured them that the disaster which had befallen them had occurred across the city. The entire resistance had been wiped out in a matter of hours.

Yet nobody seemed more strongly affected than Willow. She hadn't said a word to anyone since her stand on the roof. The best Edward got when he'd tried to approach her was a detached kind of stare that went on for several moments before she looked away. It scared him.

"This is ridiculous," Brooks said, slamming his fists on the metal bars. Pacing the cell furiously, he'd tested the door each time he reached it. He was the only one who had not sat down since they'd arrived. Edward was about to tell him to save his energy when Feelus came thundering down the corridor.

Patrice's two henchmen turned out to be just as two-faced as their boss. In fact, it was Hugo and Feelus whom Edward had first seen when his blindfold had been ripped off. The two giants, who had shown them to their rooms at Patrice's, had now been more than happy to show them to their cell—the irony of which had not been lost on Edward.

Feelus took the keys from his belt and unlocked the door, pointing to Willow and Kincaid. "The king would like to see you two," he said, his voice echoing around the tiny chamber. Then his eyes found Edward. "And you."

Everyone looked at him.

"Me?" he repeated, feeling uneasy. Feelus growled, and Edward decided that he'd better not argue. He followed Feelus and the others out the door. They marched down the corridor and stopped at the foot of a narrow staircase, where Feelus unhooked a thick iron chain from the wall.

"You've got to be kidding me," Kincaid said. Feelus smirked.

He clasped the first iron loop around Willow's neck, and then one around Edward's, the cold steel gripping him tightly. Finally, he locked Kincaid in. He then pulled out a second set of chains and cuffed their hands together. Finally, they rattled up the stairs. When they reached the top, Edward's jaw dropped.

They were standing in the front corridor of the king's palace.

Black and white marble sparkled beneath his feet, and massive windows lined the hallway, decorated with velvet curtains. A stunning view of The Line greeted them outside. On the opposite wall hung portraits of past kings and queens. Edward rolled his eyes. Even in death, they kept a watchful eye on those they had oppressed. The prisoners were marched down the hall until they came to a large staircase that fanned out at the bottom.

At the top, the staircase split off and continued up another level in both directions, but whatever lay above them would remain a mystery, as Feelus dragged them straight ahead and opened a large wooden door. Edward stumbled forward into the room.

It was long and narrow, and large windows lined each wall. Edward gazed out and could see clean across the city to where the edge of the ravine met the orange sky. Then his gaze returned to the room and settled on its main focus. Display stands were spaced out along the length of the room, each featuring a unique pistol.

There were so many guns. Each piece was neatly polished and encased in glass, the smooth wood and metal of the mechanisms sparkling at him. Beside him, Willow and Kincaid paid no notice to the collection, and Edward guessed that they had been here many times before. In fact, so engrossed by the guns was he that it wasn't until they had reached the end of the room that Edward even noticed the throne.

Or the man sitting on it.

Feelus yanked on the chain, and they stopped at the foot of a short marble staircase and looked up. King Pentheus peered down at them from his seat at the top.

He was a ratty-looking old man and sat like a vulture with his back hunched and his neck stuck out forward over an enlarged belly. His skin hung loosely around his face, which was partially hidden by a patchy grey beard.

Edward thought he looked rather silly in his thick red robes and golden crown.

Finally, the king waved a hand at his servant. "Thank you, Feelus," he croaked. The giant bowed and left the room. Pentheus eyed his prisoners through a pair of wiry spectacles, which kept slipping down his crooked nose.

"My dear," he called, keeping his eyes on them, "come out here, will you?"

A wooden door creaked open, and Edward felt his stomach roll as Patrice strode out to stand beside the throne, dressed in a delicate pink blouse and skirt. She smiled at them for a moment, and then Edward watched as she kissed the king warmly on the cheek. Despite the circumstances, he blushed and tried not to look at them. Finally, Pentheus cleared his throat and addressed them.

"Kincaid," he said, "I must say that I am so disappointed in you. Patrice and I had a little wager. I thought you'd be able to stomach killing Willow and the Teradowians, but I suppose it's better that we know where your loyalties lie."

Kincaid glared at the king, who ignored him and continued.

"And you, Willow, forever a troublemaker. Will you ever stop causing problems for me?"

"Probably not."

The king laughed. "Of course." He sighed and shook his head, and then seemed to come to a decision. When he started speaking again, it was in an almost academic tone, as though he were instructing simpletons. "You see, my beloved wife Patrice and I realised long ago that there was a problem with people like yourselves in Candosia."

Edward felt his mouth fall open upon hearing that Patrice was actually *married* to the king, and he could only imagine the shock Willow must be feeling.

"So, we orchestrated this little resistance scheme to root out possible insurgents." He sounded almost boastful. "Those who remained loyal to me once they learned the truth about the realms, we knew we could trust, and those who joined Patrice, well... We kept a very close eye on them. Things worked quite well for many years... until you Teradowians showed up, and we realised that we had to take matters more seriously.

"You did make things easy for us, of course. Letting us know exactly when and where you entered the city. I knew then that Willow must still be with you. So, we sent men to every one of her old hideouts, but... alas... you slipped away!"

The king chuckled. "Then, lo and behold, you showed up at Patrice's door, and we thought, well... here's an opportunity to get them all at once! I get to vanquish the so-called 'resistance' *and* collect the ransom on the Teradowians on the same day! Well, I'm sure you can imagine..."

The king continued to ramble, but Edward was no longer listening. Something was moving around in his pocket. He held very still, though his frown deepened, trying to work out what was happening. Then he remembered the little red stone.

But... I didn't have that with me, he thought. As a matter of fact, he realised, he had lost track of it completely in the chaos of the previous days. Suddenly, he felt a jolt, and then the stone was pushing against the seam of his pocket as though trying to make him turn. He clutched his side, hoping nobody had noticed, and dared a peek in the direction the stone seemed to be urging him towards. There was nothing out of the ordinary that he could see. The stone pushed harder then, almost seeming irritated at his lack of response.

He actually had to stick his leg out a bit to keep his balance, and Willow looked over at him like he had three heads. He shrugged, sweating under his collar. He tried to swat the stone to get it to stop, but this only made it more energised. Then he glanced over again to where the stone was urging him. It was completely empty, save the display cases... Suddenly, a devious idea struck him.

He cleared his throat.

King Pentheus glared at him. "Ah, the youngster from Teradowa. Something to say before you return home?"

Noticing absently that the stone had gone still in his pocket, Edward gestured to the case. "This is an impressive collection you have."

This got the king's attention, and he beamed at Edward. "At least you have an appreciation for fine artistry. That's something, I suppose."

Edward was inclined to point out that his majesty had made a career out of lying to millions of people, and that maybe he was not the best person to cast judgment on anyone. Instead, he simply said, "I've seen better."

The king's smile faded. *"Better?"* Edward shrugged, which only fuelled the king's indignation. "What do *you* know about weaponry or marksmanship?" He practically spat out the words. Beside him, Patrice shifted anxiously.

Edward sighed. "Well, I was a pretty good shot myself, back home."

Pentheus laughed, but Edward could see the king growing red in the face.

"I'd like to see that!" he said.

Edward rolled his eyes. "I don't know if that's a good idea. I bet you've never even fired a shot."

This sent the king over the edge. He shot out of his throne then, cursing Edward's name.

Kincaid fidgeted beside him, and Edward wondered if he had ever seen anyone insult the king before. Maybe he was predicting what would happen next.

"Never fired a shot!" The king yelled, hobbling down the stairs, his enormous gut bouncing around with each step. Patrice put her hands to her mouth and stepped nervously after her husband. Pentheus reached the bottom and stood fuming before Edward, who was amused to find that the top of the old man's head barely reached his chin. Realizing this himself, the king grunted and took two steps back up the stairs, where he stood with his hands on his hips, gut hanging down like a half-inflated balloon. "Edward Sting, the great shooting ace, eh? Strange that King Sento didn't mention your skills."

Edward scoffed. "Well, of course, he wouldn't. Would he?"

The king stared at him; then a grim smile broke across his face.

"Feelus!" he shouted. The door opened, and the giant poked his head into the room. "Bring me that pistol there," the king said, pointing to a case by the door. Feelus approached it with his hands outstretched. "No! Not that one! The next one."

The king rolled his eyes and looked apologetically at his prisoners. Finally, Feelus arrived and held out a soft purple cushion to the king, upon which sat a shining silver gun in a sleek holster.

"My newest duelling pistol," the king explained as he slowly drew it out, taking the weapon in his hands and running his thumb over the hammer. "A true flintlock, wouldn't you say, Sting?"

Edward narrowed his eyes and pretended to study the weapon. "Yes, I would."

Pentheus eyed him, apparently satisfied. "All right then. Since you're so confident, I'll make you a deal," he said.

"Tomorrow at noon, on The Line, we shall duel, you and I."

Kincaid laughed. "Have you gone completely mad?"

"I have to agree," Patrice said, grabbing the arm of her husband. "This doesn't seem like a good idea, dear."

Pentheus shook off her grip and waved his hand sharply. "Silence!" He glared at Edward. "If I win, your friends are mine to do with as I please—as is the case now, of course." He snickered. "But if *you* win… I'll set you free!"

"And my friends?"

"Yes!"

Patrice was flustered now. "Honey," she said, carefully placing her hand on his shoulder, "you have nothing to prove! These people are criminals!*"*

Willow laughed. "You've got some nerve saying that."

"Enough!" the king roared. "So, what's it going to be, Sting?"

Edward pursed his lips. He was anything but an ace shooter. In fact, he'd never fired a pistol in his life. But what choice did he have?

Just one: He was going to duel and win, or he was going to die—either here on The Line or back home at the hands of King Sento.

"I'll do it."

The king clapped his hands together. "Excellent. Tomorrow at noon."

With that, he beckoned Feelus back in, and Edward's fate was sealed. Just before the door closed, he turned and watched Pentheus spin his flintlock pistol three times forwards, twice backwards, and then slip it back into its holster. All in the blink of an eye.

*

There was a chill in the air the next morning. The sky was cloudy, and a grey shadow hung over Candosia.

Edward pulled out his pocket watch. It was eleven thirty. Most of his items had been returned to him the previous night, thrown with him into the dark cell where he had been locked up. He hadn't slept a wink. He'd spent the night pacing his cell, wondering if this would be the last night of his life.

Did Pentheus actually believe he was an ace shooter? If so, then why had he agreed to duel him? Edward didn't think it likely that a king would allow himself to be potentially killed in front of his own people—or at all for that matter.

Maybe he had seen right through Edward's lie, and this fight was nothing more than a glorified execution. Or perhaps, most frightening of all, the king was truly arrogant enough, or insane enough, to leave both their fates to the luck of the draw. Literally. Either way, what had been his alternative? Allow himself to be sent back to Teradowa, where he would certainly be killed? Refuse the challenge and simply fall upon the questionable mercy of Pentheus?

Edward's knees felt weak.

He took another step into the boulevard. Loose gravel crunched beneath his boots. The Line had been painted a bleak grey for the event. He could feel his guard's eyes digging into the back of his skull as he shuffled out into the street.

He wished they would stop. All they were doing was making him nervous. If he was going to run, he would surely have done so by now. His hand ran momentarily over his pocket, where the little red stone sat. It had been completely dormant ever since its odd behaviour the day before.

Edward wasn't sure why he had not told the others about the stone. There was no real reason not to. He didn't quite understand it, but somehow, he felt he had a bond with the stone now. Like it was a part of him.

He stopped in the middle of the boulevard.

People were starting to gather along the sides. Whether or not the crowd was here by choice, Edward did not know. He assumed he had been branded as some sort of terrorist by the king, but it was impossible to say. Somewhere in this crowd, he wondered if Willow would be watching. He hadn't seen her since leaving the throne room the previous day, after which Patrice had separated them, although she had made her feelings on his decision clear. The minute they'd been led out of the room, she had screamed at him about how stupid he was being. About how he was going to get himself killed.

A ringing endorsement.

It wasn't as if he were doing this for himself. If he won, they'd all be free to leave. Even if Willow wasn't executed alongside them, how long did she think she would last if she refused to continue doing Patrice's bidding? And what about the others? Sure, he was grasping at straws with his challenge. But when the alternative was to burn all the straws to ashes, she could bet he was going to take a chance. Across the street in the city square, the clock tower struck noon, a deep, resonant bell announcing to all that the moment had arrived.

At the sound, Edward looked around as though expecting Pentheus to jump out from behind somebody and shoot him. But nothing happened. The crowd was still gathering, and he stood alone on The Line. He unholstered the silver pistol that had been given to him upon his arrival, running his thumb over the smooth, wooden hilt and brass hammer. It was surprisingly light, and the powder—he had been assured—was the same quality as what would be used by the king.

Edward laughed, thinking that it didn't matter at all.

Suddenly on the steps of the palace, several hundred yards ahead of him, a chorus of trumpets sounded. The band began marching down The Line. Behind the band followed a group of soldiers, carrying on their shoulders a large cushion—not unlike the one Feelus had presented to the king the day before—resting upon a platform of ornately carved wooden poles, and sure enough, atop this cushion sat the man himself.

King Pentheus was adorned from head to foot in a luxurious-looking fur coat, which Edward suspected might once have belonged to a relative of the noguchi that had tried to eat him back in the forest. When the king reached The Line, and the band had finished playing, Pentheus dismounted (if one could call it that), and Edward could have sworn he heard the old man grunt with the effort from where he stood. The King of Candosia shook off his coat then to reveal his own weapon, holstered to the side of his thick leather belt—partly hidden by his gut, which hung shamelessly over it. Edward watched as the king waddled out into the middle of the boulevard and faced him.

Then a third man strode out in between them. He was slim, bald, and wrapped in a white gown. He raised his hands and beckoned for Edward's approach. Familiar with the order of things, the king was already on his way. Edward tried to look calm as he made his way over. The man bowed when the two combatants arrived.

"Good day, gentlemen," he said. "I will be officiating today's duel." Up close, the man was younger than Edward had thought and kept glancing at Pentheus. Edward guessed that he wasn't used to giving his king orders. "It is my duty to confirm that you are both aware of the stakes of this engagement?"

Edward and the king looked at each other and nodded, though Pentheus seemed to be off somewhere in his own world, his eyes darting around madly.

"Very good," the officiator said. "Then we shall go over the rules." Edward thought it was pretty simple. The loser was whomever hit the ground. "You will start back-to-back and march thirty paces. You will then wait for the first chime of quarter past noon, at which point, you will turn, draw your weapon, and fire your shot."

Edward's mind was spinning, trying to process this information.

"It is my understanding," the man said then, glancing between them, as if looking to be corrected, "that this shall be a duel to the death?"

The king nodded solemnly, and Edward followed suit, thinking that he might be sick. He had of course been aware of the terms, but to hear those four words officially spoken aloud was something else entirely. "Very well, you may take your positions."

Pentheus extended his hand and Edward shook it then they moved to the centre of the boulevard and stood back-to-back.

Edward's mind was spinning. Was he really about to do this? Thoughts flew by too quickly to grab onto. The commissioner had his arm raised and was about to order their thirty-pace march to begin.

"Wait!"

Edward had blurted this out before he actually had something to say. He could feel Pentheus's head turn sideways against his back. *Think of something.* Then it hit him.

"How do I know you won't cheat?" he said.

The king scoffed. "Well," he said, "how do I know *you* won't cheat?"

Edward thought this was fairly obvious. "Because if *I* cheat, I'll just be killed anyway."

Pentheus grunted, acknowledging the logic of the statement. After a moment, he said, "Well, I'm not going to cheat."

"Yes, but how do I know? How do I know you're not just gonna turn around while we're marching and shoot me in the back?"

The king scoffed and looked to the commissioner. Edward did the same.

The man rubbed his bald head, looking as though he'd rather be anywhere else at that moment. "I-I suppose that… whatever damage the cheater inflicts on his foe… will be done unto him as well?"

Pentheus nodded his head in approval. Edward moaned internally. It was clear that no amount of arguing was going to get him out of this.

The crowd had fallen silent. He was too late. The officiator lowered his hand, and they were ready. Edward took one heavy stepped forward, his heart pounding. Only twenty-nine more to go.

Chapter 10

Lucky Return

Willow was being watched, but she didn't really care. Patrice had released her from the dungeons that morning, letting her know that she did not want her to die with the others and that she had big plans for the future, in which she wanted Willow to play an important role. Of course, Willow had accepted her 'freedom' but as far as ever working with Patrice again was concerned…

Never going to happen. She'd die before ever knowingly becoming a part of that woman's corrupt games. If she thought she could get her on her side just because she'd spared her life, she was sorely mistaken. After years of Patrice pretending to care about her, it had turned out to all be a lie. She was nothing more than a problem to be handled. Identified as a threat and plucked from the streets to be examined like a lab rat.

She waded cautiously through the crowd. Twice that morning, she had already slipped away from the men tailing her, and was in the process of doing so again. They weren't very good at their jobs. The first time she'd shaken them, she'd gone to visit Cliff and the others in jail, and the second, she'd gone to one of her spots across the city where she'd kept a stash of weapons. She now had a pair of daggers pressed against her skin, under her tights.

The area around The Line was filling with people. Although the king himself rarely, if ever, participated in the actual duels, attendance of them all was closely monitored, and if you knew what was good for you, you showed up. And she had no doubt that Patrice expected her to do just that. She wanted her to see this. Wanted her to come to grips with the way things were.

The crowd was growing tense. She gazed up at the clock tower. It was nearly noon. A murmur passed through the crowd, and she craned her neck to see what was happening. Edward was standing in the middle of the street. Waiting. She felt her heart melt. He was standing up straight, trying his best to look confident, but she knew he must be scared. She wanted to go to him, pull him to her, run away as fast and as far as they could.

Why he'd ever thought this was a good idea was beyond her. What did he think this was going to accomplish?

He was going to die, and she was going to have to watch.

Of course, the idea of staging a rescue had occurred to her—after all, this was her fault. If she had just listened to Edward sooner, this would never have happened. Yet she had already tried to save the day once, and it had landed them all in prison. And now, short of running out and jumping in front of the bullet, there was nothing she could do. And when it was all over—when Patrice came to initiate her into a new life of lies—she would die too. She would follow Edward. Maybe they'd even see each other again someday.

The clock struck noon, the bell rang out, and a hush fell over the crowd. Out on the street, Edward was looking around expectantly. The telltale sound of trumpets boomed in the sky then, and the royal party began their approach from the palace.

Willow waited impatiently. She had seen this drill a thousand times before. The challenger always came down from the high ground of the palace with the support of the king. It was odd to see the king himself being carried forward though.

Finally, he and Edward were both on their feet and being beckoned forward by the commissioner, a young man dressed all in white to signify his impartiality. He was speaking to them now, no doubt going over the rules and looking a bit nervous in his role. Willow crept towards the edge of the crowd, not sure if she would be able to stop herself from doing something stupid.

There seemed to be some kind of hold up. Edward and the king were arguing now. Maybe this had all been another trick, and Pentheus was about to just shoot Edward in front of everyone.

She felt her pulse quicken and began to push her way through the throng more aggressively. Suddenly, something furry brushed against her ankle, and she paused. Glancing down, she gasped.

"Hikoo!" she whispered. The skulposis peered up at her with his big eyes and wagged his bushy blue tail. "What are you doing here?"

"Hikoo missed his friends," he said. "I found you by your scent, see."

Willow's mind raced, and her eyes darted back to the street. Edward and the king were back-to-back once again. She turned back to Hikoo, an idea brewing.

"Hikoo, we're in trouble. I need you to do something for me."

The creature bounced on his hind legs and nodded. She told him what to do and he slipped through her legs and disappeared.

Chapter 11

On the Winds of Decius

The ground crunched beneath Edward's boots and sweat trickled down the back of his neck with each step that he took, silently counting them out in his head... *Seventeen, eighteen, nineteen...* Each one seemed to last a lifetime. He wondered if getting shot would hurt. Would he even feel it? Or would everything just be gone in an instant. He tried to clear his mind. This wasn't what he should be thinking. After all, the king could miss... or hit him in the leg. Then it would take several more painful shots to finish him off. He didn't know which option he liked less. He took his thirtieth step and came to a halt, waiting for the tolling of the bells, but what he heard first was something else entirely.

A shrill yelp cut the air. He whirled around, hand hovering over his gun. The king was hunched over, sixty paces away, clutching his shins. His pants were torn, and blood oozed from cuts on his legs. Edward gaped at the scene. A flash of blue fur was scrambling up the king's back now, and suddenly, the man screamed again as his attacker dug its claws into the back of his neck.

Then something happened which caught Edward by surprise. Maybe it was the sight of their king on his knees, or maybe it was just years of pent-up anger, but the crowd suddenly surged out into the boulevard.

The few soldiers lining the edge of The Line fired off

gunshots, but they did little to deter the onslaught. In a moment, the street had been transformed into a battlefield. The royal guard, realizing they were hopelessly outnumbered, scattered like dogs.

Edward stared into the chaos, watching it all with mute shock and relief. A moment ago, he'd been a dead man walking, and now he was just another face in the crowd. He spotted the king, whimpering on the ground, and strode over to him with his pistol raised.

The king looked up at him. "You people are insane!" His face was covered in bloody scratches and a chunk of his left ear was missing.

He couldn't shoot the king now. It didn't seem right. He also didn't feel any responsibility to do so. One glance at the chaos around them made it clear that all the power had slipped from the old man's grasp.

"I hope you're happy," Pentheus spat.

Edward reached down and snatched the king's pistol from its holster and tucked it into his belt.

Pentheus protested feebly but kept his hands pressed to the wounds on his neck. "You're a fool, you know," he said, staring up at the barrel of Edward's gun. "You've just unleashed something that you have no idea how to control."

Edward shrugged. "It's not mine to control."

The king smirked. "You're right. It's *his*! And he will make you pay for this." He chuckled mirthlessly. "Surely you know about Lord Gorlak. Not the kind of man you displease more than once."

Oddly, Edward felt a twinge in his stomach, but he forced himself not to show it. "Who?"

Pentheus sneered. "You'll meet him soon enough... if you

make it to Regnum that is."

Edward frowned, then pressed his boot into the king's shin. Pentheus shrieked.

"If I were you," Edward said coldly, "I'd worry about myself right about now."

Then he turned and walked away into the swarm, leaving the king to whatever fate had in store for him. He shoved his way through the crowd, looking for Willow, but he couldn't get that name out of his head: Lord Gorlak… clearly the fabled wizard king that Willow had mentioned hearing rumours about. He shuddered; an uncomfortable feeling beginning to form in the back of his mind.

The crowd soon spilled out into the streets all across Dobson's Canyon, trashing the estates and manors of the nobles and ransacking shops. Across the city, buildings were burning, and smoke and the crackle of gunfire filled the air. From what he could tell, there were three main camps. The largest by far were the rioters, who were hell-bent on destroying the city. Opposing them were the soldiers—those who had stuck around—and opposing both these groups, was a smaller faction of resistance fighters who wanted to keep some sort of order so as to ensure an effective transition of power.

"Edward!"

He spun around; Willow was pushing towards him, her green eyes electric.

"Willow! How did you—"

"I was watching you. Come on! We've got to hurry!" She took his hand, and he stumbled after her. "Where's the king?"

"He's not a problem anymore," he said, and she gaped at him. "Oh, no, he's alive, though he's looked better. What happened?"

She grinned. "You didn't recognise our little friend?"

He frowned for a moment, and then his eyes widened. *"Hikoo?"* He had been so wired that he hadn't even realised it was him. "Where is he now?"

"I sent him to go free Cliff and the others."

Edward groaned. "You didn't."

She shot him a look. "He did just save your life."

Edward couldn't argue with that. They got off The Line on the far side, the palace looming off to their right. Willow turned left and dashed along the treeline, leaving the city behind them.

"Where are we going?"

"We're getting out of here. I told Hikoo to meet us at the airfield."

Edward felt his pulse quicken. "Tell me we're not riding on one of those flying creatures."

She looked at him sideways but kept going. They hurried along the edge of the boulevard until Willow took a sharp turn into the bush, and they trekked up the ravine on a steep dirt path. On either side of them, cobblestone retaining walls jutted from the ground. Edward turned and looked out over the burning city. Then a thought suddenly struck him.

"What happened to Patrice?" he said. Willow just shrugged. "You don't think they're gonna kill her, do you?" Edward didn't like Patrice, but he wasn't sure if she deserved to die.

"Come on," Willow said. "We've got to keep moving."

*

Edward poked his head up between the rocks. He and Willow were perched on a ledge that jutted out from the narrow trail. Behind them, the cliff face dropped off sharply to the ravine floor, nearly a mile below them. On the other side of the ledge, a flat platform backed onto the canyon wall. Edward scanned it. Off to the side, a wooden dock stuck out from the cliff like an open hand reaching towards the sky.

"Could they have picked a worse spot to build this thing?"

"This is where the arubbak graze," Willow said.

Edward was pretty sure that even if he was a giant flying lizard, he wouldn't want to graze on the side of a cliff.

"Okay, so what's the plan?"

Willow scowled at him. She had already told him the plan, but he had been too absorbed by the daring climb to listen.

"Once the traders return from Decius for the day, we're just going to walk right up and take their ride. They're not permitted to take any weapons with them, so they won't be armed when they get back here." They heard the scuffling of feet nearby, and they both moved over and peered back towards the trail.

"Well, it's about time," Willow said.

Cliff scowled up at her, with Brooks and Kincaid behind him, looking exhausted. "Nice to see you're alive too," he grumbled; then he looked at Edward. "Ed, that was some trick you pulled. What was I gonna do if you got yourself killed?"

"I honestly don't know."

Cliff scoffed. "I've been rotting in jail for the past two days. I nearly starved to death!" Hikoo scurried up Cliff's arm and onto the ledge.

"Master Sting, Hikoo is esteemed to be in your service again."

"Suck up," Cliff mumbled.

Edward scratched the skulposis behind the ear. "I owe you one, Hikoo. You saved my life back there." Hikoo beamed at him, his blue fur glowing purple for a moment.

One by one, they climbed up the ivy-covered wall and onto the ledge. Once they were all hidden there, Willow relayed the plan.

Cliff scratched his head. "So, we're just supposed to walk up and take off with their bird? Seems kind of risky."

"I hate to agree with him," Brooks said, "but I can see this going badly."

Willow looked unimpressed. "Well, if anyone has a better idea, I'd love to hear it, but seeing as I don't have my bow—"

"Oh!" Kincaid interrupted, looking at Cliff.

"Oh, that's right," Cliff said. He unslung his pack. A long leather-bound wrapping was sticking out of the top. "Almost forgot, we got your things," he said, pulling out Edward's sword and Willow's bow.

Willow's eyes lit up, and she slung the quiver over her shoulder.

"How?" Edward asked, running his hand over the silver blade.

"This guy's got a nose like you wouldn't believe," Cliff said, nodding at Hikoo. A throaty croak boomed over the canyon, and they glanced up to see the silhouette of a winged creature soaring over the top of the cliff. The arubbak glided overhead in a lazy circle, cutting the blue sky with its spiny tail.

Willow tightened her bowstring. "Okay, this should be a little easier now."

The giant reptile croaked again before dipping into a sharp dive. When it was just a few feet above the dock, it pulled up and landed softly, sinking its thick talons into the wood.

A man stepped out of the carriage on the animal's back and tossed a rope ladder over the side. Behind him, two more men emerged, and they began hauling out crates.

The arubbak curled its dark green wings underneath itself to make the job easier, while the first man strolled up to its large, scaley snout and started polishing it with a rag. Edward couldn't help but chuckle.

Willow waved her hand, and they crept along the ledge towards the men. When they were a few yards away, she sprang onto the airfield and raised her bow. The traders looked up, eyes wide and dropped their crates. Then Edward and the others dashed forward and quickly separated the three men from their ride. "In the good name of Candosia, step aside and retain your honour," Willow said. The three men were pale and grizzled and didn't put up a fight.

Edward strode towards the carriage, thinking that this was easier than he had thought it would be, when suddenly, the carriage door burst open again, and Patrice hobbled out, followed by Feelus and Hugo, who were both armed with muskets. They all froze.

Patrice looked terrible. Her face was dirty, and she limped towards the ladder like she had been stampeded over by a bull. Her eyes drilled into Willow as she scrambled down to the dock.

"You stupid girl. Do you have any idea what you've done? War, hunger… That's what's in store for them all now. Do you really think people will be better off being free and learning the truth? That there is no god? That the world is full of people different from themselves? Don't you understand that people *need* to believe in something! They need to feel safe and secure! For years we've protected you, and now—"

"And now they'll be free from your control."

Patrice let out a mad sort of giggle then, and Willow drew her bow. Immediately, Feelus and Hugo raised their guns to Edward's head.

"Now," she said, looking at Willow, "put that silly thing away."

Willow eyed the two giants and lowered her bow. Hugo stepped forward and wrenched it from her hands.

Patrice shook her head glumly. "We could have been so good together, you and I."

"It's over, Patrice," Edward said. "The king is finished."

"It's over when I say it's over," she spat.

Edward's mind was spinning; then he remembered the pistols that were nestled snug inside his jacket: his own and the king's.

"Now, Mr Sting," Patrice said, "you are going to pay for the trouble you've caused me."

He only had one bullet loaded in each weapon, so he'd have to be perfect.

"I was going to hand you over to Teradowa and collect the ransom, but now I think I'll kill you myself." Hugo and Feelus cocked their weapons.

In a flash, Edward drew his pistols, raising the first one to his shoulder, and fired. Hugo crumbled to the ground. He tossed that gun aside and jumped as a shot rang out beside him. Feelus had gambled and lost. Now, with a moment to spare, Edward raised the second gun and pulled the trigger.

Feelus dropped to the ground with a heavy thud.

In an instant, Kincaid and Brooks whirled on the first two traders and tackled them. The third man simply raised his hands in defeat. Patrice stared at them all for a moment, seemingly indifferent. Then she started to chuckle. She laughed until her eyes watered, and her knees gave out. Willow picked up her bow and pushed the tip of her arrow under Patrice's chin.

"Go ahead," the woman said. "Kill me. It's what I would

do."

Willow glared at her, the bowstring tight between her fingers. Then she lowered the bow. "And that's exactly why you'll live." She stepped back and joined the others.

Patrice staggered to her feet, her pale face gazing out at the burning city. "I hope it was worth it."

Edward watched her limp away and was surprised to feel almost sympathetic. He supposed that, in her own twisted way, Patrice might have loved Candosia more than anyone.

Cliff clapped his hands. "Well, this has been fun, but I think I'd like to leave now."

"Should we take these crates with us?" Edward asked, pushing the lid off one. He peered inside. "Cannonballs?" He blinked. "Why was Pentheus getting cannonballs delivered from Decius?"

Kincaid and Willow shrugged.

They lugged their bags onto the carriage and prepared to leave, but Kincaid remained on the dock.

"Come on," Edward said.

The man shook his head. "I'm afraid I can't."

They all glanced back at him. "What do you mean?" Edward asked, hopping back down.

"I am incredibly grateful for your help, Edward, but I can't leave now. Somebody needs to sort out this mess." He nodded towards the ruined city below. "Might as well be me."

Edward nodded. "I get it."

Kincaid put a hand on his shoulder. "Today, you almost took a bullet for me, and for that, you will always have a friend in Candosia."

"Thank you."

Kincaid grinned. "And by the way, that was some fine

shooting just now."

Edward blushed. "Yeah, well... I was kind of surprised it worked. I thought maybe I'd have to reload it or something." He knew that didn't make sense, but he didn't care. Kincaid surely wouldn't. They shook hands, and then Edward boarded the carriage.

Willow was in the cabin at the front window, and he stepped up beside her, glancing through the glass at the blue sky beyond.

"Are you any good at flying?"

She shrugged. "I guess we'll find out." She yanked on the thick rope that protruded from the floor, and the arubbak jerked to life. Edward clutched the wall as the creature rose and strode to the edge of the dock.

Beside him, Cliff was white as a ghost. "Is it too late to get off?" he asked, clutching his stomach. The arubbak stretched out its wings and sprang from the dock. Edward's belly rose into his throat, as they dipped over the cliff face and the canyon floor surged up in the windshield.

"Woah!" Cliff shouted.

Then a whooshing noise swept past his ears as the beast flapped its wings, and they shot into the sky. On the dock below, Kincaid shouted something, but it was too hard to make out. They were already soaring away.

*

The sky was dotted with clouds, scattered above and below them like blotches of snow. Edward's blond hair danced in the wind as he peered down at the green hills rolling by below, wondering what kind of dangers they were soaring over. He didn't know how high they were, but he guessed he wouldn't want to fall.

Beside him, Cliff was leaning over the rail, stretching out in the breeze.

"Cut that out. You're going to fall."

The chubby boy rolled his eyes. "It's fun, Ed. Try it."

Edward peered over the rail, this time at the arubbak, flapping its spiney wings.

Cliff yawned. "I'm gonna head in. All this excitement has me beat." With that, he shuffled towards the cabin. "Wake me when we get to Regnum."

Edward watched the beast for a moment longer. He envied it, so strong and free, gliding above the earth completely indifferent to the chaos below. It was while he was standing there, admiring the view, that the most peculiar thing happened.

A little bird appeared out of nowhere and perched on the rail. Edward frowned, a familiar feeling creeping into his mind. Then he saw that it was, in fact, wearing a headset, just like the bird he had seen in Candosia.

He gasped and jumped away from the rail. The bird skipped after him, observing him through its spyglass. Its head darted around like a broken toy for a moment; then the bird sprang from the rail and disappeared.

Edward dashed to the edge and peered over, but the bird had vanished. Where had it gone? They were thousands of feet in the air.

After a moment, he wandered into the cabin. Willow was at the reins, and Brooks sat at a small table, pouring over the map. Cliff saw him first.

"What's wrong, Ed?"

"I saw the bird again."

"What bird?"

"With the spyglass."

Brooks looked up from the table. "What did you say?"

Edward pointed outside, and Brooks got up and dashed out onto the deck. Edward followed him.

"It's gone. It was yellow with an orange beak, and it was wearing a spyglass on its head. I swear saw it in the forest too." Brooks' face was grim, and he rushed back into the cabin.

"What's going on?" Willow asked.

"We're being followed."

Edward felt his legs go numb. Beside him Cliff stuttered, "Followed? By whom?"

Brooks grunted and started rummaging around in his bag. Then something seemed to catch his eye. Edward followed his gaze out the window. There were two tiny black dots on the horizon, growing larger. And fast. Soon, Edward could make out what looked like wings.

Brooks whirled on Willow. "Get us on the ground!"

Willow fussed with the reins for a few moments, then shook her head. "He doesn't want to land."

Cliff shrieked. "We're doomed!" Suddenly, the cabin gave an awful shudder as the arubbak shook itself, and Edward slammed against the wall.

"Those birds are making him nervous."

Edward brushed himself off and squinted out the window. "Those aren't birds." Two massive arubbaks were speeding towards them, with figures milling about on their decks, shouting and waving their fists.

"They don't look happy," Cliff said. "And has anyone seen Hikoo?" One of the cargo containers moved, and Hikoo's head poked out.

"Stay there, Hikoo," Edward said. They took a sharp turn, and Edward sailed through the cabin, crashing into the far wall.

Outside, bullets whizzed by the deck as the newcomers opened fire on them.

"Hold on!" Willow shouted. She yanked on the rope, and the creature shot higher into the sky.

"I thought we were going down!" Cliff cried, as more iron pellets zipped by like a swarm of angry wasps.

The two arubbaks darted after them, harrying them on either side. Edward stared, wide-eyed as they rode up on their rear.

"Brace yourselves!" Willow shouted.

Their pursuers rammed into the carriage, and the sound of cracking wood filled the cabin as Edward crashed onto the floor. Pain shot through his back. He scrambled over to the window and peeked out, then ducked as an arrow ripped through the glass, showering him with broken shards and stinging his skin.

The arubbaks rose above them, and then dove again, using their giant scaly snouts like battering rams, crushing the deck and buckling it towards the far wall of the cabin. Edward struggled to his knees, feeling his heart pounding against his chest. Cliff, Brooks, and Willow lay pressed against the floor. Suddenly, the cabin creaked, and the roof was ripped away as if by the hand of God. The attackers flapped overhead, their roars filling the sky. The nearest one shrieked then and lashed out with its tail. Edward stumbled forward and fell through the cabin as their own beast dove to avoid the strike. Ahead of him, he saw the fast approach of the front window and covered his face just before he smashed through it. Broken glass thrashed his skin, shooting pain across his arms as he rolled down the deck, grasping for something to hold onto to keep from plummeting to the earth.

His fingers wrapped around the outside corner of the rail at the very brow of the deck and held on tight. Gritting his teeth, he felt his stomach jump into his chest and his whole body rise against the wind as they dropped like a rock through the air.

"Edward!" Willow shouted. She was hanging out the front window, waving the steering rope at him. It flailed around just out of reach. He could feel his fingers slipping and knew he didn't have long. Then the arubbak pulled out of its dive, and his body slammed back down, almost ripping his fingers from the rail.

Their attackers moved in for another strike, slamming into them hard. Edward released his grip on the rail and snatched the rope just as the deck crumbled away. Slowly, he pulled himself, hand over hand, towards the small portion of the carriage that was still intact. The roof and most of the walls were gone.

He heard another shriek from one of their attackers and looked back. The arubbaks were circling far overhead and Edward soon realised why; his own creature was no longer attempting to flee, rather, it was quickly descending towards the earth.

After what seemed like forever, he made it back to relative safety, and leaned against the ruined wall of the carriage, catching his breath and still clutching the rope. Cliff and Brooks lay unconscious on the floor.

Willow yanked the rope away from him and smacked him on the arm. She was crying.

"That was so stupid!"

"What?"

"What were you thinking? You're so stupid! You know that?"

Edward stared at her. "Why are you crying?"

She hit him again.

"Because you could have died!"

He gazed at her shaking form, and his heart melted. He reached out and gently touched her cheek, wiping away the tears.

He grinned. "I guess that's another one I owe you."

She sniffled and shook her head. Then he leaned over and kissed her lightly on the lips.

When he pulled back, she eyed him, her green eyes glistening, then she rested her head on his shoulder.

Edward wrapped his arms around her, savouring the warmth of her body against his as they began a slow descent, spiralling downwards through the clouds.

Chapter 12

Queen in the Castle

The treetops grew bigger as they descended, their arubbak's ear-splitting wails piercing the sky.

"I think he's hurt," Willow said. The beast dragged its left wing, searching for an opening in the trees. Eventually, it could stay aloft no longer, and they smashed into the forest. Edward stuck his hands out as branches went whipping past them. They dropped beneath the canopy, and finally, the arubbak slammed into the ground, kicking up mounds of dirt before sliding to a rest.

Edward peeked over the ruins of the carriage and staggered over to his friend, still prostrate on the creature's back.

"Cliff," he whispered, shaking his friend. There was a bloody cut on his forehead.

The boy moaned. "What happened?"

"We crashed."

He rolled onto his side. "You can say that again."

Edward turned back to Willow, who was staring glumly at the sky.

"We still have a problem," she said. The two arubbaks had returned and were now circling above the trees.

"What are they doing?"

She shrugged.

With a low groan, Brooks limped over to them. "I say we don't stick around to find out," he said, tossing his bag to the forest floor. They clambered down from the arubbak, and Edward winced as his arms grazed its scaly skin. His waistcoat was torn, and his forearms were a bloody mess.

"We need to do something about that," Willow said.

"I'm fine," he said, but her scowl sucked away his will to protest, and he slumped to the ground.

Overhead, the attackers continued to circle. He felt like a turkey waiting to be cooked. He was about to argue again when Willow dropped to her knees beside him and brushed her fingertips across his cheek. Suddenly, a new feeling coursed through his body, making him forget all about the danger for a moment. He leaned back against a tree trunk, while she rummaged through her bag and pulled out a clear vial.

"What is that?"

"It's for your arms," she said. "I made it."

"Is it gonna set me on fire?"

She smirked. "No promises." She rolled his sleeves up. "It *is* going to sting a bit."

He sighed.

She poured the liquid from the bottle out onto his arms, and he gritted his teeth. It felt like he was being stung by a thousand bees all at once. The feeling intensified until he couldn't suppress a cry of pain as spots appeared at the edge of his vision. But, after another moment, the pain was gone.

He looked down at his arms. They were raw and bruised but no longer bleeding. Pieces of glass were bubbling up out of his cuts, and one after another, were sliding off him onto the ground. When all the glass was gone, she took his arms and bandaged them tightly. He watched her work, glancing up at her face occasionally, and then their eyes met. He looked away fast, feeling his heart jump. When he looked back up a few seconds later, she seemed deep in thought. Finally, she opened her mouth to speak, but at that moment, Cliff lumbered towards them.

"Here they come!" he said.

The arubbaks were diving towards the trees above them. Edward staggered to his feet and took a deep breath. He was all out of tricks.

Brooks was leaning against their own injured arubbak, looking pale. It was obvious that he was in no shape to fight. Thick branches cracked like twigs above them as the beasts settled down on the thick canopy overhead, spreading their weight nimbly across many trees at once.

Edward squinted upward. A moment passed with only the rustle of the leaves and the groaning of overburdened tree trunks. Then rope ladders began to drop to the forest floor all around them, and people began sliding down like spiders dropping from their webs, landing on the matted dirt all around them.

They were all women, tall and brawny, with long braided hair. They continued to drop until Edward lost count, and he could only measure their number by the growing dread in the pit of his stomach.

Finally, the last woman dropped to the ground, and when she did, the others all stood up straight and still. Her cherry-red hair hung in a tight braid, and like her comrades, she wore thin plated armour and a set of sheathed daggers on her hips. She eyed Edward, like one would a rabid animal.

"You there! Today's business was already complete. Why have you returned to Decius?"

Edward blinked. "What?"

"You are from Candosia, are you not?"

He stuttered. "Well yes, but we've never even been here before! We're just passing through and—"

"You do not have permission to 'pass through' Decius. Does King Pentheus know about this?" She said this last part with an air of suspicion, like she already knew the answer. Edward glanced at the others and shrugged.

"Pentheus is no longer the king," he said. The woman chuckled, sending a course of laughter through the group.

"Think that's funny?" Cliff said, puffing out his chest. "You nearly killed us up there! What's the matter with you?"

She frowned and addressed Edward. "Who are you?"

Edward didn't think lying would make the situation any better—though, of course, he rarely did.

"My name is Edward Sting."

A murmur ran through the circle.

The woman raised her eyebrows. "So, you are the famous Edward Sting?" She strolled around him, eyeing him like a piece of meat. He stiffened as she stopped before him and crossed her arms. She was nearly as tall as him, and Edward found himself paralysed by her deep blue eyes.

"And I suppose this is your ragtag crew," she said. Her gaze fell on Willow then, and the two women exchanged a dark look.

"Well," Brooks said, limping forward, "it seems that we're not who you were looking for, so why don't we just go our separate ways?"

The woman smirked. "You must be Shanley Brooks. I'd recognise the voice of a diplomat anywhere. You'll be disappointed to learn that Pentheus sold you out the minute he discovered you had broken King Sento's trust."

Brooks' smile faded. "You would be wise to make a deal with us."

She snickered. "Sounds like a threat, but not to worry, you won't be going home anytime soon."

Edward felt the blunt end of a dagger shove him from behind. As he was led towards the rope ladder, he couldn't help but think it would be a long time before he made it to Regnum.

*

Pale desert stretched out beneath them like a giant blanket covering the earth. After leaving the forest behind, the air had become dry and hot, and now they were gliding over miles of barren, sandy wasteland. Brooks sat opposite him, hunched over on a wooden bench. Cliff, Willow, and Hikoo had been taken in the other arubbak. Edward wasn't sure if this was so they wouldn't try to escape, or if they simply didn't have enough room. Looking around the cramped cabin, he suspected it was a bit of both.

He met Brooks' eye for a moment, and the duke gave him a wink. Edward felt a little guilty. Brooks had come to his aid and been side-lined ever since they had left Teradowa. Sometimes Edward forgot that Brooks was on this journey for the same reason he was.

The woman with the cherry-red hair came through the cabin door. "Better stretch those legs boys," she said. "We're here."

Edward turned to look out the window. They were soaring low over a city. It looked as though someone had taken a square grid and dropped it in the middle of the desert. The result was a patchwork of slums and weathered-looking buildings, beyond which a giant dome loomed near the horizon, with marble columns lining its exterior. Beside it sat a glassy lake. Edward thought it looked like an arena of some sort. The city, arena and lake all sat in the shadow of a lush mountainside.

Edward soaked it in as they raced past. There was something

very intentional about the city and the mountain. Then his eyes settled in the direction they were flying. Set back on a hill, a castle loomed over the city, cracked brick and stone giving it an aged appearance. The arubbak croaked as it sailed over towering stone spires and circled the nearest wing of the castle. Then a large shimmering platform came into view below them, and they landed gently. Edward was shoved to his feet and led from the cabin, his boots hitting the landing pad with a light tap.

"Watch it!"

He glanced over across the platform to where Cliff and Willow were being dragged from the other carriage. They were marched under a tall archway, and the temperature dropped as they entered the shade of the castle. Then the light dimmed as they stepped into a short tunnel. On the other side, Edward's jaw dropped. The hall they found themselves in was enormous; its high vaulted ceiling was tall enough to house a forest and shone like the night sky. Colourful patterns crisscrossed the lines in the ceiling and crept down the walls like vines in a jungle. To his left, a sweeping staircase led outside.

"Keep moving!" the woman snapped.

Edward stumbled forward. The room itself was practically empty except for a round pink sofa at its far end, on which a woman lounged. She was dressed in a green silk dress and golden jewellery hung from her ears and around her neck. A man stood beside her, fanning her with a giant leaf of some sort. Edward and the others were marched right up to the sofa and stopped before the woman. He could see now that she was very young, perhaps even younger than him. She had steely blue eyes and long, blonde hair that hung down in a pair of braids. She was leaning back on her hands and smiling at Edward.

"You have got to be Edward Sting. You're *just* what I

imagined. Tall… strong…" She giggled. "I didn't expect you to be blond though."

Edward rolled on the balls of his feet, while the woman with the cherry-red hair leaned against the wall, looking amused.

"You flatter me," he said.

The girl hopped off the sofa and strolled over to him, stopping when she was mere inches away.

"I admit, I didn't think I'd get the chance to meet you." She sounded breathless. "There were rumours that you ran into trouble." She stroked his chin. "I even heard you were in prison!"

Edward twisted away from her touch. "You seem to know an awful lot about me, but I don't think we've ever met."

She laughed. "Of course. Allow me to introduce myself. I am Sofia Andron, Queen of Decius." Edward couldn't hide his shock. He forced himself to bow.

"Please." Sofia laughed again. "I know you don't respect royalty."

A little yellow bird flew through the window and landed on Sofia's shoulder. She stroked its back. "You see, I've been watching you closely, Edward,"

Edward eyed the bird. "Yes, it appears you have."

She gave him a coy grin, like a child caught misbehaving. "Don't be upset. I think you're wonderful, you see." She ran a finger over his jaw. "I don't know if there's anyone else like you." He could feel her breath on his neck as she spoke, her pink lips just inches from his skin.

He jerked his head away. "Listen, why don't you just tell us what you want or let us go?" She stepped back, and something different came into her eyes. Was it hurt?

Suddenly, there was a loud clank, and the door to the chamber burst open. A tall man with a grey beard strode in, a thick, red cape billowing out behind him, and all the guards suddenly stood at attention. He was red in the face and looked as though smoke might come pouring out of his ears.

"Sofia!" he snapped, striding towards them. Beside him, an older woman struggled to keep up, nervously ringing her hands. "You've got to stop this, you silly girl!"

Sofia shrank behind Edward.

"But, Pa—"

"No." He raised a finger. "I've let you go too far this time. From now on, you'll do as I say. Am I understood?"

Sofia sighed. "Yes, Papa."

"And no more birds! All you use them for is nonsense like this."

Sofia stomped her feet. "But, Papa, you can't!"

"I can, and I will."

"Oh, Anax," the woman said. "It does no harm."

"It certainly does no good either!" Anax said.

Sofia crossed her arms. "Well, what am I supposed to do all day?"

Her father scoffed. "I'll tell you what. You're going to learn to conduct yourself like a proper princess should. And where's Eclipse?"

The red-haired woman stepped forward. "Here, my king."

Anax blinked as if startled by her appearance then pointed his finger. "I know you encourage this behaviour. But enough! No more games. From either of you!" He glanced back at his daughter. "Now go on. There's business to discuss."

Sofia gave her father one last dirty look and stormed out of the room.

The king shook his head. "You'll have to forgive me. My daughter has a kind heart, but she's more trouble than she's worth."

Edward supposed that must be quite a lot of trouble. The king looked down the line at Cliff, Brooks, and Willow and gestured to Eclipse, who nodded. One of the other guards stepped forward and uncuffed them. Edward rubbed his sore wrists.

"So," Anax said, dropping onto the sofa, "I suppose I should welcome you to my kingdom. I am Anax Andron, ruler of Decius... and anyone within its borders," he added pointedly. "This is my wife, Claudia Andron," he said, smiling up at the woman standing stoically by the sofa. "Since we all know who *you* are, why don't you start by telling me what has become of my friend Pentheus?"

Edward hesitated. "King Pentheus no longer rules Candosia."

Andron raised his bushy eyebrows. "Is that so?" He narrowed his eyes. "Last I heard, he was giddy over having quelled a rebellion... which included you."

Edward pursed his lips. He didn't want to divulge too much information, as he wasn't sure how much Andron knew. "He wasn't as successful as he let on."

The king seemed to consider this, then burst with laughter. "Serves him right, the old fool! That man couldn't tell a bandoro from his own gut." Andron laughed until he was red in the face again, and tears streamed down his cheeks.

Edward relaxed. If there was one thing that put a selfish man in a good mood, it was the misfortune of his enemies.

"And the new king?" Andron asked.

Edward grinned, thinking of Kincaid. "I think you'll find him quite reasonable."

The king dusted off his robes. "Good," he said, regaining his composure. "That's Candosia all right, a new king every week! I need somebody I can work with."

Brooks cleared his throat. "And what about us? Can you work with us?"

The king glared at him, his good humour seemingly exhausted. "I don't care what your business is, but you came into my realm uninvited, and so now, you are of concern to me."

"If you let us go," Edward said, "we'll be gone by sunset, and you'll never hear from us again."

The king smiled humourlessly. "I wish it were that easy, but I need to trust somebody before I can take their word, and I don't trust you, Mr Sting. Not after the noise you've caused."

Brooks scoffed. "This is ridiculous," he said, but the king shot him a look.

"Ridiculous is it, Shanley? I could always send you back to Teradowa if you prefer. I'm sure Sento has some questions he'd like answered. And the reward would surely be worth it."

Edward cleared his throat. "How can we make you trust us?"

"It's not easy," Andron said, gazing at the ceiling. "I'd like to let you go. Truly. Knowing what you do about the realms, it's in my best interest for you to be as far away from my people as possible."

At this, Edward could see Willow's fists clench. For a moment, he thought she was going to leap at the king.

"What is it that you want?" Edward said, growing weary of being toyed with.

Andron crossed his legs. "There is one thing. Seeing as I'm doing you a favour, not turning you in, perhaps you could do me one in return." He looked at Edward with a cheeky smile now. "We have a little competition coming up here in Decius, Mr Sting, and there are one or two wealthy gentlemen interested in being represented therein."

Edward dreaded what was coming next. He fervently wished the king would stop talking.

Andron tapped the tips of his fingers together. "See, with your... popular status, your involvement could make the games more exciting for those individuals privy to your adventures."

"Of course, it would," Edward murmured.

*

"No! Absolutely not." Willow glared up at him, hands on her hips. They were standing on the steps leading out of King Andron's throne room. Torches flickered along the path, illuminating the dark courtyard.

"What was I supposed to do?"

"We should be exposing him for the fraud he is! It's not right the way he treats these people! They're just like you and me!"

"And how exactly did you plan on exposing him?"

Willow crossed her arms. It wasn't that Edward thought she was wrong; he simply didn't see any alternative. Andron had been quick to point out the large bounty that King Sento had placed on them and how easy it would be for him to just send them home and collect the money. Still, he didn't like this game the king was playing. He obviously wanted to keep them around a bit longer. But why?

Edward sighed. "Look, it's just a little competition."

Willow frowned. "It's not going to be what you think. For all we know, he's lying, and you're going to end up dead."

Edward laughed. "That makes me feel better."

"You know what I mean," she said. "This is just like the last time you tried to talk your way out of danger. People aren't so lucky twice."

"I know." Edward met her gaze. "But I can't go back to Teradowa." The firelight flickered across her green eyes then, and he wanted to say something but couldn't. Instead, he wrapped his arms around her. Her body felt good against his own.

"We're trapped," she whispered.

Footsteps echoed from above. They broke apart as Cliff came thumping down the stairs with Hikoo on his shoulder. Brooks limped along behind them.

Cliff yanked Hikoo off his back. "Found this one sneaking around the castle."

Willow smiled. "You have a way of getting around, Hikoo."

"Hikoo must always be ready to help his friends." The skulposis dropped at Edward's feet, stuck his hind leg behind his ear, and scratched vigorously.

"We'd better get moving, Ed," Cliff said. "Sounds like some fancy aristocrat is waiting for us."

Brooks cleared his throat and glared at Cliff. "We must be cautious. We will no doubt be watched."

Cliff shrugged. "At least this Andron seems all right." Edward didn't like his friend's blind optimism, but he was too tired to argue. "And that princess," Cliff said. "She's got an eye for you." Edward sputtered and looked at Willow, who averted his gaze.

"What?" Cliff asked. "I wouldn't be surprised if the king wanted you to marry her."

"You're right. We should get moving," Edward said, keen to change the subject.

"Where we headed anyway?" Cliff asked.

Edward had completely forgotten about the instructions the king had given him. He rummaged through his jacket pocket, his fingers briefly finding the stone, and pulled out the folded paper he had been given.

Opening it, he scanned the page and could see now why the king had not just told him where to go. The directions were so confusing that he had to read them over several times.

They were to travel a very specific route through the city to the mountainside estate of King Andron's so-called 'friend of the crown.'

"I'll send a bird ahead; he'll be expecting you!" he'd said.

Edward shoved the paper back into his pocket, and they began their trek.

An hour later, they finally reached the edge of the city. Even in the relative darkness, Edward could tell this was no place he'd want to live. Crumbling, ramshackle buildings lined their route, and the fumes of an old, decrepit sewer system wafted through the streets. The few people that they passed hobbled around like deflated souls with a mad look in their eyes.

Cliff shuddered. "How can people live like this?"

Edward wished he had an answer. The city soon fell away, and they passed the stadium. It was even bigger up close. The marble columns towered overhead, and between each pillar stood statues of past champions, guarding the entrances. Edward squinted up at the stone figures.

Each of them held a small oval object, but he couldn't make out what they were supposed to be.

As they passed, dark clouds floated ominously in from the lake, and it felt as though the columns were going to topple and crush them. A horrible feeling suddenly gripped Edward, but they continued on. As the arena and the glassy lake faded behind them, they were confronted by the mountain ahead. It wasn't a large mountain, as mountains go, and it had several lights flickering across the face of it.

A steep but narrow road would allow them access to a lightly forested ridge far above. Edward thought his legs might give out as they climbed, but he managed to go on. Eventually, they arrived at a fork in the road. As per the letter's instructions, they went left, and soon after, ascended a shimmering staircase and knocked on the front door of a handsome estate. Brooks was white as a ghost and leaned on the porch. Edward could feel his own legs wobbling and thought he might pass out. In fact, the only person who didn't seem on the verge of death was Willow. She peered through the glass panes on either side of the door, eyes narrow with suspicion. After several moments, Edward knocked again.

Cliff panted. "Don't tell me this guy is asleep." As if on cue, heavy footsteps boomed from deep in the house. Then the lock clicked, and the door swung open.

A man in a bathrobe smiled at them. He had an empty glass in one hand and a bottle in the other.

"My friends," he said, "your timing is absolutely fabulous! Please, come in!"

They shambled through the door. A large rug decorated the front hall, from which a grand staircase extended to the second floor.

"I was pleased to hear from Anax about you," the man said, refilling his glass from the bottle. He led them through the front hall to a lounge with large decorative windows overlooking the mountain. "Please have a seat," he said, slipping behind the bar.

Edward dropped gratefully onto a couch.

"To think that I have the mighty Edward Sting, defier of kings, competing for *me!*" Then he winked. "Of course, we'll have to keep that to ourselves publicly." He gazed at their dumbfounded faces and laughed. "You must be wondering who

I am. My name is Hidalgo Stern. I am a close friend of King Andron and a sponsor of the Tikki Tournament."

"So, you're rich?" Cliff said.

"I am."

"And how did you get all that money?"

Hidalgo smiled. He was younger than the king, with grey eyes and a wide jaw. "I do favours for the right people."

"Like the king?" Edward suggested.

Hidalgo chuckled and poured out several glasses. "Anax said you weren't the most trusting people."

"Can you blame us?"

"No, certainly not, my boy." Their host shuffled around from the bar and set the glasses down on the coffee table. "Fiddleberry beer?" he asked, pushing the glasses across the table.

"No thanks."

Hidalgo eyed him. "It's not laced with poison or anything," he said.

"We'll pass," Edward said firmly.

Hidalgo gazed across the coffee table at him, his thick black hair hanging just above his dark eyes. He studied Edward for a moment. "Do you know why I love Decius, my boy?"

Edward shook his head.

"It's because here… you can make whatever kind of life you want. I wasn't born wealthy; I was born down there." He pointed back towards the front hall, beyond which lay the city. "In the slums." He took another swig of his drink. "But when I discovered the truth about the realms, I didn't pout about it. I used it to my advantage." His face darkened. "This isn't some trick. We're not monsters. You do what we want, and we'll return the favour."

He set his glass on the table with a clank and leaned back in his chair. Edward shifted uncomfortably. He didn't believe a word Hidalgo had said. As far as he was concerned, they had sprung themselves from one prison just to end up in another, only with nicer cells.

Edward cleared his throat. "You'll have to forgive us, but it's been a very long day, and if you have some beds somewhere, I think we could all use a rest."

Hidalgo chuckled, returning to his carefree persona. "Of course. You've come a long way." He summoned a servant and whispered some instructions to him.

As they followed the man upstairs, Edward wondered what kind of monsters would visit him in his sleep.

Chapter 13

Royal Intrigue

Edward spent the next week at Hidalgo's estate training on the mountain. He was well rested and fed, and his host kept him on a strict regimen. For eight hours a day, he was hurling javelins, swinging swords, and racing up and down the mountain. The hills behind the estate were briming with trails and creeks and cool wallows, and Edward got to know them like the back of his hand. He could close his eyes and see the route in his mind. When he wasn't traversing the mountain, he was at the house, learning hand-to-hand combat.

"Am I really going to have to fight somebody?"

"That's the fun of it, my boy! Nobody knows! It's different each year. So, we must prepare for anything."

For hours at a time, Hidalgo would lounge in the shade and watch Edward baking in the sun, kicking and punching bags of sand. By only the second day, blisters had broken out across his hands, and his bones ached. Cliff, for his part, was enjoying their stay. His role was to ensure that Edward was sticking to his exercise program when Hidalgo was off the estate 'on business'.

"Just think," Cliff would say, after Edward staggered in from scaling the mountain, drenched in sweat, "when this is over, you'll be in amazing shape!"

By the end of the week, Edward's whole body hurt, and he was beginning to think he might drop dead from fatigue. He wondered if that would be enough to exempt him from competing.

"Have you heard anything from Brooks?" he asked, during an afternoon sword-fighting drill on Hidalgo's patio. He hadn't seen the duke all week. The day after they'd arrived, Brooks had been whisked off to stay with some other dignitary until the tournament was over. Edward suspected that the king didn't want them plotting anything against him, so it was probably a wise decision.

"I haven't heard anything. Although, before he left, he did tell us he'd try to let us know before he made any moves."

Edward sighed. He was beginning to feel more and more useless, like a show pig getting primed for the fair. He tossed his wooden sword aside and dropped into the shade of the house. A cool breeze was drifting over the mountain, sending the sweet aroma of Hidalgo's gardens across the patio.

"You look tired, Ed."

He was. He hadn't been sleeping well. The red stone was keeping him up. He would wake up in the middle of the night to find it glowing like a star on his bedside table. He'd tried everything but couldn't get it to stop. On top of that, every time he closed his eyes, he would hear Pentheus's voice, hissing that name: *Lord Gorlak*. He couldn't get the mysterious King of Regnum out of his head. Shortly after they'd arrived at Hidalgo's, he had told his friends what Pentheus had said, but neither Cliff nor Willow—Brooks had already been whisked away—knew anything about Lord Gorlak beyond vague rumours like the one Willow had shared back in the woods of Candosia. Other than the fact Pentheus seemed to be afraid of him, Edward was at a loss. A name was, after all, only a name…

He stared at a spot on the ground, wondering why it

unnerved him so badly.

"You should rest, Ed. Hidalgo won't be back for hours."

Edward glanced up at Cliff, having forgotten his friend was even there.

"Where's Willow?" he asked suddenly.

Cliff shrugged. "Who knows with her?"

Edward got to his feet and shuffled towards the house as fast as his sore body would allow. He just wanted to hear her voice; he needed to calm down. His footsteps echoed on the shiny floor as he entered the side wing, and he was just passing the front hall when a voice called out to him.

"Mr Sting."

He whirled around. A man dressed in blue robes was standing in the doorway.

"What?"

The man cleared his throat. "You have a visitor."

"Huh?"

The man pursed his lips. "There is someone here to see you, sir."

Edward shook his head. "I think you must be mistaken."

"I'm afraid not, sir. She is waiting for you in your room."

"She?"

The man shot him a knowing smile and left. Edward watched him go and was about to continue on his way, but then he hesitated, glancing upstairs. After a moment, he bounded up the steps.

The door to his room was closed, and so he knocked.

"Come in," a woman's voice called out. He opened the door.

Sofia leaned casually by the window.

She was gazing outside at the afternoon sun, her blonde braids swaying in the wind.

Edward froze in the doorway. "Princess, what are you doing here?"

She smiled. "Why don't you come in?"

"I'm actually a little busy right now, but—"

"I insist," she said, more emphatically. He stepped inside but kept the door open. "How's your training going?" she asked, breaking away from the window.

"Fine." He shuffled around the bed to keep his distance.

"I'm looking forward to seeing you in the tournament."

"I hope I don't disappoint."

She laughed. "I'm sure you won't." She bit her lip as though she wanted to say something. Suddenly a blue blur shot out from under the bed. Sofia shrieked, and Hikoo dashed up Edward's back and clung to his shoulder.

"Hey, buddy," Edward said, scratching his ear.

Sofia's eyes were wide. "What is that?" she asked, moving closer and poking Hikoo with her finger.

"He's a skulposis. They're native to Candosia… I think."

She grinned, entranced by Hikoo, and then took his whiskers gently between her fingers, causing him to sneeze. She giggled. "He's fantastic."

"Didn't your birds ever tell you about them?" he asked, more aggressively than he'd meant to.

Sofia blushed. "I'm sorry about that," she said. "I've never actually left Decius. With my birds, I can see the whole world. In a way, at least."

Edward suddenly felt a twinge of sympathy for the girl. He grinned. "You could always just do what I did and run away."

She laughed. "My father would kill me. Besides, I could never do what you did." She grazed his arm with her fingertips. "The famous Edward Sting."

"So I keep hearing."

"Well, you are. At least among my father's friends." She put a finger on his chest, but Edward's mind was racing. Maybe Andron wouldn't have to turn them over to Sento. If his name was thrown around enough, the king could easily find them all on his own.

She reached out then and cradled his jaw in her soft hands, pulling his face towards hers. "But my father doesn't appreciate you like I do." She pressed her lips to his and sighed.

He didn't mean to kiss her back. He didn't mean to be here at all, but it was happening. Her pink lips tasted sweet, and her flowery perfume filled his senses, making them dull.

Break it off. Break it off right now!

Then he noticed her, out of the corner of his eye, standing in the doorway.

"Willow!" he said, pulling free of the kiss. "I-I was just coming to find you." She stared at the ground for a moment; then her eyes flickered up, and he saw in them something he'd never seen before. It only lasted a second, and then she turned and dashed back down the hall.

"Willow, wait!" He jerked free of Sofia and rushed out of the room. But it was too late, she was gone.

*

"Straighten your back." Hidalgo took another sip of his swizzleberry juice and examined Edward's stance from the shade of his patio.

"There. Better?"

Hidalgo stroked his chin. "It's perfect, my boy."

Edward was standing on a podium in the courtyard while a

servant measured him. Hidalgo had told him it was important for contestants to wear flashy armour to get the attention of the crowd.

Hidalgo dropped into his chair. "Remember, the audience needs to fall in love with you."

Cliff lounged nearby, stirring the ice cubs in his glass. "He's right, Ed."

Edward rolled his eyes. The chubby boy had adapted to the aristocratic lifestyle without skipping a beat.

Hidalgo frowned. "Edward, my boy, you don't seem focused."

The truth was that he was the farthest thing from focused. Besides the fact that the Tikki Tournament was only hours away, he hadn't seen Willow in two days.

"He's just worried about our friend; I keep telling him to relax. She'll be fine."

Edward lifted his head as a servant brought a measuring tape up under his chin.

"It is strange though," Cliff added, "why she would just up and leave like that."

Edward knew exactly why she had left, and he didn't blame her one bit.

Hidalgo nodded, trying to look concerned, though the effort seemed a strain. "I'll have my people look for her."

"Thanks," Edward said dryly. He was sure Hidalgo already had plenty of people looking for her. A man strolled out of the house and handed Hidalgo a folded piece of paper.

"Ah, it seems my correspondent from the press has arrived," he said, rubbing his hands together, getting up, and dashing into the house.

"What?"

Cliff put up his hand. "It's all right. I'll take care of it."

"Cliff, we can't be talking to the press! We're on the run!"

Cliff grumbled. "What does it matter anyway? We're out of here tomorrow."

Edward sighed. "It's just something Sofia said to me."

Cliff stopped mid drink. "The princess was here?"

He nodded.

Cliff whistled. "When's the wedding?"

Edward stepped off the raised platform he'd been placed on for his fitting. "Listen," he said. "We need to be careful; we shouldn't draw any more attention to ourselves with this bounty out on us." He was already uncomfortable with how widely his name had been spread around the upper echelons of Decian society and he was sure that Andron held power over the newspapers. It was probably his idea to have them visit Edward to stir up excitement for his upper-class friends. But why did he care so much about the tournament anyway? Hidalgo re-emerged from the house, followed by a squat man with a balding head and a gut like a bag of sand.

"Gentleman, this is Carl Mint from the *Decius Post.*"

Edward shook his hand. He smelled like smoke and bad cologne.

"It's fabulous to meet you, Mr Sting." The newsman man pulled a pad and pen from his brown waistcoat. Edward shot Cliff a look, and his friend groaned.

"Sorry, Carl," Cliff said. "We don't have anything to say."

"My friend," Mint said, putting his arm around Cliff's shoulder, "surely, you must!" He turned him jovially to face his friend. "He's an unknown contestant! The underdog! Folks love an underdog."

Edward furrowed his brow. "What do you mean an unknown

contestant? I thought I was famous around here."

Mint laughed. "I mean that you've never fought in the Tikki Tournament before."

"Fought?"

Mint exchanged looks with Hidalgo, who shook his head, stepping between them quickly.

"He's just confused, my boy! He's a reporter, They're a wacky sort."

Edward whirled on him. "You'd better tell me exactly what's going on, right now!"

Hidalgo chuckled nervously. "Nothing. Really. He only means that you're new is all." Edward grabbed him by the shirt collar and pinned him to the wall. He swallowed hard. "Okay... Okay, I may have been a little dishonest with you about the fight."

"So, it *is* a fight?"

"To the death."

Cliff grumbled. "Why, you lousy piece of—what happened to *we're not monsters, do what we want, and we'll help you out*?"

Edward felt his temperature rising. Squeezing Hidalgo's collar tightly in his clenched fists, he practically lifted him off his feet. Beside them, Carl Mint scribbled furiously in his notebook. Hidalgo squeezed his eyes shut, anticipating a blow, but after a moment, though he didn't release him, Edward lowered him back down, disgusted with the whole thing and knowing that there was no point. The frightened man opened his eye a crack, relief washing over his face.

"But you'll win, my boy!" Hidalgo said, emboldened. "I know you will!"

"And what's in it for you if he does?" Cliff snarled.

Hidalgo glanced between them and sighed. "The king uses

the Tikki Tournament as a way of choosing members of his inner circle... from among the sponsors."

Edward blinked. "Are you telling me that I'm going to risk my life so that you might get a promotion?" His fingers slipped around Hidalgo's throat now.

The man gasped. "When you say it like that, it sounds terrible."

"It *is* terrible."

"Look," he said, trembling, "I'm on your side, but if you back out now, I'll have no choice but to tell the king."

Edward stopped. He was right. There was nothing he could say and nothing he could do to stop what was going to happen.

"So, what do you say, Edward, my boy? Shall we win this thing together?"

Edward scoffed and let the man go. Hidalgo crumpled to the ground, rubbing his neck.

"Right then," Mint said, jamming his notebook back in his bag. "I think I've got enough!" He looked at Edward. "And don't worry about that business with the bounty, kid. I'll only be using your stage name in my article: The Stinger!" He slapped Edward on the shoulder. "Good luck!"

Edward watched him go, thinking that even he wasn't lucky enough to cheat death yet again.

Chapter 14

The Egg

Willow was leaning back on the barstool with her feet up on the table. The shadows of her hood concealed her face but still allowed her to watch the flow of traffic coming through the door.

Not one person was smiling.

She didn't blame them. The dingy bar was poorly lit and smelled as though something were rotting in the kitchen. It didn't seem like the kind of place one visited if things were going well.

It hadn't been difficult to find a place to sleep in the city. The first night, she had fallen asleep on a rooftop in a quiet area of the slums. The weather was warm, and the stars were out. She liked falling asleep under the stars. It reminded her of her treehouse in the summertime, when the sky was lit with countless sparkling lights that peeked through the trees and kept her company while she slept.

The second night, she'd found an abandoned building on the outskirts of the city and slept surrounded by broken glass. Not ideal, but much safer than being out in the open. She knew that the longer she was gone, the more people would be looking for her. However warm and welcoming Hidalgo had tried to seem, he was sure to betray them, and she wasn't going to be lulled into trusting that he wouldn't.

That wasn't a mistake she would ever make again.

It hadn't taken her long to figure out what she wanted to

know. Information was easy enough to come by down here. People were too stupid to keep secrets. The trick was picking the right people. The losers. The ones that had fallen from grace—that had thrown their hats in the ring and been rejected and eventually forgotten. She smirked. Maybe in a few years, Hidalgo Stern would come walking through that door. It was people like him that she needed. They had the information, and after a couple of drinks, they were happy to share it. Yet they hid themselves well. Better to be forgotten than to share too much and disappear for good.

She drummed her fingers on the table. Those people were good at hiding, but she was better at finding them; she'd made a career out of it—or would have. A couple of conversations in scummy bars like this, and she had gotten the big picture. The so-called *friendly tournament* Edward had eagerly signed up for was anything but friendly, and a fight to the death wasn't something she could let him walk into without a way out. It wasn't going to be easy though. Even if he discovered the truth before the tournament started, there would be nothing he could do. Hidalgo would threaten to involve the king, and that would be the end of it. And all of it simply so that Hidalgo could gain political capital. The whole thing made her sick.

And the worst part was that it was her fault.

She had known Andron wasn't to be trusted, and yet she hadn't been able to talk Edward out of this plan. She had put them all in danger in Candosia, and now she had blown her chance to make up for it. Of course, it wasn't entirely her fault. She knew that. It *had* been Edward's plan after all.

And she couldn't trust him anymore.

She had decided to forget about what she'd seen in his bedroom, knowing that emotions only clouded her judgment. But a part of her still wondered if the king had sent Sofia there that day, just to get in Edward's head. Maybe she wanted to believe that. It didn't seem all that likely. But then, Edward must have invited her in of his own accord, which... Willow was no princess, she knew that. She didn't talk like one, and she certainly didn't act like one, but she had thought that maybe...

She finished her drink and ordered another. She wasn't looking for anyone in particular, but when the right person came in, she knew it instantly. He stumbled through the door eager to chat but lacking any friends. The man sauntered through the bar, slurring his words and stumbling into people. When he was a few feet away, Willow removed her feet from the table and pulled her hood back.

"Thirsty?" she asked, her voice dripping with sweetness.

The man looked down at her. He had bloodshot eyes and was missing some teeth. "Hey there, sweetheart," he said, dropping into the seat across from her. "You sure are pretty."

Willow pretended to be flattered. There was just one piece of information she still needed. She pushed her fiddleberry beer across the table. The man gulped it down and nodded.

"Are you going to be watching the tournament today?"

"Course," he said.

"It's all very exciting, isn't it?"

He grinned. "If you're into violence."

Willow put her elbows on the table and leaned forward. "I've never really understood the point, you know?"

"Whaddya mean?"

She hesitated. "What could be worth killing for?"

The man scratched his stubble. "Ain't you ever been?"

She shook her head. "I'm from out of town."

The man grunted, taking her answer for exactly what it was:

vague.

"Well," he said, scratching his head now, "I guess what you're talking 'bout is the egg." He paused to take another drink. "Every year, one of the king's big flying beasties lays an egg. Just one," he said, raising a single finger. "And that's what them boys are always fightin' over." He shrugged. "Worth plenty, I'd guess. But everybody knows that—"

"Like I said, I'm from out of town." She rose from her seat and was heading for the door before he could ask for her name. She had a lot of work to do.

*

The castle seemed deserted. The king was either very stupid or very devious. She was hoping for the former, but as always, preparing for the latter. From her perch high in the tallest tree within proximity of her target, Willow could see clear above the outer stone wall and into the courtyard. At the corner of the wall stood the target: the smooth spire of the guard tower. There had been no activity for the past half an hour.

She rummaged through her bag and pulled out the rope she had stowed away when they'd left Candosia. Bracing herself between two branches, she tied one end to an arrow and stuck the other under her boot, leaving a large coil of rope in between. One of the windows in the tower was open, and she aimed just above the wooden frame. Nocking the arrow on the string, she pulled it back to her jaw, and let go. The arrow sailed through the air, carrying the rope with it, and wedged deep into the tower just above the open window.

She couldn't help but smile. The thrill when she fired an arrow never faded. The rush of energy was like fuel for her body.

It was as though each arrow had her back and wouldn't let anything hurt her.

She grabbed the rope's end from under her boot and climbed higher into the tree until she was a good distance above the window. Then she tied the rope around a thick branch, slid her bow over top of it, and planted both feet on the branch, taking a deep breath and staring for a moment at the ground below. Finally, she launched herself from the tree and slid through the air along the rope towards the tower, tucking in her feet as the thing grew in her vision and ducking straight through the open window, landing with a thud on her back.

The room was small and a large lantern hung from the ceiling. Willow dusted herself off and peered down into the yard. The lawn was split down the centre by a stone path leading to the castle gates. A gardener was tending to a bed of flowers nearby. Willow watched as a pair of guards approached and exchanged a few words with him; then they disappeared around the corner.

She waited for a moment, but no one else appeared. It was time to move. She skipped down the spiral stairs, muffling her footfalls as best she could. At the bottom, she counted to one hundred and waited. The old man was still out there pulling weeds, but the guards did not return. She sprang from the tower and dashed across the yard towards the corner of the castle, keeping an eye on the gardener. After what seemed like eternity, she made it safely, and paused to catch her breath.

Willow remembered the area very well from the day they'd arrived in Decius. Up ahead would be the platform their arubbaks had landed on. If what she was looking for was not there, she would be out of luck.

Pulling an arrow from her quiver, she loaded her bow and crept slowly along the wall, careful to keep in the shadows of the tall castle. She was almost to the platform when she heard voices up ahead. She froze, recognizing one of the voices as belonging to the red-headed guard, Eclipse. Willow sprinted forward and ducked under the steps leading to the platform just as footfalls sounded above her.

Eclipse was speaking, she sounded concerned. "Please, do not get involved."

"I won't go," the other said. It was a woman.

"My lady, you must. You don't want to upset your father."

Willow squinted through the cracks in the steps. The second woman was Sofia. A mix of emotions suddenly welled up inside her.

"I don't care. What he's doing isn't fair!"

Eclipse put a hand on Sofia's shoulder. "I'm only looking out for you, my lady. This is for the best."

Sofia trembled. "But why is he making them fight?" She was red in the face. "They're going to kill each other!"

Eclipse gripped Sofia by the arm and whispered something that Willow couldn't make out. Then the princess yanked her arm away and stormed off. Eclipse glanced back at the platform briefly and then trailed after her.

Willow waited until they had been gone for several minutes before emerging and scrambling up the steps, trying to ignore the growing panic inside her. She had no doubt who Sofia had been talking about. When she reached the platform, relief washed over her.

Thirty yards away, three arubbaks were dozing on the marble surface, one huge adult and two juveniles, both a few years old, at least, and large enough. Their green, wrinkly bellies rose and fell softly as they breathed. There were no guards in sight. Apparently, the king assumed that nobody was crazy enough to do what she was about to do.

She crept steadily forward, her eyes locked on the sleeping giants and her hand gripping her bow. The two smaller creatures were curled up on either side of the large one, which she suspected was their mother. As it shifted in its sleep, Willow held her breath for a moment, and then pressed on. She was only a few yards away now. The hot steam from its snout thickened the air, and the sound of its snoring reverberated in her ears.

She dared another step, and then the arubbak's eyelid rolled back, and a dark pupil focused on her. The beast growled and sprang to life, rearing up on its hind legs. Willow felt her senses go numb. She stumbled and fell to the ground, her heart pounding in her chest. Fumbling with her bow, she drew back an arrow just as the creature reached its full height, towering over her and threatening to crush her beneath its front claws.

"Please!" she cried, gripping the bowstring so tightly she could hardly feel her fingers. "Please! I-I need your help!"

The animal scrunched up its snout then and bared its teeth, slowly backing away and dropping back to all fours, but not before Willow noticed a fleshy pouch on her pale belly, almost invisible against the expanse of its flesh, but sagging slightly with the weight of some object. With its enormous watery eyes, the arubbak looked at her. As though a rock pitted in her stomach, Willow suddenly felt the magnitude of what she was about to ask.

"If you don't help me, my friends will die."

The arubbak tilted its head and a whine escaped its throat. Behind them, the beast's young stirred impatiently. Their mother chirped once, and they fell silent. Then she turned back to Willow, her massive eyes peering down at her, seeing everything.

Willow's hands were shaking. She didn't want to let the arrow go. Didn't want to rob another being of their mother. She couldn't...

She slowly lowered her bow and let the tension off the string, never taking her eyes from the arubbak. It seemed to know, somehow, what she wanted. "I'll take care of it!" she said then, gesturing to the creature's pouch. "I promise, as though it were my own. And I'll bring it back to you if I can, I swear on my life!"

The creature was still for a moment and then huffed loudly, turned and shuffled away.

Willow sighed, utterly drained and exhausted, then staggered to her feet and hobbled back towards the stairs. It had been worth a try. She'd almost reached the steps when she felt a light tap on her shoulder and turned around. The arubbak's long snout hovered beside her, and cradled in its mouth was a lightly speckled, milky white egg.

Willow felt her heart leap and stretched out her hand. The mother placed the egg carefully in her open palm and looked deep into her eyes.

Tentatively, Willow reached out with her free hand and laid it on the arubbak's forehead. "Thank you."

The beast whined and slowly beat its wings.

Carefully slipping the egg into her bag, she thanked the creature again, and then sprinted back down the stairs, hoping that she wasn't too late to put her gift to good use.

Chapter 15

The Tikki Tournament

Edward put his hand on the cold stone door and pushed it open. The roar of the crowd echoed off the walls of the tunnel and made him sick. He put a hand on the damp wall and wretched.

Cliff frowned. "Are you sure you can do this?"

Edward nodded and took a deep breath. The smell of fiddleberry beer and sweat hung in the air. Cliff put his arm around him, and together, they hobbled up the passage. At the far end of the tunnel, Carl Mint wrote feverishly in his notebook, and Hidalgo waited anxiously.

"There's absolutely nothing to fret about, my boy. You're going to do great."

"Even if you don't, you're going to make one hell of a story," Mint said. Then he winked. "Especially on the insider's edition. Picture it." He swept his hands through the air, imagining the headline: "EDWARD STING MEETS HIS MAKER AT THE TIKKI TOURNAMENT."

Edward shrugged at the enigmatic newsman. "You can print whatever you want when we're gone." His baby-blue armour felt cold against his skin, and he felt ridiculous in it. He wiped nervous sweat from his brow. "Let's do this, I guess."

Hidalgo clapped him on the back. "That's the attitude!" Edward glared at him, and Hidalgo quickly retracted his arm.

The noise from the audience grew to a crescendo as they

exited the tunnel and entered the stadium proper, somewhere about halfway between ground level and the upper seats, reserved for the nobles, in full sight of the excited throng, some of whom surged to their feet at the sight of him.

Edward looked around. The stands were teeming with countless excited bodies, many bumbling around and bumping into each other as they tried to find their seats. In the upper levels, the elites of Decius lounged in private balconies and peered down upon the masses with indifferent expressions.

The huge arena floor below was in the shape of an oval and blanketed in sand, with a small, dense forest in one area looking as though it had been plucked from the wild and artificially planted there. Around the stadium, other contestants were arriving through their own separate tunnels. The crowd cheered as each one emerged. Edward couldn't quite believe what he was seeing. They all reminded him of Hugo, Patrice's bumbling but enormous lackey, although these men looked much smarter. He felt his nerves heighten.

"And *this* is supposed to be Ed's competition?" Cliff snarled, looking at the sheer size of the other competitors. "You said he'd win easily!"

"He will!" Hidalgo said, putting up his hands. "Trust me. Nobody trains a fighter like I do."

Cliff scoffed. "You'll say anything at this point."

Edward waved his hand. "It's fine, Cliff. We can do this." He turned to Hidalgo. "So with your position, all I have to do is fight one guy, right? Then let the others kill each other?"

"Yes well… if you win your fight, you'll have to fight again to be crowned champion."

A horn sounded before Edward could respond, and Hidalgo ushered him along towards a set of narrow steps leading down to his gate. As Edward descended, he almost turned back to say something to Cliff, but there was no point, and he didn't know what he would say anyway.

The stairs ended, and he stepped into a dark chamber, at the front of which was an archway that faced into the arena, closed off with an iron gate. He peered through the bars. It was a strange thing, he decided, being so close to death but unsure if it would find him. He yearned for a sliver of hope, even if it was misguided. He wasn't brave enough to consider the alternative. He would fight all right—even kill if it came to that, though the thought didn't inspire any more confidence in him. Either way, he decided that he would die before giving anyone the satisfaction of begging for mercy. A hand fell on his shoulder from behind. He spun around, drawing his sword.

Sofia gasped and jumped back. "Edward!"

He let his weapon drop to his side, but his adrenaline remained. He couldn't believe she had followed him here.

"You've got a lot of nerve coming to see me."

She looked pale, and dark circles shadowed her eyes. "I'm sorry. I *wanted* to tell you. I did."

He shook his head. "If you wanted to, you would have." He couldn't even look at her.

Sofia choked. "It's not that simple. My father thought you… you might try to escape if you found out—"

"Found out I was entering a death match?" he laughed hysterically. "What? Didn't think I'd enjoy being gutted in front of thousands of people?"

"Edward, please." She was trembling now, but he'd had enough.

"I bet you were just itching to see me fight. To see if the *famous* Edward Sting could pull off another miraculous trick."

She shook her head, and a few tears trickled down her cheek. What did she have to cry about? He was the one who was about to be fighting for his life.

"There's something else—"

"I don't want to hear it," he spat. "You're nothing but a spoiled princess, and you came between me and my friend." He felt his anger swell at the memory of what had happened in his bedroom.

She sniffled. "But you need to—"

"You should go," he snapped, clenching his fists. She swayed on the spot, her lip trembling. "I mean it."

With one last sorrowful look, she backed away, turned towards the door, and ran off. Edward picked up his sword and tried to get Sofia out of his mind. More footsteps on the stairs made him glance back.

Hidalgo emerged, looking giddy. "It's almost time!" he said, pointing out the gate. The crowd was on its feet, watching a man in a booth on the very highest tier of the stadium who strolled out to a podium and put his hands above his head.

Suddenly, a voice boomed around the arena, so clear that Edward would have thought the man was standing next to him. "Ladies and gentlemen, welcome to the four hundred and sixty-seventh annual Tikki Tournament!"

The orator waited as cheers erupted around the stadium. Across the arena from Edward, an iron gate slid open, and then another one. "For our first event, from the swamps of Kalisam, may I introduce... *the mighty Zel!*" A hairy man strode out of the first gate, brandishing an iron club. He wore a loincloth over his midsection but no armour. He hoisted his club over his head, displaying it for the crowd. A few boos drifted down from the stadium.

"A Kalisam fighter won the tournament last year," Hidalgo explained.

"Why doesn't he have any armour?"

"Poor soul, he's probably being offered up for slaughter. I bet he's Lord Pine's contestant. Slimy little fellow was probably bought off by someone."

The orator's voiced boomed again. "And facing Zel, your hometown fighter, ladies and gentlemen, please welcome the fantastic... *Dr Glopenstone!*" The crowd cheered as Dr Glopenstone strode onto his platform. He wore thick green armour strapped tightly to his bulging chest and arms and wielded a sword and shield.

"He's a two-time champion. This'll be a quick fight."

The two contestants climbed down from their platforms and into the arena. Whether it was over-confidence or stupidity, they chose not to use any of the natural cover around them and instead met in the centre of the arena in an open patch of sand. A deep gong sounded, and Edward heard the orator's voice again.

"Let the tournament begin!"

Edward put his hands on the rusty metal gate and watched as the barbarians started circling each other. Zel took a couple clumsy jabs that either missed or were easily deflected, and the crowd began to boo his efforts.

Then Glopenstone lashed out and struck a blow to Zel's leg. The hairy man staggered backwards. The crowd cheered. Zel recovered quickly and drove at Glopenstone, smacking him across the face with his club. The hometown fighter collapsed to the ground, gripping a bloody gash on his cheek. A nervous murmur ran through the stadium as Zel raised his club for another strike on the wounded man, but Glopenstone rolled sideways at the last second, kicking Zel in his injured leg. The man from

Kalisam crumbled to the ground, and Glopenstone rose to his feet, jabbing his sword into the sand beside Zel's head.

Zel fumbled with his club and dodged another blow but was ill-fated on the third. Edward winced as Glopenstone plunged his blade into Zel's soft belly, and the man sprawled lifeless in the sand. The crowd exploded in cheers, and Glopenstone raised his fists in triumph.

"Too bad," Hidalgo said. "Could have made a good fighter someday."

Edward stared at him in disgust. The body was dragged away, and the next fighters came out. As the event dragged on Edward thought it very strange that nobody chose to use the forest for camouflage; instead, they fought out in the open, flailing about in the sand like manic instruments of pain.

The crowd too played a large part in each battle, seeming almost to be in command of the fighters. Egged on by fiddleberry beer and mayhem, they picked favourites and cheered them on to victory. The killing didn't seem to bother them either. Perhaps they were too drunk to care. Edward thought about the Assembly, and how King Sento demanded participation. Looking out at the rumbling crowd, he found it hard to believe that these people had been forced to attend.

A particularly grimy battle ended when the victor plunged his sword into the midsection of his opponent and staked him to the ground. As the body was carried away, Edward heard a grinding sound that made him jolt backwards. Then his eyes went wide as he watched his own gate screech open. His pit master—a hairy, wrinkly faced man—put his hand on Edward's shoulder.

"You're up, kid."

Across the arena, a menacing-looking man stood on a platform with his hands on his hips. He had a long pointy nose and small eyes. His armour was light, and his lean body was covered in scars. Edward's heart started pounding.

Hidalgo beamed at him. "You can take him. I'll be right here when you come back." He extended his hand, and Edward shook it, and for the briefest of moments, he found that he really did want to win the tournament for him. As he climbed down the ladder, Hidalgo called out to him with an urgent look, as though he had forgotten to mention something, but his words were too hard to make out against the roar of the stadium.

The orator's voice boomed in his ears. "Next... from the wild hills of North Biller, I give you... the extraordinary... *Chazil!*" The audience roared, and Edward felt his stomach roll as Chazil dropped into the sand across the arena.

"And making his Tikki Tournament debut, known far and wide... loved by some and feared by others, here he is, folks! *The Stinger!*"

To Edward's surprise, as he climbed nervously down into the arena, the crowd erupted into even louder cheers, and from the upper tiers of the stadium, dignitaries and aristocrats alike rose from their seats and peered at him through spyglasses and spectacles as though he were an animal at a zoo.

Beads of sweat broke out on his forehead, and his breathing came in short bursts. Chazil was waiting for him in the centre of the pit. Although obviously strong, he was also almost decrepit looking. Old wounds were tattooed across his face and arms like ugly cracks in his skin, and his tiny, dark eyes sunk into Edward. Then the gong chimed, and Chazil charged at him.

Edward was surprised by his speed. The man was upon him before he could even raise his sword, and he had to duck in order to avoid being splayed open. The crowd gasped, and Chazil snarled.

Edward shimmied away and fumbled with his weapon. He raised it to block another strike, and the clink of metal smacking against metal rang in his ears. He shot his boot out then and kicked Chazil in the gut, sending him rearing backwards into the sand. Edward jumped forward and lashed out, swinging his blade near Chazil's chin, but the barbarian dodged the blow and struck Edward in the jaw with his fist.

Pain shot through his face, and his vision went blurry. He hit the sand then, and his helmet rolled away. Cries from the audience made Edward glance up just in time to see Chazil raise his sword above his head. He rolled away as the sword drove into the sand beside him. Staggering back to his feet, Edward dashed towards the trees.

The orator's voice called out from above: "The Stinger has entered the forest, folks, and you know what that means: *It's Tikki Time!*"

The crowd buzzed with newfound excitement, and a dark feeling crept into Edward's mind. As he slipped between the trees, the forest blocked out both the sun and the noise from the stadium; it was eerily still, almost as though he had left the fight and the arena behind entirely. Then a voice growled somewhere behind him.

"Show yourself! Chazil is hungry for blood!"

Edward's heart thumped in his chest. Chazil was weaving through the trees behind him. Quickly, he scampered up a tree and hid himself among the branches. Chazil strolled up to the tree and paused underneath, seeming to sniff the air before peering up at Edward with a nasty grin.

"Come on down from there."

Edward gasped as the barbarian pitched his sword up into the tree, catching him right between two plates of armour and slicing his shoulder. He cried out and clutched his wound, a thin smattering of blood trickled out and fell onto Chazil's face, who spat in disgust.

"If you won't come down, then I'm coming up."

The man had just reached out and grabbed the trunk of the tree when there was a rustling behind him and suddenly a worm-like creature popped out of the dirt. It had giant pincers underneath its gaping mouth, and countless serrated teeth lined the inside of its jaws.

Chazil screamed as the beast hissed and slithered towards him. He raised his sword, but it was too late. The creature grabbed him by the midsection and quickly devoured him in a flash of frenzied movement. Edward stared wide-eyed as the beast feasted on the last of Chazil's body, until all that was left of the man was a red stain in the dirt. Panic setting in, he glanced around. The tree beside him wasn't too far away.

He swung from the branch and landed in the next tree before dropping to the ground and sprinting for the edge of the forest. The worm creature looked up and gave a dreadful hiss, then slid after him. Even with Edward's head start, he could hear the thick, tube-like body gaining on him as he sped through the trees. It nipped at his heels, its warm breath seeping into his back. It was nearly upon him when Edward slid out of the forest, kicking up sand.

Behind him, the worm reared up, shrieked at the sunlight and disappeared back into the forest.

"What a finish!" the orator called. "The bloodthirsty Tikki has chosen its victim, folks, and *The Stinger wins!*" The crowd erupted in applause, and Edward felt his whole body turn to rubber as the rush of what he had just seen started to wear off. He hobbled across the sand and climbed back to his platform, where

Hidalgo was absolutely bubbling with energy.

"I knew you could do it! I *knew* it! What did I say? I never doubted you for a second!"

Edward dropped down onto the wooden bench near the gate and sighed. "Maybe I *can* win."

"Of course, you can, my boy!" There was a noise on the stairs, and a servant appeared, carrying a note. He handed it to the pit master, and then quickly left. The man scanned the letter, then glanced at Edward. "Better get ready, kid, 'cause you're going back out."

Hidalgo frowned. "So soon?"

Just then, the orator's voice called out over the crowd again, and Edward's heart dropped.

"By decree of the king, *The Stinger* will have the chance to win the tournament right now against the favoured champion! Ladies and gentlemen, may I introduce you to... *the Mysterious Night Demon!*"

A gate opened across the arena, and Brooks strode out onto his platform.

Hidalgo stuttered. "Wait a minute!" He grabbed the pit master's shoulder. "What's going on? I was told the duke wouldn't be fighting. There's been a mistake!" The other man merely shrugged.

Edward glared at Hidalgo.

"My boy, I had nothing to do with this. I swear!"

"I don't think it matters at this point." He glanced at the pit master, who was growing impatient; it was clear the man lived by the opening and closing of the gate, and nothing would change that.

He crept out to the edge and stared into the arena. Brooks now stood expectantly in the middle of the pit. So, this was

Andron's endgame: to pit him against Brooks. He rubbed his temples. Maybe it wasn't too late to—

With a laugh from the pit master, Edward felt the wind rushing suddenly past his face. He'd been kicked off the ledge. The deep sand broke his fall and flew into his eyes and mouth. He got up, staggering forward, as all around him, the audience chanted his name. His armour suddenly felt unbelievably heavy.

Up in the highest tier of the stands, he spotted the king's booth. He could just make out Andron and was thankful that he could not see the expression on the king's face. By the time he reached Brooks, he was gasping once more for breath.

"Brooks!" The duke was just standing there, frowning at the sand.

He didn't know what to say. There must be something they could do; he just couldn't think of what it might be.

Brooks looked at his feet, the daggers in his hands hanging loose at his sides.

"What now?" Edward asked.

Brooks raised his chin. He was paler than usual, the familiar coolness gone from his eyes now. "There's nothing. We have to fight." Edward shook his head. He could feel his knees shaking and smell the blood-stained sand. "I'm sorry, I-I don't think there's anything we can do Sting. You must kill me."

"What?" Edward said, trying to fight off the panic that was seizing his heart.

"You have to. If you do, the king will let you live. I'm sure of it."

Edward scoffed. How could he be so sure? And even if true, that wouldn't make this right. They were nothing more than pawns to the king. To all of them. He threw his sword into the sand. "I won't do it."

Brooks stared down at the sword. The crowd was beginning to boo them. They wanted a fight. "Pick that up."

"No!"

Brooks' sallow features darkened. "What of your grandfather, Sting? What of your friends? What will become of them if you don't do this?"

Edward felt tears run down his cheeks. He felt his spirit start to wither and die. All his life, he had hated Brooks, and here he was offering himself up—offering to die so that he might live.

"Edward."

He glanced up. The duke was smiling at him. "It's not your fault."

Somehow, Edward didn't believe him, but he reached down and picked up his sword.

Chapter 16

Over the Ledge

Willow raced through the tunnel, the archway at the end growing closer as the sound of thousands of screaming voices shook the walls around her. Finally, she emerged, squinting against the sunlight, and scanned the stadium for Cliff. He was standing outside a tunnel entrance on the tier below her.

She rushed along the ledge until she was directly above him and then flipped over the railing onto the platform.

Cliff gasped. "Willow?" He looked anxious.

"We have to hurry. Edward and Brooks are in trouble."

Cliff opened his mouth to speak, but at that moment, Hidalgo came bounding towards them. He stopped short and bent over, resting his hands on his knees.

Willow raised her bow. "Did you know?"

He panted. "What?"

"About the fight. Edward and Brooks. Did you know?"

Hidalgo scoffed. "What purpose would that serve me? What good would it do?"

She brought the point of her arrow beneath the man's quivering chin.

Cliff grabbed her by the arm. "Forget about him. Look."

She followed his gaze. Edward was walking into the middle of the arena, where Brooks was already waiting for him.

She lowered her bow and let it fall to the ground, then

gripped the rail. They were too late.

"I didn't know anything about this. I swear," Hidalgo repeated. "You have to believe me. The king does whatever he wants."

"Get out of our way," she said, shoving past him.

He looked between them. "What are you going to do?"

She reached into her bag and pulled out the speckled egg. "I'm going to put a stop to this."

Hidalgo gasped. "Where did you get that?"

"What's it to you?" Cliff said.

"It's mine!"

"Not yet," Willow said and turned to go.

"Wait! You can't," he pleaded. "You're under my supervision! I'll be ruined!"

"I'm not going to let them die just to protect you!"

Hidalgo frowned. "Well then... I'm sorry." His hand flashed into his jacket and came out gripping a pistol. His arm shaking, he raised it to Willow's head. "I really am sorry. I know you care about him, but I can't let you do this."

Willow froze but then her eyes flitted past him. In his haste, Hidalgo had forgotten about Cliff. Now the chubby boy slid to the ground and retrieved her bow.

She raised her hands. "You're not evil, Hidalgo. You don't have to play the king's game."

He laughed. "You don't know what you're talking about. We're *all* playing a game, even the King." Cliff was on his feet again, behind the man, gripping the bow now.

"I'm sorry to hear that," she said.

With one swift motion, Cliff smacked Hidalgo on the back of the head. The man looked shocked for a moment and then his eyes rolled back into his skull and he slumped to the ground unconscious.

Cliff looked between the bow and Hidalgo in disbelief. "What should we do with him?"

Willow thought for a moment, looking out at Edward and Brooks, who were now talking in the middle of the arena. Then she glanced across the platform, her eyes settling on the countless antsy spectators sitting just below, literally begging for a fight to start…

She grinned. "Bring him here." Cliff dragged him over to her, and together, they hoisted him onto the rail that separated the platform from the stands.

Hidalgo lolled in their grasp and came out of his daze.

"Wait!" he shouted, staring over the rail.

Cliff chuckled. "Don't worry, my boy. I'm sure you'll do marvellous." They pitched him over the edge, and Hidalgo Stern vanished into a sea of angry bodies. Cliff shrugged. "Or maybe he won't."

"Come on," Willow said, and they broke into a sprint.

Chapter 17

Rumours in the Ballroom

Edward gripped his sword. Brooks stood defencelessly in front of him. It was clear he wasn't going to put up a fight. He probably wanted to make it quick.

Brooks raised his daggers just above his waist, offering most of his body as a target. "You can do this," he said.

Edward swallowed hard and drew his sword back.

"Ed!"

He spun around. Willow and Cliff were bounding across the sand towards them. The crowd, who had been steadily booing—though it appeared a scuffle had broken out near one of the platforms—now erupted in indignation at this fresh interruption.

His friends reached him, and Cliff bent over panting. Willow gave Edward a fleeting glance and then held something up.

"Stop!" Cliff cried straightening himself, apparently unaware in his exhaustion that the fight hadn't even begun.

Edward smiled. "It's good to see you guys." The casual phrase sounded out of place, but he didn't care. It *was* good to see them, even if it didn't seem to help his situation.

Cliff opened his mouth, still hungry for air. "She... has the ..."

He frowned. "What?"

"The egg," Willow finished, holding it out. Edward inspected the object in her hand more closely. It was milky white with black speckles. "It's what you're all fighting over."

He furrowed his brow. "So... we're saved?"

She sighed and strode past him. The crowd was on its feet now, throwing garbage into the arena and cursing the tournament crashers. King Andron rose from his throne and stood at the edge of his balcony. Then he smacked his staff into a nearby gong, and the crowd quieted.

Willow strode past Brooks without a second look and glared up at the king.

"You dare to interrupt our tournament?" Andron said, his voice booming around the stadium, the pleasant, business-like tone Edward remembered now gone. Willow raised the egg above her head, showing it to the crowd, and a nervous murmur ran through the arena. The king had to strike the gong again to quiet them.

"A little premature to be presenting the trophy, don't you think?" he asked. The crowd laughed, but Edward could tell that Willow had made the king uncomfortable.

Willow hesitated. "I'll destroy it."

Andron smirked. "No, you won't."

Edward glanced at Willow, and he could see that Andron was right. Whatever this egg was, it wasn't something Willow was prepared to destroy.

The king pressed on, seeing Willow's resolve bend, and like a dealer with a stacked deck, played his next card. "In fact, why don't we open up these flood gates and let the people decide what to do about you?"

That got the crowd excited again, but it also gave Edward an idea. He stepped in front of Willow. "I've got a better idea," he said. "Why don't I tell everyone all of your big secrets?"

Edward could see the king's smile fade. He had made one

fatal mistake: He had given Edward an audience.

A murmur ran through the crowd at Edward's suggestion, and the king smacked the gong again, with more malice this time. "Enough," he said, his voice booming. "You will return the egg safely to me."

Edward rubbed his chin. "In exchange for what?"

The king sighed tiredly. "For now, let's say *your lives*... and you should consider yourself lucky." Edward looked at Willow, whose expression was etched in stone, then at Brooks, who was still in a state of shock, and finally at Cliff, who offered him a weak smile. Edward nodded.

Their lives would do just fine.

*

Edward's boots were shining for the first time since he'd left Teradowa. They gleamed like stars on the marble floor. Much to his surprise, Andron had been true to his word. They had been allowed to return to Hidalgo's estate and collect their things (including a particularly excited skulposis) and then been escorted back to the castle, where they'd been given clean clothes and good food, all in the span of just a few hours.

He and the others now stood, awaiting their fate, in the same throne room where they had first met the king. Edward still wasn't sure if they were going to make it out of Decius, but he liked their odds a lot better than he had that morning. Willow hadn't said much to him since the arena—about his kiss with the princess or anything else. But Edward supposed it was a good sign that she had come back at all.

He glanced around the room. It looked nearly the same as it had several weeks earlier, except now there was a golden throne where the pink sofa had once been.

The side door swung open, and a dozen of the king's warriors filed into the chamber, including Eclipse. Behind them, Sofia shuffled through the door, looking tired, and finally, King Andron himself. The king eyed them as he stormed over to the throne, his face contorted in disgust.

He was sore about the tournament, that was for sure. Edward had decided that he hated the man. He didn't hate many people, but looking at Andron now, seeing what a cold-hearted fraud he had turned out to be, what he felt was definitely hate.

"So here we are," the king said, taking his seat. Sofia beside him, staring at the ground with her shoulders hunched.

"You have until sundown to get out of Decius," Andron announced.

Edward frowned. Had the king really brought them all here just to tell them that they were free to go?

"I don't care what direction you go in. I just want you out."

Cliff laughed dryly. "The feeling could not be more mutual."

Edward cleared his throat. "Maybe you can tell us why you even bothered having us fight each other. I mean, you must have known we'd find out you were lying about everything."

"Actually, no. I was assured that you wouldn't find out, but that is another matter, which is being handled. Besides, what did you expect? My people want to be entertained, and I like to entertain them. As for you two fighting each other, there was a last-minute bet placed, and my hands were tied. I'm sorry."

"Apology accepted," Cliff said. They all turned to go.

"Just one other thing," the king said, his lips curling into a wicked smirk. He pointed to Hikoo. "That... *thing*... stays with me."

Cliff scoffed. "Hikoo stays with us."

The king laughed. "Well, in that case, you could all stay here... forever." He looked over at the warriors lining the wall. Edward closed his eyes. So, this was why they were here. For the king to humiliate them one last time. They had taken something of his, and so now, he would do the same.

"Are you really that petty?" Brooks said.

"Not at all, you see," the king continued, "the creature is a gift... for the princess."

Edward felt a twinge in his stomach. His eyes darted to Sofia, but she would not meet his gaze. Two warriors stepped towards Cliff to retrieve Hikoo.

"Stop!" Cliff cried. Hikoo wriggled on his shoulder, his eyes the size of the moon. "You can't have him!" Cliff squirmed, wrestling with the guards.

"Yes, they can," Edward said quietly. "Let him go, Cliff."

His friend turned on him. "What?"

Andron was practically giddy.

The warriors wrenched the shaking skulposis away from Cliff, and Edward forced himself to watch as Hikoo was dragged from the room. The door closed behind them with a resounding thud, and Andron clapped. "Well," he said, crossing his hands on his lap, "I think we're done here."

Edward glared at him. "Yes, I think we are."

The day was quickly fading by the time they were outside the castle gates, and clouds were billowing on the horizon, casting pink streaks across the sky. When they were out of earshot of the castle walls, Cliff whirled on Edward.

"What was that? We can't let them take Hikoo!"

Edward rolled his eyes. "Of course not, but there was nothing we could do in there."

Brooks cleared his throat. The duke had regained his

coolness after the incident in the arena and having recovered his black cloak—which hung once again off his lean frame—he was looking much like his old self. "Why even bother with the creature? We're free to go and doing anything else is too risky."

Edward sighed. "We all owe Hikoo our lives. We can't just abandon him now."

Brooks crossed his arms. "Then I expect you have a plan, Sting?"

"I do." A smile was creeping across Edward's face. He was beginning to get a feeling—a funny little feeling he'd had only once before. And he wondered if he might find something else hiding in the castle.

*

Darkness blanketed the sky. Neither star nor moon illuminated the yard; the conditions were perfect. Edward chuckled to himself. If there really was a god, he was on their side tonight. About thirty yards ahead and around the corner, he could hear the buzz of guests arriving through the front gates of the castle. Decius's most rich and powerful dignitaries were milling up the steps to the main hall of King Andron's palace.

"I'd just like to say once more," Cliff whispered from behind him, "that this is a *very* bad idea."

Edward lolled his head against the wall. "So, I've heard." Behind them, Willow attached a small grappling tip to the end of an arrow, which in turn was tethered to a rope. "If you'd like," Edward whispered to Cliff, "you can try the front door."

Cliff poked his head around the corner at the heavily guarded courtyard and crossed his arms. "Of course, the night we do this, the king has to throw a party."

Brooks came lurking out of the darkness. "It's all clear out back." He glanced at Willow, who was putting the finishing touches on her grapple. "You sure she can make this shot?"

"I guess we'll find out." Cliff said.

Willow shot them both a look.

"As long as you two do your part, you'll have nothing to worry about." She finished her rigging and pulled back her bowstring.

"Okay, here goes nothing." They had picked a dark window on the second floor, which by some miracle was open. The side of the castle was a patchwork of stone and cracked brick in the dark; however, Edward guessed they would have no more than a twelve-foot climb.

Willow let the arrow fly. It sailed straight upward and stuck in the window frame, but on the wrong side, shattering the left windowpane in the process and sending shards of glass raining down on them.

"That'll let them know we're here!" Cliff said, wiping glass off his shoulders.

Willow glared at him. "It's a hard shot," she said, her voice hoarse, "but you're welcome to take it next time."

"It's all right," Edward said softly. She glared at him, and he fell silent.

"Will it hold us?" Brooks asked.

Willow shrugged. "Only one way to find out." She yanked hard on the rope, but the arrow remained wedged in the wood. "I'd say it will hold *most* of us," she said, peering pointedly at Cliff. The fat boy blushed.

She quickly started to climb. In less than a minute, she was through the window. Brooks followed her, then Edward, and finally Cliff came shimmying up the wall.

The room was dark, and Edward sensed it was quite small. He felt around until he discovered a candle on a table, pulled out his matches, and lit the wick. He blinked as his eyes adjusted. The room *was* small and filled with wooden crates. Boxes were stacked against three walls and piled randomly in the corners, as though whomever had put them there wasn't too concerned about organization. Edward walked up to a box and squinted at the print on the top: MUSKETS. His eyes trailed to the next box. Again, only one word was printed: GUNPOWDER.

"You know what this is?" Cliff asked, glancing nervously between the boxes. "This is a weapons stash."

Willow shook her head. "But why would Andron store all this in the castle?"

Edward didn't know, but he felt uneasy. His mind was flickering back to the shipment of cannonballs they had discovered while leaving Candosia.

"Maybe he doesn't want everyone to know he has this much firepower," Cliff answered.

"It doesn't matter," Brooks said. "What matters is getting this done quickly."

Edward nodded. "Right," he said, focusing his thoughts. "Everyone, suit up." When he had first thought of this plan, the others had raised concerns, but Edward was convinced that, once they were in the castle, nobody would look twice at them in the crowd. So, they had stolen outfits from the estate of Hidalgo Stern after leaving the castle that afternoon. As he stripped off his cloak, he wondered what had become of the man after his unfortunate fall…

He unlatched his sword and set it on a box. If all went according to plan, they would be leaving through the same window once they'd gotten what they came for. He removed his holster, hesitated, and then tucked the gun under his belt. Just in case. Then he stripped off his ratty old navy-blue jacket and put on Hidalgo's fresh green waistcoat. Finally, he rummaged in his bag for the black tricorn he had taken to complete the makeover. In a few moments, he, Cliff, and Brooks looked as high class and fashionable as any aristocrat in Decius.

Willow came through the door and glanced at Edward. "Your hat is crooked."

"Huh?"

She rolled her eyes and set it straight, then brushed off his jacket.

"That's better."

"Thanks," he said, a dazed feeling coming over him. He wanted to blurt out all the thoughts bottled up inside him but couldn't find the words.

"Well?" she said, giving him a sideways glance. "Give a girl some privacy."

"Oh right." He shuffled awkwardly out the door. Outside, the hallway was well lit, and a thick rug ran the length of the corridor. Cliff was leaning against the wall, breathing fast.

"Relax," Brooks said.

Instead, Cliff began again, listing off all of the terrible things that could go wrong, but Edward wasn't listening. His mind kept drifting back to Willow. He shook his head, trying to focus on the task at hand. Finally, the door clicked open, and she stepped into the hallway.

The dress she had chosen must have belonged to a woman from Hidalgo's younger years because it fit her perfectly. It was bright red and clung to her chest and waist. Her jet-black hair was undone and fell in loose waves over her shoulders.

Edward stared at her until he realised that he had been doing so for too long and forced himself to look away. "Okay," he said, clearing his throat, "we're just four people enjoying the party. Whoever finds out where Hikoo is being kept, find the rest of us first. Nobody goes off searching alone. This place is crawling with soldiers." They strode down the corridor until they reached a staircase.

Downstairs, music drifted through the halls, and a waiter passed by carrying a platter of some kind of green meat. Edward glanced at the others, shrugged, and followed the man. A pair of large wooden doors swung open, and they emerged into the ballroom. The massive space encapsulated two-floors of the castle. Edward figured that they must be right below the king's throne room.

Guests were everywhere; some were dancing, while others sat at tables, dining and chatting. Small groups of men were clumped at the bar, sipping wine and discussing business. Edward felt a breeze and noticed that the balcony doors were open to the warm night air. Opposite the balcony sat a stage, on which a quartet of violinists were playing a lovely piece. Edward paused for a moment. He recognised the music. It was a song of celebration often performed in Teradowa.

He scoffed; they even traded their precious music. Suddenly, he realised that he was standing alone. The others had dispersed and were already indistinguishable among the crowd. He strolled farther into the room, and when a server passed by, he took a glass of wine off his tray. He sipped it and let the bitter liquid calm his nerves. There was a clinking of glasses then, and suddenly, everyone quieted. Andron was standing on the stage at a small podium, with a glass in his hand, making a toast.

"I'd like to thank everyone for another successful tournament," cheers erupted from the crowd, "and may the gods bless our holy realm." Pretentious laughter made its way around the room, and everyone raised their glass. Edward's body filled with rage, and he felt sick to his stomach. How dare these people live so lavishly, and mock those they lie to? He drained his glass and went straight to the bar, where he sat down and leaned on the counter, rubbing his temples.

A hand fell on his shoulder, and he spun around. Hidalgo Stern peered at him, his black hair a ruffled mess.

"Hey, kid," he said quietly, trying to smile but his lip was split, and his face was so bruised and puffy that his eyes were nearly swollen shut. He limped around Edward and took a seat at the bar. "Suit looks good on you," he said, admiring Edward's jacket. Then he waved down the bartender, chuckling. "Not the first time it's been wore to a party here."

"Well, it'll likely be the last, I'm afraid."

He grunted. "I believe you." The bartender brought his drink, and he gulped it down.

Edward eyed the man intently.

"After your stunt at the tournament, Andron wasn't too happy with me."

"Guess you didn't get that promotion?"

Hidalgo shrugged. "Dreams die every day in this city. Listen, I want you to know, I didn't know about the bet. Honestly."

Edward nodded. "I believe you."

The nobleman smiled, this seemed to set him at ease. Edward was about to leave the man to his sorrow when a thought struck him. "Hidalgo." The older man turned. "Why was Andron sending cannonballs to Candosia?"

He shook his head. "I don't know."

"You said you helped him with those things, didn't you?"

He sighed. "Yes, but I don't know anything about that."

"Why not?"

He shrugged. "Everything comes from Regnum."

Edward stared at him. "What?"

Hidalgo's swollen eyes suddenly shifted around the bar. "All the weapons anyway." He looked longingly at Edward's drink, and Edward pushed it over to him. "Look, I know what you and your friends are up to, so I'll give you a word of warning: He who rules Regnum, rules the realms."

Edward hesitated. "You mean Lord Gorlak?"

Hidalgo sputtered. "How do you know that name?"

"Pentheus told me."

"Best not to go repeating that," he whispered.

Edward's mind raced. "What do you know about him? What powers does he have?"

Hidalgo shrugged. "He keeps the kings in line, sends weapons and soldiers… But make no mistake, Andron and the others… they're just pawns."

Edward rubbed his forehead. So much was beginning to make sense. The reason for all the secrecy between the realms, it wasn't because of the kings.

It was Lord Gorlak.

Hidalgo put a hand on Edward's shoulder. "I'm sorry, kid." His eyes glistened, and Edward thought he might cry. "You and I are the same, you know. Both used and cast aside."

The man rummaged in his jacket. "Here," he said, pulling out the speckled egg from the tournament. "As you might have guessed, I was denied this little trophy, so naturally, I stole it." He pushed the egg into Edward's hand. "God knows you've earned it more than I have."

Edward took the egg. It felt warm against his skin. "Thank

you."

Placing the egg into an inner pocket of his jacket, he left Hidalgo at the bar and started across the ballroom, careful to keep his face shielded from the stage. An eerie feeling was growing in the back of his mind.

So it was Lord Gorlak pulling the strings. But why? There was still something missing. He was about halfway across the room when Willow appeared at his side.

"You look excited."

He smiled, eager to share what he'd learned. "I've just had a very interesting conversation with our friend Hidalgo Stern."

Willow raised her eyebrows. "Oh?"

He held out his hand, forgetting everything else for a moment. "Care for a dance?"

She hesitated, then took his hand. "Was he upset?" she asked, wrapping her arms around his neck.

"About you pitching him over the balcony? I can't imagine why he would be." He fell into step with the music, glad to see he hadn't lost his touch. "Turns out, he and Andron are no longer that close."

"There's a shock."

Edward pulled her closer. "There's more." He told her what Hidalgo had said about the weapons and the mysterious ruler of Regnum.

"So that explains all the cannonballs," she said.

"And what about Lord Gorlak? Are you sure you never heard anything else about him?"

Willow shook her head. "Like I said before, only rumours... stories about strange powers. I never even learned his name. Pentheus didn't like to talk about him with anyone."

Edward closed his eyes, deciding that there was nothing

more they could learn tonight. Willow's hair wisped around his face, tickling his cheeks. Even now, miles from the forest, she smelled of sweet flowers and pine.

"Listen," he said, searching for words, "what you saw with Sofia... It wasn't like that."

She glanced away. "You don't need to explain yourself. I've been alone for a long time, and I'm okay with that."

He shook his head and gently took her chin between his fingers. "You're not alone. I'll make sure you never are again."

She rolled her eyes, but colour rushed into her cheeks.

He grinned. "I'm serious. I don't know what I'd do without you."

"That's because you'd be dead already."

He gazed into her green eyes. Those were always her tell—the weak point in her armoured shell. He brushed aside a lock of black hair then and kissed her.

When he pulled away, she seemed hesitant to speak.

"What?"

"You know... Sofia's not a bad girl."

Edward frowned. "What do you mean?"

"Didn't I tell you? When I went to get the egg, I overheard her and Eclipse talking. She didn't know about the fight. Between you and Brooks, I mean."

Edward's mind flashed back to his interactions with her. He had assumed she was working with her father the whole time. Certainly, that was why she had come to his room... to get in his head. Right? Could she truly be just a naïve, young princess? Suddenly, a wave of guilt washed over him. That was what she had been trying to tell him in the tunnel before the tournament. She had been trying to warn him, and he had screamed in her face.

He thought back to that afternoon, in the throne room after the tournament, and how she wouldn't even look at him. She wasn't angry, he realised suddenly. She was ashamed.

"I think," Willow said, "that in the end, she had no choice."

Edward stopped dancing abruptly and grabbed her by the shoulders. "That's it!" It was suddenly so clear.

"What?" Willow said.

"I know how to get Hikoo back."

Chapter 18

Fire in the Hole

Sofia was seated near the end of the stage, separated from her father by several members of his inner circle and her mother. She was picking at a plate of delicious-looking meat with a sour expression on her face.

Edward crept along the edge of the room. Keeping a close eye on Andron, he moved from one pillar to the next beneath the second-floor balcony until he reached the stairs and crouched down behind them.

The side of the stage was only a few yards away now. For a moment, he thought of Brooks and Cliff. Perhaps he and Willow should have told them before putting this new plan into action. Then he brushed the thought aside. Once he had Hikoo, they'd meet back up at the second-floor window.

Edward gazed across the ballroom and waited. Suddenly, in the far corner of the room, a young woman collapsed on a dining table, sending glassware spilling across the floor. Several partygoers gasped and went to her aid. Edward grinned at Willow's performance. It was exactly what he needed. As soon as Andron's attention was caught by the scene, he sprang from his position and dashed to the edge of the stage.

"Sofia," he whispered. She turned and locked eyes with him, and her jaw dropped. He put his finger to his lips and motioned for her to come over. She bit her lip, glancing hesitantly back at her father.

Edward's heart raced, but finally, she scooted off her chair and crawled over to him.

"Edward!" she whispered. She wore a sleeveless pink dress that made her blonde hair and pale features pop.

"Shh," he said, keeping his eyes on King Andron, who was now back in conversation with a man beside him. "I need your help." He helped her off the stage and sprinted down the hallway, dragging Sofia with him.

"What are you doing here?" she asked when they stopped, her eyes wide. "If my father finds out, he'll kill you."

"Don't worry. He's not going to." He took her by the arm and led her down a hallway off the main corridor until they found themselves alone. "Listen, I'm sorry for the way I treated you. I know you were just trying to help me."

Her eyes flitted away, and she rubbed her bare arms. "It's okay, Edward," she said. "You should be upset with me."

"No, I was wrong. You had no choice, but if your father does find out you helped me tonight…"

She blushed. "I'm not going to tell him. Don't worry."

Edward nodded. "But if he does, will he punish you?"

She sighed. "No, Mama will take care of it. What do you need?"

"I came back for Hikoo. Do you know where he is?"

Sofia set her jaw. "Yes. Come with me." Now it was Edward's turn to follow.

They sauntered back towards the ballroom, careful to not seem at all rushed, until they reached the stairs. On the second floor, they emerged into another identical hallway, decorated with tapestries. Edward gazed out into the dark, empty yard; he could see how someone could get bored living here.

Sofia stopped in front of a closed door at the end of the hall. "This is my room," she said, turning the lock.

The room was large and circular, and Edward guessed they were in one of the spires on the corner of the castle. Pink curtains hung from the windows and around the bed, giving the room a cozy glow.

A blue, furry shape leapt off one of the windowsills and dashed over to Edward.

"Hikoo!" he cried, scooping the skulposis into his arms.

He laughed as Hikoo nibbled at his ear. "Master Sting came back for Hikoo."

"Of course."

Seeing Edward cuddle the creature, Sofia suddenly burst into tears. "Oh, Edward, I swear I didn't ask him to do it! I tried to stop him, but he wouldn't even look at me after he found out I went to see you in the tunnel. I'm sorry." She sat on the edge of her bed and wiped her cheek. Edward sat down next to her and put a hand on her shoulder.

"It's all right. Someday, it will be your turn to run Decius, and something tells me that you'll do a much better job than your father."

She sniffled. "He's not a bad man. I know he's not, but… sometimes, he can treat people terribly."

Edward nodded. Sofia was young. She had plenty of time to decide what her father was and was not. He got up and faced her. "Now, I've really got to go."

"I don't think so," a voice said from behind him. Edward whirled around.

Andron stood in the doorway, his pistol raised.

Sofia gasped. "Papa?"

"Not so fast," he said, as Edward reached into his waistband.

"I don't remember inviting you tonight, Mr Sting." He stepped into the room and yanked Edward's weapon from his belt.

"Papa, what are you *doing*?"

"That'll do, darling," the king said. "You're lucky I don't have one of these aimed at you."

Edward was furious with himself. How could he have let this happen?

Andron smirked. "I knew you'd come back. A part of me was hoping you would. You just had to be the hero. I kindly allow you to leave, and that's not enough for you." He shoved Edward towards the door.

Sofia rushed after them. "Papa, please stop."

"You may as well come too, sweetheart. Keep you from causing me any more trouble."

Edward marched down the hall with Andron's pistol digging into his back.

"Where are we going?"

"Where I tell you," the king hissed. "Shout and you're dead. We don't need to ruin a perfectly good party over this." Edward held his tongue; behind them, Sofia whimpered.

"And where is your little friend now?" the king whispered in his ear. "He has abandoned you." It was true, and Edward hadn't even noticed.

Hikoo was gone.

They marched right past the staircase that had brought them to the second floor. Instead, Andron led them farther down the hall and stopped outside an open door on the right, through which a steep passage sloped downward into darkness.

He pushed Edward ahead. "You first."

As he descended into the dark, the air became stale and musty. He stuck his hand out and felt cold stone. Behind him came the thumping of the king's boots and the frantic clicking of Sofia's heels. Finally, the ground levelled, and a dimly lit, corridor carved out the darkness. Arches in the ceiling were cracked and crumbling.

Andron jabbed him with the gun. "Walk."

Edward crept forward, the rock had been hollowed out in spots and turned into cells with iron bars. All of the cells were empty. He braced himself for a fight as they marched. He wasn't going to become some skeleton, collecting dust in a dungeon.

After a few moments, Andron stopped. "Well, this seems as good a spot as any."

In a flash, Edward whirled around and kicked the king's feet out from under him, grateful now for Hidalgo's training. The man cried out and fell, the gun flying from his hand, landing on the floor several feet away. Andron reached to retrieve it, but Edward was quicker, snatching up the pistol and turning it on its former master.

"Don't move," he said, savouring the look on the king's face. He reached down and rummaged through the man's deep pockets, retrieving the silver pistol that Andron had just confiscated from him. He tucked one in his belt and held onto the other. Sofia stood nearby, gaping at them in disbelief.

Edward was about to say something to her when he heard the noise. So faint and distant that he might not have even noticed it, if he hadn't heard it before—once in a forest and then again in a watery cave. Wordless music drifted towards him from the darkness—soft and familiar—calling to him.

A thrill shot through his body.

"What is it?" Sofia said.

Edward gazed down the tunnel. "You don't hear that?"

"Hear what?"

Suddenly, something seemed to drop into his pocket. He felt its weight and knew what it was instantly. He began frantically groping along the walls of the tunnel.

Sofia shook her head. "What are you doing?"

The king staggered to his feet. "He's gone mad, darling. I knew they were crazy, the whole lot of them,"

"It has to be here…" he muttered.

"Edward, what are you *talking* about?"

He pulled the stone from his pocket. "This!" Its red glow lit up the tunnel like a star in the empty void of space.

Andron gasped. "Where in God's name did you get *that?*"

Edward hesitated. "I found it in Candosia… Do you know what it is?"

The king's eyes were gleaming. "I didn't believe it was real."

"What is it, Papa?"

"A legend. Told to me as a boy by my father. The Heart of the Realm, he called it."

"What legend?" Edward said, completely forgetting the urgency of the moment. The king rubbed his hands together, his violent intentions apparently forgotten in the presence of the stone.

"The story goes that, long ago, one king ruled over all the land and the kingdom was called Akmenadon. Every year, he demanded gifts from the people." Edward listened intently. "One year, a peasant came to the king and presented him with a stone, saying that it contained the secrets of immortality and ultimate power. He also gave the king a warning: 'The stone can also bestow a terrible fate on those who are unwise.' The king laughed and demanded the peasant return with a real gift. But soon, the prophecy came true. The king lived beyond his years and wielded tremendous powers, but..." Andron smirked. "He became greedy. His once loyal children turned against him and demanded control over the stone. Eventually, a terrible war broke out, and the stone was shattered. But five fragments remained. They were taken by the king's children who left the kingdom and created realms of their own. It's said the power of the stones kept the natural worlds from meeting, and only under the will of man could anything cross between them."

"What happened to the king?" Sofia said.

"Without the power of the stone, the old man, filled with remorse, withered and died. His five sons, bitter with one another, closed their borders. Never to be opened again." The king chuckled dryly. "Only then did they realise that, without all the pieces of the stone, the fragments were largely powerless. So, they hid them away where they could never be found... save for one king."

Edward frowned. "Who?"

Andron's face darkened. "The King of Regnum refused to give up his fragment, and unlocking its power became his obsession. The legend says that his stone has been passed down from one ruler of Regnum to the next as they try to discover its secrets."

"Regnum," Edward whispered.

Andron snickered. "You're on a fool's errand, Mr Sting. Nobody returns from that dreadful wasteland."

"Because of Lord Gorlak?"

The king's smiled vanished. "I see you think you know what you're up against. Well, let me assure you that you don't. He sees things before they happen. No matter what you do, you'll play right into his hands."

Edward scoffed. "We'll see."

"What kind of powers do the stones have, Papa?" Sofia asked.

The king shrugged. "It's just a legend." Then he gazed back at the stone in Edward's hand. "But it looks like this one might be true."

Edward raised his pistol again and the king's smirk faded; then he turned again towards the far end of the tunnel. A deep sense of foreboding was crawling into the back of his mind. He closed his eyes and held out the stone towards the darkness ahead… and heard the music begin once more, almost instantly.

"There!" He pointed.

"What?" Sofia said.

"Didn't you hear that?"

The princess and her father exchanged looks.

Edward took off down the tunnel. "Come on!" The three of them dashed into the darkness, following the glow of the stone. At the end, they came face to face with a narrow brick wall. Edward frowned; it couldn't be a dead end. He felt his hand vibrate, and the stone shot out of his grasp. It stuck to the wall like a magnet and began to glow so brightly that he was momentarily blinded. Edward squinted towards the wall, and his jaw dropped.

"Oh my god," Andron said.

Steam was rising from the wall as brick after brick melted away. Thick sediment oozed down the sides of a growing hole, and in a moment, the wall was completely gone. Edward peered into the darkness on the other side, feeling the heat emanating from the floor and ceiling of the narrow opening. Beyond the gap, a stone staircase led sharply downward. He picked up the stone tentatively, finding it perfectly cool, then motioned to Andron with the pistol.

"You first."

"Down there?" The king swallowed hard and then shimmied sideways through the gap. Edward followed him and helped Sofia through after him. Unlit torches lined the walls. Edward waved his pistol towards the king. "Got a match?"

Andron rummaged in his pocket and lit the first torch. Suddenly, the staircase was brightened by the glow of countless tiny flames, as torch after torch burst to life. Edward studied Andron's stunned look and decided that the king was just as surprised as he was.

He turned to Sofia. "You can stay up here."

She shook her head. "No way." She took off her heels and tossed them aside.

Edward nodded and poked the king in the back. "Lead the way."

They descended the stairs. Cobwebs littered each step, and the walls were coarse and coated in dust. The temperature soon dropped, and Edward could hear Sofia's teeth chattering.

After about ten minutes, the ground levelled out, and they stood on another small platform in front of a heavy wooden door that had been fitted into the carved stone around it.

"We must be deep underground," the king said.

Edward approached the door and gripped the ancient brass handle. It was unlocked. With no small amount of effort, he yanked it open—revealing a tiny room that had been carved out of the earth and propped up by wooden beams—and gestured for Sofia and her father to precede him. Sofia plucked a torch from the wall and stepped inside.

The air inside was dry and musty, and Edward jumped as the heavy door slammed shut behind them.

The king gazed around in awe. "It's some kind of vault.

Sitting right under my feet all this time!"

"But where's the treasure, Papa?"

Then Edward saw it. A small iron box sat on the floor in the centre of the room. Sofia put her hands over her mouth. "Do you think that's..." Her voice trailed off.

Edward brushed by her, feeling the stone vibrating in his hands. Pushing his pistol into his belt beside its companion, he knelt down and undid the clasp on the lid. Inside the box was a small stone nestled on a cushion. As soon as it was exposed, its red glow pierced the dark room. Edward scooped it up and heard that deep, hollow sound emanating from it like music to his ears.

Suddenly, something hard struck him from behind. He hit the floor and felt the air leave his lungs. The king stood over him, his eyes flush with rage and a rough piece of timber in his hands. He put his boot on Edward's neck.

"Fool," he snarled, bending down and snatching the stones out of Edward's hand.

The king's boot was crushing Edward's windpipe, and his vision began to blur. He thought he might pass out.

"Sofia, bring the torch!" Andron snapped. The princess hesitated, her eyes lingering on Edward. "Sofia!"

She scurried across the room to his side.

The king smiled wickedly in the orange light. "Well, Mr Sting, you have proven far more useful than I ever could have imagined." He finally removed his boot from Edward's throat and backed away towards the door. Edward rolled onto his side, gasping for air.

"To think," Andron snickered, "you actually expected to keep these for yourself."

Edward staggered to his feet, rage building inside him.

"Give those back!" he shouted.

"I don't think so."

"You said it yourself, they're powerless."

The king scoffed. "Only if you have one, but now I have two, and if the stories are true, I shall soon have the rest. Then *nobody* will give me orders!" His lips curled into a psychotic grin.

Suddenly, Edward realised what the king had forgotten. He drew one of the two guns still wedged in his belt and raised it to Andron's head.

The king's smirk vanished. Then, in a blur, he grabbed Sofia around the neck and threw her in front of him, shielding himself.

The princess shrieked. "Papa?"

"Go ahead, boy! You wouldn't dare."

"Papa, please!" Sofia squirmed in her father's iron grip, and the torch slipped from her fingers.

Then several things happened very quickly. Hot embers spilled across the floor, towards the base of the nearest support beam. Edward watched in horror as the ancient wood suddenly burst into flames. The fire began to spread around the room, devouring the wooden structure.

The king sneered. "So long, Mr Sting." He turned to the door, grabbed the handle, and pushed.

It didn't open.

He pushed again, harder this time. Nothing.

Edward put his gun away then and rushed to the door as thick smoke began to billow near the ceiling. The door handle was ancient, and rust had destroyed the locking mechanism.

"It must have broken when the door slammed."

Andron went pale.

"You mean we're trapped!" Sofia cried.

Sweat was breaking out on Edward's forehead. They had mere minutes to escape. He hammered his shoulder against the door, trying to force it open. No luck. Panic began to set in.

He pulled back and slammed into it again and again until he felt lightheaded. Sweat poured off him now, and the crackle of flames boomed in his ears. The ceiling moaned. In a few moments, the supports would collapse, and they'd be crushed beneath falling stone.

The door was just too heavy. Slamming into it wasn't going to work. He squinted through the haze of smoke. There was nothing with them in the room except the iron box. He dashed over to it. Pulling out his gun, he pulled back the steel hammer on top of the barrel and emptied the priming pan into the box. Then he dashed back to the door and set the box down at its base. His skin felt as though it were melting and sweat stung his eyes. Beside him, Andron leaned on Sofia, his eyes starting to fall closed.

The princess coughed. "Hurry!" she pleaded, shaking her father and trying to keep him conscious.

Edward ripped off a small piece of his waistcoat and held it to the flames. When it was burning, he snatched it back and stuck the unlit end in the powder before closing and latching the lid.

"Get back!" He grabbed Sofia's hand and pushed Andron ahead of them. The explosion knocked them to ground and blew the door off its hinges. Sofia cried with joy and stumbled towards the opening, half dragging her father behind her. The roof began to rumble overhead as Edward staggered to his feet, his ears ringing.

He managed to dive out the door just as the rock began to cave in behind him, sealing the vault for good.

*

Together, Edward and Sofia helped the barely conscious king back up the darkened stairway towards the relative safety of the dungeon tunnels. They arrived at last, passing through the entranceway the stone had revealed, and headed back down the tunnel, but in only a few steps, the king succumbed to exhaustion and collapsed in their arms. Edward set the unconscious man down against the wall.

"Will he be okay?" Sofia asked.

He nodded, reaching into his pocket and pulling out a canteen of water. "Give him this when he wakes up." Sofia took the bottle.

Edward strolled over to the other side of the tunnel and inspected the cell there. It had a functioning door with a bolt that was rusty but still strong. Nodding, he went back over to the king and dragged him inside, laying him down. Then he rummaged through the king's pockets and recovered the stones. Sitting quietly against the far wall of the tunnel, Sofia watched him closely.

Edward glanced over at her. She looked very small sitting there in her tattered dress, darkened with soot, and her bare feet. She had forgotten to pick up her heels on the way back. He scratched his head absently.

"It's probably best if you come in here too. That way you can say that I forced you." She nodded and shuffled past him into the cell.

He sighed. "He shouldn't treat you that way, you know."

She shrugged. "He isn't always like that."

"Well, you deserve better. Will he be upset with you?"

Sofia laughed. "Probably, but Mama will keep him from doing anything he regrets."

Edward shook his head. He was beginning to sense a pattern

with Sofia and her parents. "Will someone find you down here?"

"Oh yes, they're probably already looking."

He nodded. "Well, I'd better be going." He hesitated by the cell door, then bent down and kissed her lightly on the cheek. "It has been an honour knowing you, *my lady.*"

Even in the dim light, he could see a tiny smile spread across her face. The cell door clanked shut then, and as he sped back up the tunnel, he felt rather good about things, as though some clarity had come to something previously unknown.

Back in the airy halls of the castle, the party surged on. Edward dusted off his jacket and strode down the hallway towards the ballroom. Deep violin cords drifted through the corridor, and he broke into a brisk walk, hoping that everyone would be waiting for him at the second-floor window. He rounded the corner by the stairs and bumped straight into a guard in a red uniform. The two men exchanged looks; then Edward dared a glance towards the stage and locked eyes with Claudia Andron. It was only a fleeting glance, but it was enough.

"Stop him!" she cried.

The guard reached for Edward, but he sidestepped his grasp and punched the man hard in the jaw. Then he bounded up the stairs, two at a time, his heart pounding in his chest. At the top, he dashed along the balcony as shouts began to fill the air below. He rounded the corner near the second-floor window—

"Woah!" he said, as he almost crashed into Willow.

"Edward!" she gasped. "Where have you been? We've been looking all over for you. Hikoo said you were in danger."

"I'll explain later," he said, taking her by the hand. "What's going on?" she asked, as he dragged her down the hallway. Edward just kept running; all their work tonight would be for nothing if they were caught. He stopped short as soldiers appeared at the far end of the corridor and opened fire. Bullets whistled passed them, and they dove for cover behind a pillar.

"I see you made some friends," Willow said.

Edward drew his remaining pistol and fired off several shots around the corner. The door to the weapons depot lay on the opposite side of the hallway only a short distance away, but it may as well have been miles.

"We're going to have to run for it." Suddenly, the crackle of gunfire started up from the opposite end of the hall as more soldiers swarmed the corridor. Edward ducked as several bullets ricocheted off the pillar behind him.

He stuck out his arm to return fire, and pain shot through his upper body. He gritted his teeth and suppressed a scream.

Willow's hand pressed him back against the pillar. "You're shot," she said over the whine of gunfire. The bullet had struck his lower shoulder, and a small circle of blood was growing beneath his waistcoat. "Hold still," she said, taking the gun.

But the powder was spent. She tossed it aside. Soldiers were creeping along the corridor on either side, closing the distance between them. Finally, the door to the weapons depot burst open, and Brooks emerged, brandishing an odd-looking weapon. He let off a flurry of shots in both directions. One struck a man in the front of the pack and his musket suddenly disintegrated. The next thing Edward knew, he was on his feet, and his head was swimming. His arm was around Willow, and they were stumbling across the hallway. The little ball of hot metal felt like it was digging deeper into his flesh with every movement of his body.

When they were halfway to the door, he felt the same burning sensation strike his side, and he collapsed onto Willow, as dark spots formed at the edge of his vision.

"Edward!" somebody shouted, but they were far away.

He hit the ground and felt hands grip him and drag him towards the door...

Then he was sitting on a wooden crate. Brooks was there, shouting something; then he was on his feet again. Somebody had their arm under his shoulder and was helping him towards a window. His body twitched, and he opened his mouth, but the pain made words impossible; instead, he nodded, trying to make the others understand. He knew he would have to climb out himself.

With one leg over the sill, he braced himself against the stabbing pain in his side and swung the other leg over. Taking hold of the rope, he began to rappel down the wall. The motion sent waves of pain through his whole body, and three quarters of the way down, he let go and fell to the earth.

Dazed and barely able to breathe, he became aware of two bandoros sniffing his head. He sat up painfully.

"Ed!"

Edward could just make out the silhouette of his friend sitting atop one of the creatures.

"Get in," Cliff said, gesturing frantically behind him.

Edward looked back and saw that a wagon had been harnessed to the mighty beasts. Groaning, he managed to climb to his feet and roll over its side and landed on something soft. A sweet aroma wafted up to his nostrils. *Fruit?* Then Willow came swinging over the side of the wagon after him, and they took off.

The cool breeze felt incredible on his skin after nearly being burned alive. They raced past the castle until it faded from view and was replaced by rolling hills. As Edward lay in the wagon, gazing up at the starry sky, a tiny object crossed his view. It fluttered down from the trees and landed beside him.

It was a bird. It flapped its little yellow wings, then turned and winked at him. Edward smiled vaguely and watched the bird fly away.

Then he passed out.

Chapter 19

The Saint Elmer

"Edward, you have to stay awake,"

He rubbed his eyes. Willow's face was hovering over him. She was leaning against the back of the wagon with his head cradled in her lap. He tried to sit up and felt the bullets pinch into his flesh.

"Don't move."

He groaned and lay back in defeat. In the distance, the faint shouts of men filled the air. "Where are we?"

Willow gazed out at the dark woods. "I don't know." The wagon hit a bump, and Edward yelped.

"Sorry, Ed!" Cliff called over his shoulder. "Hang in there! We'll get you out of here!"

His chest was starting to feel tight, and he gasped for breath. "I don't feel great…"

Willow frowned. "We've got to get those bullets out of you." She sifted through her bag. "I think you've been poisoned."

"What?"

"In Candosia, we used bullets that dissolved inside the body, spreading poison… Something tells me Andron would love that idea."

Feeling more awake suddenly, if nothing else, Edward yanked his waistcoat off, ignoring the searing pain in his side. His blood-soaked shirt was dry now but felt cold against his skin.

"Where is it?" Willow said, rummaging through her bag. Edward's eyes were fluttering open and closed, and he was having trouble following what was going on.

"I hate to interrupt, but we've got trouble," Cliff called back.

Willow's eyes darted up from her work. Two chariots were slicing through the woods, hot on their heels.

"Hold on," she said to Edward, but he was starting to feel awfully nauseous. Willow grabbed her bow and unleashed a slew of arrows, striking the man in the first chariot in the chest. It veered off the path and slammed into a tree. The man in the second chariot raised a crossbow then, the end of which glowed orange.

"Look out!" Edward shouted as Willow drew another arrow. He slammed into her and pulled her down to the floor of the wagon just as a flaming arrow struck the wood behind them, setting it ablaze.

Hikoo poked his head out of the fruit. "Fire! Fire!" He scampered onto Edward's shoulder.

Brooks—who Edward hadn't even notice until now—suddenly ripped off his cloak as flames licked up the wagon's walls, and attempted to snuff them out. Another arrow whizzed by overhead; Edward could no longer contain his stomach, and he leaned over the edge of the wagon and vomited.

"Here it is!" Willow said, pulling a small vial out of her bag. Edward eyed the green liquid inside. "Drink it." He took the vial and gulped its contents down; it tasted horrible.

"What was that?"

She smiled. "You don't want to know, but it's all I have, so try not to get shot again."

"Maybe you shouldn't have shoved me in front of all those bullets then?"

She rolled her eyes. "You're lucky I didn't leave you there."

"If you two are done, I suggest you duck." Brooks was scowling at them. His charred cloak was on the floor of the wagon, and he gripped a dagger in one hand. The second chariot was closing in behind them, close enough that he could make out the expression of both the driver and the archer beside him. Brooks' dagger cut through the air and sunk into their bandoro's skull. The animal collapsed, pitching the men into the bush.

Willow shot him a look. "You didn't have to kill it."

"You have your way, I have mine," he snarled.

"What matters is that we're safe," Edward muttered. He could barely keep his eyes open now and leaned back in Willow's lap, finally allowing himself to feel the fatigue that had been chasing him the past few weeks. His muscles were stiff, and his bones ached, but they had made it. With every passing moment, the cries of outrage behind them grew more and more distant until finally... he couldn't hear anything at all.

*

Edward's eyes cracked open, and he squinted at the daylight. Streaks of sunlight peeked through a thin canopy of trees above him. He sat up in the back of the wagon and stretched, working a knot out of his neck. His chest was sore where Willow had stitched him up, and his side didn't feel much better. Beside him, Willow was passed out with her head on her bag, her chest rising and falling slowly. He smiled. They had stopped in a clearing surrounded by thin trees that stood straight and tall, their branches vanishing into low-hanging mist.

He climbed out of the wagon and felt his feet sink into the ground. He saw that Brooks and Cliff were nuzzled up together against the bandoros, and he chuckled, wishing he could capture the moment. He thought about waking them but decided against it. Instead, he strolled off into the trees. The air felt different here. It seemed... salty?

Up ahead, a flash of movement caught his eye, and he crept forward, peering through the trees. The woods were calm, then a sharp crack pierced the air high above, followed by a human shriek. He jerked around. A man was dangling precariously from a tree top a short distance away. Then the tree split, and the top half came tumbling down, delivering the man to the earth with an uncivilised thud. Edward stared at the man who was still clinging motionless to the broken trunk like a marshmallow on a stick; finally, a soft groan escaped his lips.

Edward let out a sigh of relief.

"Are you okay?" he asked, fairly certain that the man was not one of Andron's soldiers. Though nothing could have prepared him for when the man rolled over and it was Enzo who stared up at him dumbly.

The bounty hunter blinked. "Lynus?"

"What?" Edward said, his mind racing. "Oh, right."

"What er you doin' in Decius?"

"Why don't you tell me why you're here first? In fact, why don't you tell me why you were up in a tree, spying on me?"

Enzo struggled to his feet and dusted off his burly shoulders. "We're... uh... doin' a job."

"We?"

He turned and hollered into the woods. "Boys, git out here." Several bearded faces popped up from the undergrowth, and Truss, Cal, and Derek peered at Edward through grimy, dirt-covered faces.

"Lynus?" Truss scratched his beard. "What are you doing in

Decius?"

Edward buried his face in his hands. "I'd like to ask you the same thing."

Enzo blushed. "Well, that's the thing see? We... uh... we thought you were Edward Sting."

Edward sighed. "I think you'd better come with me."

*

Edward rushed through the bush, the four eager bounty hunters bounding jauntily behind him. When they reached the camp, his fears were confirmed.

Neil was already there, wrestling with Brooks in the sand. Edward caught only snippets of the incessant curses that were flying between them. Cliff stood nearby, watching the tangle of limbs that was the two men turn up dust. Willow was perched in the wagon, pure confusion on her face. Edward hurried over and jumped between them.

"Enough!" he shouted.

Brooks gathered himself and brushed off his cloak.

"I knew it all along!" Neil said, foaming at the mouth. "You're not chasing them! You're helping them!"

Brooks sneered. "You're an awful long way from home, Neil. Can't go crying to Sento."

"So are you." The bounty hunter spat. "And when he finds out—"

"He's not going to," Edward said.

Everyone looked at him. "I *am* Edward Sting."

Although Enzo and the others gasped, Neil's lips turned up in a devilish smile. "Of course, you are. Well, the road trip is over, boys and lady." He leered at Willow. "Come on down here, sweetheart."

Edward caught Brooks' eye and he could see the duke fuming, his hand hovering over his dagger. He shot him a look. He just needed a few minutes. Neil was never going to believe their lies, but then again, that's not what he really cared about.

Edward cleared his throat. "What if it's not over?"

The bounty hunter's smile faded. "Don't be stupid, kid." He raised the dagger in his hand. "The king didn't say nothing 'bout you being alive when we brought you in."

"We'd like to hire you."

Neil laughed. "No way you can pay me more than the king."

Brooks clenched his fists. "And I'd rather die than give him a cent."

"We can pay you more than you think," Edward said, stepping between them.

Neil inclined his head. "And how's that?"

"You see, we're not just on the run. We're on our way to Regnum." A murmur ran through the outfit.

"You're crazy," Truss said.

Edward shook his head. "You and I both know the kings are bound to Regnum for their survival. Think about how much money it must be hoarding."

Neil peered at him with his one good eye. "And you're going to rob them?"

"Why not?"

He chuckled "And what are you gonna do about *him?*"

Edward's stomach churned. "You mean Lord Gorlak?"

Neil nodded.

"Let us worry about that. If you get us to Regnum, I can double your money."

The man paused for a moment, stroking his shaggy chin.

"That's a lot of risk for me."

"We'll triple it then."

"If you don't, you're a dead man."

"Fine."

Neil laughed and shook his head. "You are crazy." He turned to his crew. "What do you say, boys?" A course of hoots finalised their decision.

Edward turned to Brooks, whose expression was grave. They began packing up their remaining supplies. Cal and Derek were sent back to the bounty hunters' camp and returned an hour later with five bandoros, all loaded down with food and equipment.

Neil directed them to put the food and gear in the wagon. "We'll ride in pairs."

By the time the sun was sinking beneath the trees that afternoon, they were ready to depart. Edward mounted the last bandoro. Willow was up ahead, riding behind Enzo. As they took off, she glanced back and gave him a look as though to say, 'I hope you know what you're doing'.

*

Edward had never seen so much water. It stretched to the horizon like a giant blue blanket, covering the world. The sound of the surf crashing on the sandy shore set his mind at ease. Growing up in Teradowa, he had never seen an ocean like this. The only water they had was the Great River, with its spinning Vortex.

Farther down the beach, Truss and Enzo were lounging in the sand—snoozing no doubt. Brooks had gone hunting with Neil, Derek, and Cal. The distrust between Neil and the duke ensured that neither one would take his eye off the other. Thus, only Willow and Cliff were left to poke around in the loose sand with him and wait.

According to Neil, a ship was going to arrive and drop anchor as soon as tonight to take them to Tydor, or rather, across it. The sea before them was, in fact, the fourth realm itself, as Neil had explained, demarcated by the shores of Decius on one side and Regnum on the other. Edward had to trust him in this, and about the vast archipelago that Neil claimed existed somewhere along the way, as his map was frustratingly blank in that regard. Apparently, the scoundrel had sailed throughout Tydor many times before and knew where to be, and when, if one wanted a quick charter.

Cliff peered down the beach, biting his lip.

"Why don't you relax?" Edward said. "Everything will be fine."

"How can you possibly know that?" his friend said sharply.

Willow was also looking at him doubtfully. Suddenly, Edward realised that, in all the excitement of the past day, he had neglected to tell them about the second stone—or the first, for that matter—and what he had seen and learned under Andron's castle. He decided he'd better come clean; it was clear now that there was more going on than they knew.

He told them everything. About finding the stone in Candosia and how it had given him the idea to challenge Pentheus to a duel. How he would get a strange feeling whenever the stones were nearby and hear music. He also told them about the secret chamber beneath Andron's castle and how he had almost been burned alive.

"Let's see these stones," Cliff said when he was finished.

Edward shook his head. "It's not like that. I can't just pull them out whenever I want. They just sort of appear in my pocket." He stared at their blank faces. "You don't believe me, do you?"

"Just because we don't understand doesn't mean it's not true," Willow said.

"If it is true, Ed, then you better hold on to those rocks."

"So, do you think Lord Gorlak has something to do with the stones appearing?" Willow said.

Edward shrugged. "I'd say he's up to something."

Willow shook her head. "That story Andron told you... it does sound familiar."

She gazed out to sea, her eyes betraying nothing. Finally, she turned back. "I think these stones might be the key to everything, Edward. To saving your grandpa, and maybe, something much bigger."

Edward felt excitement rising inside him, like pure energy charging up his spine. "I wonder what Brooks will make of all this," he said. Cliff and Willow exchanged looks.

"What?"

Cliff cleared his throat. "I don't know if we should tell him."

Edward furrowed his brow. "Why not?"

His friend sighed. "Think about it, Ed. He left Teradowa because he wants to see Sento dethroned, right? You really think if he had unlimited power, he'd use it for good?" Cliff shook his head. "You and I both know that's not true."

"Brooks came with us because he cares about my grandfather. He was his friend."

"Even so," Willow said, "if Lord Gorlak is controlling the realms, then surely Brooks would know something about it. Why wouldn't he tell us himself?"

Edward took a step back; could his friends not see that Brooks had proven himself? "Why would he know anything?

You didn't," he said, pointing at Willow.

She put her hand on his arm. "Edward—" But he jerked it free.

"Something's not right, Ed. That's all we're saying."

"He's trying to help." He said, trying to keep his voice calm. Here was a man who had just offered to sacrifice himself for them, to die so that they could have a chance at living, and now they were accusing him of being dishonest? He had let them in on his secret, and in return, they had dishonoured a man they owed their lives to. Edward turned on his heels and stormed down the beach.

"Edward!" Willow called.

They didn't understand. Family was more important than some stupid stones and nobody, least of all Brooks, would disagree with that.

Dusk was settling over the water, casting an orange glow across the waves. As he trudged through the sand, he noticed a set of white sails jutting up from the horizon. An uncomfortable feeling rose inside him, at the thought of going to sea in his present state of mind. By the time he reached Enzo and Truss, Neil and the others were striding out of the forest. Cal and Derek walked beside one another, a large rodent dangling between them on a stick.

"Nothing like fresh kexle for dinner by the seaside, eh, kid?" Neil boasted.

Cal and Derek dropped the prize down in the sand. The kexle was covered in green scales except for a strip of brown fur along its spine and covering its head.

"The finest meat this side of Nodington Valley!"

The men started building a fire as Brooks strode up, looking tired. Hikoo leapt off his shoulder and scampered through the sand to Edward.

"Boy, that little guy could find a bottle of swizzleberry juice in a herd of bandoros," Neil said. "He gets the first taste!"

*

They sat around the fire, munching on the last of the roasted kexle meat, which Edward had to admit was delicious. Eventually, Willow and Cliff rejoined them, but much to Cliff's dismay, the kexle had already been picked clean. Silently, the group watched as the approaching ship finally anchored offshore and a wooden rowboat was lowered into the water.

As it approached, Edward could make out a lean, muscular young man with tanned skin, standing in the stern, shouting out orders.

"Easy now!"

The four grizzly looking men manning the oars strained against the sea, seemingly making their way towards a rocky outcrop above the water. The skipper brought them around it, slicing through the water like a knife through butter. "Hold it!" he yelled. The boat zig-zagged to the south this time, right towards the rock face. It spun around the rock, so close that Edward thought they would hit it, but they didn't. Instead, they cut cleanly through the surf and glided to a gentle stop in the sand.

Neil clapped. "You always know how to make an entrance, Kip."

The lean man, Kip, leapt smoothly out of the boat and bowed to the group. He was as tall as Edward with the same sandy blond hair that contrasted greatly with his tanned skin. The only clothes he wore were a pair of ratty shorts, cut just above the knee. He glanced at the travellers sitting around the fire. "More of you than I was expecting,"

"Business partners," Neil said, gesturing to Edward.

Kip nodded. He seemed accustomed to not asking questions. "Well, we'll have to take two trips."

Neil motioned for Cal, Derek, and Truss to stay behind with Cliff and Willow. He obviously wanted to keep an eye on his new allies, but that didn't bother Edward; he wasn't sure if he was ready to confront his friends just yet. He climbed into the rowboat between Neil and Enzo, and they took off from the shore with a jolt. Edward looked out at the large vessel anchored ahead of them. He had never really sailed before, and certainly not on an ocean. He was suddenly filled with anxiety. The water beneath them was dark, and giant whirlpools spun away from the oars as they made their way out to sea. Sitting in the boat felt like balancing on a pendulum. He gripped the sides and looked straight ahead.

Enzo chuckled. "First time at sea?"

"Yes."

"You'll git used to it. Just try not to think about all the beasties swimming around underneath us." Edward wished he hadn't said that.

The outline of the ship grew larger in the gathering darkness until they were so close that Edward could hear the shouts of the crew on deck. The boat they were in now felt tiny, rocking in the surf as they approached. The ship was huge. Its wood was faded and weathered but didn't show any signs of rot. Near the bow the words, 'The Saint Elmer', had been carved and painted. Edward squinted, beneath the name a longer inscription was written in crude lettering: 'Those who protect what they keep will be given that which they seek.'

"Closer now," Kip said, motioning them forward.

The boat lurched, and Edward's whole body tensed. Then a rope ladder came flying over the side of the ship and thumped against its hull. Kip got up first and climbed nimbly skyward until he disappeared over the railing of *The Saint Elmer*. When it was Edward's turn, he stood up, feeling nauseous, and for a moment wondered if he hadn't seen the last of his kexle, but he gathered himself and grabbed the damp rope. The surf rolled beneath them, crashing into the ship and showering him with mist as he climbed.

He reached the top and swung his legs over, landing on all fours on the deck before staggering to his feet. All around, sailors were gazing curiously at him. Most of them looked like Kip, tall and lean with tanned skin, but they weren't as well kept. Their bodies were covered in dirt and sweat, and their shorts—those that wore shirts were few and far between—were tattered and patched. An older man parted from the crowd. He had dark skin and wore a red waistcoat and a wide-brimmed hat.

"All right, lads, that'll do!" he shouted at the crew. "You'll have to excuse 'em. We weren't expecting you. Welcome aboard *The Saint Elmer*. I'm Cap'n Sanchez."

Edward had barely opened his mouth to reply when Neil came thundering up beside him and clapped Sanchez on the back.

"There he is! The most fearsome buccaneer in all of Tydor!"

The old man grinned, revealing handsome wrinkles in his sea-weathered face. He glanced back at Edward and Brooks who had sauntered up. "Neil didn't tell me he would be bringing guests, but you are more than welcome on my ship."

"Ah!" Neil said. "These are my newest associates, all the way from Teradowa. They're going to make me rich!" Then he whispered something into Sanchez's ear.

The captain smirked. "First time seeing the realms?" he asked Edward.

He nodded.

"Well, this must all be very strange to you."

"I'm beginning to expect it."

"Not to worry." The captain winked. "You're in good hands now."

"The best," Neil said as he fanned out his jacket, dispersing his pungent odour.

Edward noticed, with some amusement, the disgusted looks on the faces of the crew.

"Kip," the captain said, as his first mate appeared, "how's the water?"

He tapped his knuckles on the rail. "Just the way I like it, sir. There's another party on the beach." The captain nodded, and the sailor excused himself.

"So," Sanchez said, "the usual route, Neil?"

Neil shook his head. "Sting here has business in Regnum."

Sanchez took this in stride, his face betraying nothing. "Of course. We'll have you across in a couple of days." The old sailor gestured to the crew, busy raising the boom and the main sails. "These lads know this pond like a queen knows her pearls."

Edward felt much better than he had earlier in the day. There was something about Captain Sanchez that he liked.

"Come on, my friends," he said to Edward and Brooks. "Let me show you to your quarters." They followed him amidships to a square hatch in the deck, which he threw open to reveal a set of steps. They descended below decks to a narrow corridor. "We offer a wide range of rooms here on the *Elmer* that can accommodate even very lavish tastes." Edward peered in the first few doors they passed, which were ajar, but caught only flashes of colours. "Of course, if there's anything you need, please don't hesitate to ring your bell."

Edward furrowed his brow, then to his amazement, looked down to find a small brass bell clutched between his fingers. Captain Sanchez stopped before a pair of rooms, one on either side of the hall. "Did you gentleman enjoy the ocean breeze this evening?"

Edward shrugged. "I guess,"

Captain Sanchez nodded. "I see." Reaching into the folds of his coat, he produced a cane and gave the door to his left two quick taps. Then, satisfied, he put the cane away.

"There we are." He opened the door. The room was circular and very spacious. A bed with a curved headboard rested opposite a rich oak dresser and a mirror. Terrace doors were drawn open on the far side, allowing the cool evening breeze to drift in. Edward frowned; he didn't recall seeing any balconies from the rowboat. Sanchez strolled towards the open doors and smiled into the tropical night air. "I hope you find this to your liking, but of course, you have your bell."

"Thanks."

He turned to Brooks. "My liege, I think you'll find yourself more at home next door."

Expressing his disdain for the perceived mockery with his usual grumble, Brooks followed the captain into the hall. When they had gone, Edward dropped onto the bed and felt himself sink into the mattress. He checked the time on his pocket watch and rolled the circular object between his fingers. In the quiet of the room, he felt his anger leave him. Cliff and Willow's hearts were in the right place; he knew that, even if he didn't agree with them about Brooks. He closed his eyes, and without even planning on it, soon found himself dozing off.

*

He woke to a knock at the door. Rubbing his eyes, he glanced outside. It was still dark. He climbed out of bed and shuffled over to the door, cracking it open.

"Willow?" he said, throwing the door open. She brushed past him without a word. "What are you doing here?" He watched her pace around the room, feeling a little indignant.

"Nice room. Hm, I was wondering if I was the only one with a terrace."

"Yeah," Edward said, scratching his head. "Listen, I'm actually glad you're here. I've been thinking, and I'm not mad anymore."

She laughed. "Is that right?"

"Yes."

She crossed her arms. "I've been doing some thinking too."

"Oh?"

"And I think you're lucky Cliff and I don't abandon you right now."

"What do you mean?"

"Your friend has been nothing but good to you, he's stuck by you, he's nearly died for you and as soon as he says something you don't like, you turn your back on him, without even hearing him out."

"Well, I—"

"And then there's me. A girl who has put her trust in you, who has sacrificed a lot to be here and you're just going to walk away from me?" She scoffed, closing the distance between them. "That's what *I* ought to be doing."

He scooped his bell off the dresser, fidgeting with it in order to avoid her gaze.

"But of course, if I left, you'd be dead in a week."

"Only giving me a week, eh?"

"Face it, you're in way over your head." She was mere inches away now.

"Then why don't you leave?" For a moment, he thought he'd misspoke, but then she bit her lip. He grinned. "You don't have to answer. I think I know why."

"Do you, now?"

"Yes. You don't leave because... no matter what you say... you're too damn in love with me." He tossed his bell up in the air and caught it then. She eyed him for a moment.

"You gonna drop that thing or what?"

It was not a question, rather a demand. He let the bell fall to the carpet. She slipped her arms around him, and their lips locked. Her touch flipped a switch in him, and he was instantly wide awake. His whole body came alive at the taste of her lips, the feeling of her body against his. Together, they dropped onto the bed.

He ran his hands through her hair and heard her sigh, feeling her warm breath on his cheek as she took his hands in hers and led them down her hips and then back up to her chest.

He suddenly felt himself falling. Falling fast. With every passionate breath that left her body, he fell deeper into an irreversible trance. She whispered in his ear, and he fell even farther. In a matter of a few breathless moments, his world was turned upside down...

When it was over, he lay very still, with her dozing on his chest. He didn't dare move. He didn't want to move. Not for the rest of his life.

Chapter 20

A Parting Gift

Salty air swelled in Edward's lungs the next morning. Gone was any trace of the lush tropical aroma they had enjoyed on the coast of Decius. The sky was now as clear as the water they cut through. On the horizon, the ocean blurred and mixed with the heavens like two lost twins reuniting.

Edward broke away from the rail and from his thoughts, although he could not keep the smile from his face. He hadn't stopped thinking about Willow since the night before. All his confusion and strife from the past few weeks had melted away. Cliff sat on a large barrel in the corner, stroking Hikoo behind the ear. The skulposis hadn't stopped shaking since coming aboard. Edward had never met a creature so petrified of water.

"What's on your mind, Ed?"

He shrugged. "Nothing,"

All had been forgiven, of course. Although he still didn't like the accusations his friends had brought against Brooks, he had agreed, for the time being, not to tell the duke about the stones or Lord Gorlak.

Edward rummaged in his pockets at the thought and was disappointed to find that the stones were not there. He wanted to show Cliff, just to prove he wasn't crazy. He knew he wasn't. He had no doubt that, the next time he needed them, the stones would appear.

"It's easy to lose your thoughts out here," said Kip. He was at the helm, his sandy hair dancing in front of his eyes. He brushed it aside.

"Do you enjoy sailing?" Edward asked. It was a dumb question, but he felt like making conversation. Kip pulled a lever and then stepped away from the wheel. The three of them—four including Hikoo—were on the bridge at the back of the ship, while the crew lounged about below.

"It's all I've ever known," he said, gazing out at the water.

"What do you mean?"

Kip laughed. "I've been on the water my whole life."

"Don't you have a family?"

He smiled. "I did, a long time ago, but the crew is my family now."

"What about your parents?" Cliff asked.

"They belong to the islands, but not me. I was chosen for the sea."

Edward furrowed his brow. "Chosen? But why live your whole life at sea?"

"Because my king asked me to. See, we have a job to do… or at least we did."

Cliff shook his head. "But not anymore?"

"There's no kingdom anymore," Kip said. "Not really. Just crews like ours." Edward and Cliff exchanged looks, but Kip just leaned against the wheel and yawned.

"So, Tydor doesn't have a king?"

"Not for a very long time," he said, shrugging. "Can't have a king without a kingdom." Cliff scratched his head and stopped petting Hikoo, much to the creature's dismay.

"It's not so bad… as long as we look out for each other." Seeing their confused faces, the helmsman continued. "Captain

Sanchez is a warrior. We'll fight to the last if we have to. Besides," he snickered, "it's not like having a king has been so great for *you*."

Edward couldn't argue with that. "So, what happened to yours?"

Kip's expression became grim, and he looked out to sea. "I'm not sure. We used to keep in touch regularly and then one day, everything went silent. But we've kept on sailing ever since."

*

Edward spent the afternoon watching the waves roll by and listening to Kip tell stories from his days on the water. He seemed to have an endless supply of them. A woman who had an affair with Captain Sanchez while sailing with her husband. A drunken tribe leader who'd taken control of the helm and almost scuttled them. When asked whether Tydor had any gods, Kip simply shrugged. "If we do, I haven't met them yet."

Edward admired Kip's carefree attitude, even envied it. He imagined himself living on the open ocean, having epic adventures. He grinned at the thought, but a part of him knew it was a fantasy. Whatever Kip got out of sailing, it came at the expense of something else.

The sun was bleeding into the water by the time he left the deck, soaking the ocean in an orange glow. He found Willow below decks, sharpening her arrows and cleaning her bow.

"Hi."

She turned around. "Where have you been all day?"

"Talking to Kip."

She ran her hand up the seam of his waistcoat and stopped

at a bump in one of its inner pockets. "What's this?"

"Oh, I completely forgot about that," he said, pulling out Hidalgo's egg. It was a miracle it hadn't been destroyed in their escape.

Willow gasped. "Where did you get that?"

"Hidalgo gave it to me at the palace. He stole it from the king."

She yanked it from his hands. "It doesn't belong to us."

Edward chuckled indignantly. "What? You want to give it back to that arubbak that nearly killed us?"

"That's its mother, and I promised her I'd keep it safe."

Edward sighed. "So, what are you gonna do with it?"

She paused, and then her eyes lit up. "I'll give it to Hikoo to protect. It'll give him something to do, and it'll be a lot safer with him then it will be in your pocket."

Edward watched her storm off, thinking that egg would be at the bottom of the ocean by the end of the day.

*

Not a moment after the sun had set, Captain Sanchez gathered them all up for the most impressive feast Edward had ever seen. The dining room was adorned with velvet finishings and illuminated by candlelit chandeliers. Neil and his men were already at the bottom of their wine glasses and engrossed in a terribly unfunny story when Edward and the others arrived. Sanchez and Kip greeted them.

"Where's the rest of the crew?" Edward asked.

"Gave 'em the night off."

Edward thought that was odd. Surely the crew had to eat too, even if they were off duty. Now that he thought about it, he hadn't seen anyone else for hours. Fine wines accompanied their meal, which consisted of fresh fiddle berries, vegetables, bread, and some sort of white, flaky meat in a rich savoury sauce.

"Lagora fish," Kip said from across the table. Edward glanced up in time to see Cliff devour his whole fillet and serve himself seconds. He took a bite and found it surprisingly sweet.

Sanchez sipped from his glass. "So, Edward, is this your first time going to Regnum?"

Edward nodded. "Have you ever been?"

The captain shook his head. "I've heard the stories, of course. This journey you're on… it's not to be taken lightly. Lord Gorlak rules like a tyrant."

Edward exchanged uneasy looks with Cliff and Willow, then glanced at Brooks. The duke's expression betrayed nothing. He sat at the end of the table as still as a statue.

"Lord Gorlak?" Edward asked, trying to sound innocent.

"The King of Regnum," Sanchez said, nodding. "But he's not your average king. Of course, nobody knows what he's really like. Nobody that's met him has ever come back."

At this, Neil snickered and ran his finger under his chin. Captain Sanchez narrowed his eyes, then looked back at Edward. "Does that scare you, lad?"

Sensing he was being tested, Edward paused. "No. It doesn't. Stories are often exaggerated until they're nothing but myth."

Sanchez smirked. "You're right about that."

Neil grunted. "Maybe Sting will be the first. Rob 'em blind and git outta there, eh? Besides, you're the first that's ever sailed there with Sanchez. Ain't that right, Cap'n?"

Sanchez licked his lips. "That's right." He took a mouthful of his lagora fish, looking deep in thought. "Except for that older fellow."

Edward's ears perked up. "What older fellow?"

"About six months ago, a man comes aboard, says he wants to be taken to Regnum."

Edward's mind raced. That would have been about the time his grandfather left. "Did he tell you his name?"

Sanchez shook his head. "No. Didn't say much at all actually."

Edward was about to respond when they heard an explosion outside, followed by a tremendous splash. Kip leapt from his seat and dashed out the door, reappearing a moment later.

"Captain, two ships off our stern!"

Sanchez cursed. "Raise the crew!" He sprang from his seat, and Edward and the others followed him out on deck. The crew was somehow already out in full force, barking orders at each other and wheeling squeaky old cannons into battle positions.

Cliff stood aghast. "B-But how—"

"All hands, prepare for battle!" Sanchez shouted as he pushed passed them.

"Come on," Edward said, taking Willow by the hand. They bounded up the steps to the bridge, with Cliff huffing and puffing close behind. Sanchez was at the helm.

"What's happening?" Edward asked.

The captain sighed. "Pirates."

Edward gazed out to sea, and sure enough, there were the silhouettes of two ships, gliding out of the mist behind them.

"What's going on?" It was Brooks, who had followed them up, red in the face.

"I'd like to know the same thing," Neil declared. "Pirates, Captain? We've never run into pirates before."

Captain Sanchez grumbled. "We had to change our normal

course to get to Regnum. There's no way around it."

"Why?" Neil demanded.

"There's only one way in, past the mountains to the south, but to get there, we cross through waters that are... contested. I didn't think they would dare follow us so close to Regnum. If they keep firing, they'll awaken the Doorman." Edward didn't like the sound of that.

Cliff growled. "And *what* is the Doorman?"

"Just pray you don't find out."

There was another explosion out in the darkness, followed by a crack belowdecks. Edward's feet left the deck for a moment; then he slammed into the railing. Peering breathlessly over the side, he saw that there was a hole in the hull, just above the waterline.

"We're hit!"

"I'm going to try and go between them." No sooner had Sanchez put his hands on the wheel than the two ships tacked their sails and surged towards them, blocking them in on either side.

"Oh God," Willow muttered. The barbaric cries of the pirates filled the air as they unleashed a barrage of cannon fire. Spent gunpowder stung Edward's nose as the cannons erupted, one after the other in a violent rhythm. The deck cracked and imploded beneath them then as a shot connected, ripping through the wood. Edward reached out as the bridge collapsed but missed the rail, plunging through the deck and smashing into the dining table in the room below.

Sharp pain shot through his still-healing wounds.

"Look out!" came a shout from above.

He rolled out of the way just as Cliff came plummeting through the hole after him. His chubby friend slammed into the wood and cracked the table in half. They hobbled to their feet as quickly as they could and ran back out on deck. Edward stopped short, gasping. The world was on fire. Men rushed about, hollering between each other, and smoke covered the sky, blocking out the stars. Splintered wood littered the deck. A candle stick rolled by Edward on its way to the stern.

"We're tilted," Edward said, his voice sounding far calmer than he felt. "I think we're going to sink."

Cliff swallowed. "What do we do?" His face was pale in the moonlight.

They both jumped out of their skin as the *Elmer's* own cannons began their answering volleys, the sound battering Edward's eardrums.

"Edward!" Willow came dashing down from the bridge. He followed her gaze back up to the helm, where Sanchez was laughing manically, a crazed look in his eye. He recalled his conversation with Kip about the captain's policy of fighting to the last man.

"Let's get our things together. We may need to abandon the ship."

Another volley of cannon fire smashed into the ship, lifting huge, jagged splinters from the deck, and Edward stumbled and gripped the rail. Then came the sound of wood groaning, and the forward mast lurched sideways. Suddenly the boom came swinging around and Edward gasped as he was struck on the side of the head. He tumbled through the broken deck, smacking his wounded shoulder off something before falling for what seemed like an eternity.

Finally, his body slammed down onto solid wood, knocking the air out of his lungs. As he struggled to sit up, he shook his head. Not surprisingly, his vision was blurry. What he did find surprising was the quiet. The rumblings from above seemed a million miles away. Dragging himself to his feet, he stumbled as fast as he could down the dark corridor, only faintly aware of someone calling his name. A feeling of discovery was creeping into his body again, as it had twice before now. Finding his room, he tore it apart, flipping everything in sight upside down. He took a deep breath. If there *was* a stone here, he needed to be calm and listen for it.

He reemerged in the hallway. The floor rocked beneath him as another cannonball tore through the hull and burst through the wall ahead of him. He held up his arms and felt shards of wood dig into his exposed skin. Then the whole ship lurched, and the deck ahead of him crumpled, sending him sliding deep into the belly of the ship. He landed in ankle-deep water.

They were sinking.

Water was pouring in from a hole in the stern. He could see it now, only a short distance away. It seeped through a crack in the hull like an old habit that died hard, speeding their demise. Outside, the percussive booming continued as the pirates moved in for the kill, and another cannonball smashed through the wall behind Edward, a shard of broken wood striking his shoulder now and ripping apart his bullet wound. He stumbled forward then, hitting his head on an iron beam and collapsing into the water.

What had he come down here for? He could not remember; he was beginning to see spots at the edge of his vision again, only now they were not going away. Perhaps this was a fitting end to his foolish attempt at being a hero. He would drown. So what? Life would go on.

"Hey, kid."

He gazed up into the dim light. Kip was smiling down at

him, but there was something different about him... He seemed almost to glow.

"Was it worth it?"

Edward shook his head. "Was what worth it?"

"I know who you are. And I know what you seek. But if you failed... if it all ended right now... would it have been worth it?"

He squinted up at Kip's form, positive he was hallucinating. "I... I hope so."

Kip grinned. "You have a noble heart. Captain Sanchez believes in you. He thinks you can bear the responsibility."

Edward frowned. "I don't understand."

Kip crossed his arms the way a teacher might when faced with a dissatisfactory answer. "Those who protect what they keep will be given that which they seek."

Edward stared at him, an eerie realization slowly dawning.

"We protect what we keep, Edward. My only question for you is this: Can you do the same?"

"You protect the stone!" Part of his delirium was lifting now, or maybe he had given in to it. "Yes. I can... *I will.*"

Kip's expression was grave. "Your journey is not going to be easy. Do not give your answer too quickly, as there will be no taking it back."

He thought back on everything that had led him to this point, everything he had survived since leaving Teradowa: the secrecy, deceit, and manipulation... the violence and mayhem. It was all because he had made a choice. One that he and now his friends and God knows who else would have to live with. But it was his responsibility and his alone.

"I will protect the stone," he said solemnly, "and do whatever needs to be done. I swear."

Kip's smile returned. "I see the captain was right about you."

Edward frowned; he was still missing something. "But how

did you come by the stone?"

"Our job—given to us by our king, so long ago that none remain to even share the tale—was to protect that which he had cherished most. We have done that for a thousand years... but now it is up to you. It is not our place to help you in your struggle."

"But... why give *me* the stone?"

"Our king is long dead; he lives now only in our memories. But we are tired, Edward. We have lived long. Too long. It's time for someone else to do the job. Someone good. So, I ask one final time... Can you protect what you keep?"

Edward struggled against the pain in his body and set his jaw. "I will."

"Then why don't you check your pocket."

Edward reached into his waistcoat and pulled out Captain Sanchez's brass bell. He furrowed his brow.

Kip winked. "If you need anything, don't hesitate to ring."

Edward shook the bell, and to his surprise, a simple chime met his ears. Closing his eyes, he cleared his thoughts. He only wanted one thing. He put all of his focus on it, and then opened his eyes and tipped the bell over.

A small red stone fell into his palm.

Kip beamed down at him. "Thank you, Edward Sting. You have given us what we seek. I'd hold onto that if I were you."

"I won't let you down. I promise." Kip turned and started to walk away.

"Kip," he called, as a thought occurred to him.

The sailor turned around. "Yes?"

"What was it like... before the stones?"

Kip smiled again, and there was a sparkle in his bright blue eyes.

"It was like a dream."

Chapter 21

Visions of the Past

"Edward!"

His eyes fluttered open. Willow was crouching over him in the slowly rising water. "You're hurt."

He groaned as she pulled back his shirt. The skin had been broken once more around his bullet wound, and blood was trickling across his chest.

She rummaged in her pockets. "Just give me a minute." The water was nearly at his waist. "Here," Willow said, pulling out a bandage. The ship lurched forward, and she stumbled into the bulkhead, dropping the bandages into the water, where they were carried swiftly through a break in the hull and out to sea.

"It's okay. I have more."

"There's no time." He gritted his teeth and pushed off the wall, ignoring the blinding pain in his shoulder and the countless other stinging cuts and bruises. They began wading through the cold water, tiny waves lapping against his chest now, towards the front of the ship, but the sea was moving faster than they were. It scooped up pictures from the walls and extinguished candles as it sped by, plunging them into darkness. By the time they reached the stairs, the water was above Willow's head. She swam alongside Edward, who pushed on, paddling through the water with his one good arm, his chin held up just out of reach of the cold, black surface. Together, they stumbled up the stairs, shivering, and finally emerged on the next deck, but the floor was so slanted that it was hard to stand.

"Here," Willow said, stopping at another narrow set of steps. "This is the only way up." She bounded up the stairs with Edward trailing behind, gasping for breath. His head was still spinning but adrenaline fuelled his every move. They emerged into the cool night, which bit harshly at his wet skin.

The deck was riddled with holes and burning debris. The stern was completely submerged, and water was creeping up the deck towards them. The pirates, anchored to either side of them, seemed to have realised that their job was done and were now watching *The Saint Elmer* burn as it dropped lower and lower into the waves, laughing and chanting something he couldn't make out. They'd clearly never intended to board their ship.

Edward shook his head. *They just sank us for the fun of it—*

"Ed!" Cliff shouted, appearing at his side. "They're gone! Captain Sanchez and the whole crew! They just..." The stout young man seemed almost at a loss for words. "They just vanished!"

Behind Cliff, Neil was barking orders at his own crew as they hauled wooden crates onto a rowboat. "Careful with that," he snapped as Cal dropped a case of jewels and fine silver into the boat.

Edward stormed over. "Where do you think you're going!"

Neil laughed. "I case you haven't noticed, kid, the ship is sinking."

"We had a deal!" Edward said, pointing a finger at him. "You help get us to Regnum or you don't get paid!"

Neil looked at him in disbelief. "Do you think I care about our deal or the money at this point? Keep it! Keep it all!"

"And what's all that?" Cliff asked, stepping forward and

pointing to their loot. "You're robbing Captain Sanchez? Your friend? After everything he—"

"Consider it my compensation!" the man snapped. "Besides, it's not like the old man needs it now."

"Those should go down with the ship," Edward said, an odd sense of loyalty settling over him.

Neil's hand flashed to his belt and came back with a pistol. "You want to take them from me, kid, be my guest." Edward's muscles tensed, but he took a step back.

"So, what is the plan then, Neil," Brooks said, smirking at his old nemesis. "You going to row all the way to Regnum?"

Neil glanced between them, then settled his gaze on Edward and shook his head. "If *you* want to be a hero, take your fat friend and your lass and go. But you'll have to find your own ride because if you think I'm going anywhere near that place, you're crazy." He dropped into the boat, his pistol still raised, as Enzo cut them free. The sinking vessel was so low in the water now that the boat practically slipped right into the surf, and the men quickly began rowing away.

Edward looked around at the tattered ruins of *The Saint Elmer* as cold seawater pooled around his ankles. He took a step back, but there was no escaping it. There was nowhere to go. The pirates' war cries and chants drifted across the gap between the ships, taunting them. Neil's boat was getting smaller and smaller as they made their escape with their stolen riches, becoming little more than a dark shape in the distance, recognisable only by their haughty voices carried on the wind.

Then something strange happened. The moonlight on the water nearby began to ripple. Edward blinked, not sure if it was real. He splashed over to the rail and looked closer.

"What is it?" Cliff asked, nervously.

The ripple was growing more obvious now, moving past the ship with a low crest in its centre. Then came a low-pitched call from just beneath the surface of the water. The pirates stopped chanting. The voices on the little rowboat ceased. Even the wind died away into stillness. Suddenly, a shape shot out of the water from directly beneath the rowboat, and captured it in a vice-like jaw. The boat was then lifted into the air with a bellowing roar loud enough to cause ripples of its own, and yet not loud enough to drown out the terrified screams of Neil and the others. The jaws snapped shut then, engulfing the boat and the screams ceased. All was still and calm for a moment, the black form of the mighty creature hung silhouetted against the pale moonlight. Then the creature sank back into the water, sending waves out in all directions.

After a moment, the water stilled, and there was nothing left to be seen.

Cliffs whole body shook. "W-what was th-that?"

Edward felt a completely new sense of terror run through his body. "I think we just met the Doorman."

Across the water, the pirates completely forgot about the sinking ship. Men were suddenly rushing about on deck, shouting in panicked voices and resetting the sails.

Then Edward saw the second ripple.

The others saw it too this time. They waded over to the rail, and in the gleaming light of the moon, watched as the scaly back of a massive creature glided past just under the surface, spanning the entire length of the sinking ship. Its dorsal fin broke the surface for a moment, then it disappeared, vanishing into the depths.

Somehow, Edward knew it wasn't gone for good, and he was soon proven right. The low call seemed to come from deeper below this time—perhaps in response to the shouts and frantic movement aboard the pirate ships—bringing with it a rippling wake that moved across the still water and sent the pirates into a frenzy now. Straight away, the men on the nearest ship pushed the long oars out, their blades splashing down into the water in the hopes of hastening their escape, but it was too late. The creature launched itself from the water and slammed into the ship, snapping it in two. Men plummeted from the deck into the waiting belly of the beast. The crumbling stern and bow, no longer joined, disappeared beneath the waves, taking with them the horrified screams of the pirate crew.

The men on board the second ship stared in silence at the spot where their fellow pirates had just been.

After several moments, Cliff let out a hoarse whisper. "Do you think it's gone?"

The pirates seemed to be having the same thought, as a nervous murmur had broken out on the ship, though the crew seemed frozen in place, afraid of drawing any further attention to themselves.

"We've got bigger problems," Edward said. The water was now almost to his knees. They retreated to the highest point on the deck, now only a few feet above water. He looked around desperately for some other skiff or rowboat that might have floated up from its mooring, but they had all been scuttled. Then an idea hit him that made him shiver.

"We have to get on that other ship," he said.

Cliff gasped. "What?"

"Either that or we drown."

The others glanced at each other. Even Brooks seemed to be out of ideas.

"How?" Cliff asked.

"We'll have to swim, but we can't make a sound... I think that's what attracts it."

In the moonlight, Edward could see all the colour drain from his friend's face.

"Edward, are you sure?" Willow said, frowning pointedly at his injured arm and shoulder.

Edward shrugged. It was a bad idea. But it was the only one he had, and he wasn't about to die out here. Hikoo, who had been hiding in Cliff's pack, poked his head out.

"Master Sting, must we?"

Edward grimaced at the fear in the skulposis' wide brown eyes. "You just stay put in there, Hikoo. You'll be safe." He hoped he sounded more confident than he felt—for all their sakes.

The bow of the *Elmer* was now almost level with the water. He moved to the edge and gazed down for a moment at the cold black surface. Around them, the darkness had been steadily deepening for some time now as more and more of the burning vessel dipped beneath the waves, until finally not a single ember remained.

Edward looked up then and watched as the moon itself seemed to be extinguished, disappearing behind a bank of thick clouds overhead. The distant lights from the remaining pirate ship appeared to float untethered to the blackness that now surrounded it. Taking a deep breath, Edward slipped down into the abyss.

The water was so cold and stung his skin so ferociously that he almost turned back, but he knew that doing so would doom them all. The weight of his sword and pistols, which he had gotten used to carrying, was unbearable now, as though bags of rocks were dragging him down. Behind him, the prow of *The*

Saint Elmer finally dipped beneath the waves and disappeared. There was no turning back now.

He began swimming, ignoring the searing pain in his shoulder. The flickering lights of the pirate ship loomed ahead like a mother waiting for her children. Edward had never wanted to get somewhere so desperately. He tried to focus on those lights but was consumed by the mental image of that enormous beast, lurking in the blackness beneath him, suddenly rising from the depths to swallow them whole.

Finally, after what felt like an eternity, he reached their destination, his outstretched hand making grateful contact with the pirate ship's rough wooden hull. The others arrived a moment later, teeth chattering and breathless. Willow had her bow and quiver looped over her shoulder, and Brooks' dagger was in his hand—apparently in expectation of an altercation with the pirates, though that seemed to Edward the least of their worries at present.

"Now what?" Cliff whispered. "How are we supposed to get up there?"

"I don't know..." he admitted breathlessly, looking both ways down the length of the hull and seeing nothing helpful. "I was hoping there'd be a ladder or something." He supposed they would need to circle the ship, looking for some way in, but even the thought practically brought tears to his eyes. Although the cold seemed to have numbed the pain of his injuries, it had also sapped most of his remaining strength. He didn't know how much longer he could keep himself afloat.

"We'll have to look for something," Brooks said through gritted teeth. "We won't last much longer out here."

As the current pushed them towards the boat's stern, the duke started paddling in that direction as the others followed behind. They soon turned the corner.

"There," Edward said, pointing upwards. A small balcony, much lower than the main deck, jutted out from the rear of the ship, surrounded by a low railing.

Probably the captain's quarters, he thought.

"Do you think you could get us up there, Willow? With an arrow maybe?"

For a moment, she looked at him like he'd gone mad but then she swam nimbly past him and grabbed hold of the ship's hull.

"Let me," he said, as she attempted to yank a stubborn arrow from her quiver. He pulled it out and handed it over her shoulder to her.

She tilted her head and wriggled sideways along the hull until her bow came unslung.

"Hold this," she said to Cliff. "And *don't* drop it." She stuck the arrow between her teeth and her free hand disappeared under water. It came back a moment later with a coiled rope from her belt. Tying it off on the arrow, she took the bow back from Cliff. Finally, she took a deep breath and nocked the arrow even as her mouth and nose dipped below the surface. But then she was up again, free and clear of the water. Cliff was behind her, bracing her to the hull.

The boy smiled. "A little extra weight goes a long way sometimes." Holding most of the bow above water now, she drew the string taut and fired at the balcony overhead—luckily, it wasn't a long shot—the arrow wedged itself into the crook between a rail post and the deck. Then the climbing began. One by one, they shimmied up to the balcony and collapsed in a heap (very quietly, of course) to catch their breath.

Edward crept up to the elegantly carved doors in front of them and put his ear to the wood. He could just make out the voices of two men arguing inside.

"We need to get out of here," one said. He sounded panicked.

"If we lower the oars, we will awaken it again," the other responded, trying to sound reasonable. "And the air's gone still at the moment, if you hadn't noticed."

Edward stepped away from the door.

"What's going on?" Brooks whispered.

"There are two men arguing in there. One wants to drop the oars and make a break for it."

Cliff's jaw dropped. "Is he mad?"

"You have a plan, Sting?"

"I do, but it's risky," Edward said. He reached into his pocket and pulled out his pistol.

Willow narrowed her eyes. "What are you gonna do?"

Edward grinned, a sense of urgency falling over him. "Just follow my lead."

With that, he burst through the doors. Inside, the two pirates—well-dressed but scruffy and unkept—nearly jumped out of their skin.

"Good evening," Edward said, raising his pistol.

"Who are you?" asked the older one, who wore a red waistcoat and looked to be the captain.

Edward sneered. "That was our ship you sank."

Willow raised her bow. Brooks brandished his daggers, and Cliff puffed out his chest.

The man laughed. "You don't look much like sailors."

"Well, we are." Edward strode smoothly towards the man but in his groggy, exhausted state, caught his toe on the edge of a chair, and landed hard on the rug. Spitting out some blood, he staggered back to his feet.

The captain roared with laughter. Filled with rage, Edward rushed forward and grabbed him by the jacket collar. The man was a few inches shorter than Edward and was taken by surprise.

"We're in charge now," he said, pressing the pistol to the man's temple. The first mate broke for the door, but Brooks lunged at the man and tackled him.

With his arms around the captain's neck, and gun still firm against his head, Edward marched him towards the cabin doors.

"What are you doing?" Willow asked.

He kept walking. She wouldn't like it if he told her. He shoved the captain out into the hall and up a short flight of stairs before emerging on deck near the helm. On the lower deck, the crew milled about, glancing nervously at the sea.

They all stopped when they saw Edward and his hostage.

"Listen up!" he shouted, his voice booming. "We summoned that monster! We summoned it because you attacked us!" He could see that he had their full attention. "At daybreak, you're going to take us to Regnum, and if you don't, I swear it'll be the last sunrise you ever see!"

With that, he turned back around with his prisoner, disappearing down the stairs and into the cabin, and shut the door behind them.

*

The next morning, Edward sat in the captain's chair with his feet up on a glossy wood table. He inhaled sharply as Willow finished stitching up his various cuts and punctures. Again.

"I thought I told you to stop getting hurt."

"Guess I just couldn't help myself."

"Apparently you also can't help going crazy." He gave her a

sideways glance.

"She's right, Ed," Cliff said from the corner of the cabin. He had raided the captain's pantry and was stuffing his mouth with a loaf of bread he'd found. "That was some bluff last night."

"It worked, didn't it?"

It was true, at the first sight of dawn the crew and set sail and they'd been speeding towards Regnum for the past several hours with the captain and first mate stowed safely in the brig under Brooks' watchful eye. It occurred to Edward that he had not yet shared his discovery of the third stone with Willow and Cliff. He quickly recounted his experience in the belly of *The Saint Elmer*.

Cliff shuddered. "So that means that Kip was a thousand years old." He shook his head. "No wonder he had so many stories."

"Do you realise what this means?" Willow said.

"It means the legend Andron told me is true."

"Yes, but also, Kip *gave* you that stone."

They stared at her blankly.

She sighed. "He wanted *you* to have it. You, specifically. Why? And how come you're the only one who's been able to find them in a thousand years?"

Edward hadn't considered that. In the case of the first two stones, at least, he had assumed he'd found them somewhat by accident.

"You think Ed is connected to them somehow?"

Willow shrugged. "Remember what you told us about the water in that cave in Candosia and the music? The music that seemed to call to you?"

After a moment of thought, Cliff spoke up. "Let's see them."

Glad that they had yet to vanish from his possession once again, and suspecting they'd played at least some role in their luck the previous night, Edward pulled out the three small red stones and placed them on the table.

"What about the Teradowa stone? Don't you need all five in order to use them?"

"Yes, but I never found that one," Edward said. Willow furrowed her brow. "What?"

She hesitated. "Do you think Lord Gorlak could be trying to find these stones too?"

Edward and Cliff exchanged looks.

"If what you heard from Andron is true," she continued, "who knows what he'd do with that sort of power? Even without them, it seems like he's got all the realms under his thumb. With them, he could rule them unchallenged. And do whatever he wants to the people!"

Edward stroked his chin. "It would certainly explain all the weapons we saw being delivered to Candosia and Decius. He could be preparing for whatever comes next."

Cliff swallowed the last bite of his bread. "That's right. Didn't Hidalgo tell you all of those shipments come from Regnum?"

"And soldiers," Willow added.

Edward was feeling more and more unnerved but refused to let it show. Any fear they sensed in him would only make things worse for his friends. He owed them better than that.

"It doesn't matter anyway," he said, "Gorlak would need all five stones, and nobody's found the Teradowa stone yet."

Cliff nodded. "And we have three of them right here."

"That still leaves one unaccounted for," Willow said, her expression dark.

"Hidden in Regnum?" Cliff said.

"Andron told Edward that the King of Regnum never hid his

stone. Instead, it was passed down from one king to the next, so it's probably safe to assume Gorlak has that one."

She looked up at Edward, her eyes burrowing into him, and he met her gaze, refusing to falter in the face of the uncertainty welling inside him, a task that became near impossible at her next words: "Do you think he's after the other stones because he's finally unlocked the full secrets of their power?"

They heard someone approach the cabin door then, and Edward quickly swept the stones back into his pocket. Brooks strode in, dusting off his cloak.

"The pirates have informed me that we are approaching Regnum and they are preparing to drop anchor."

"Already?" Cliff said.

"They won't go any closer to the shore."

Edward rose and wandered out onto the balcony. Sure enough, a rocky terrestrial plain stretched across the horizon.

"We'll have to take a boat."

Shortly before noon, laden with as much food and supplies as they could carry, the four left the ship under the wary eye of the pirates and began rowing towards the shore. The water was bright blue and warm. A surge of anticipation rose inside of Edward as the shore grew slowly closer. A part of him still couldn't believe they'd made it this far. In front of him, Willow rowed on the opposite side of the boat. He watched the sinuous movement of her body beneath her tunic, the motion of her shoulders as she pulled her oar stretching the leather strap of the quiver across her back. Her jet-black hair was tied tight in a long braid once more, and he found his mind drifting back once again to the night they'd shared on *The Saint Elmer*. He yearned for her and... for the sense of adventure he felt when he was with her.

It wasn't a childish craving for excitement though, rather an eagerness to take on the challenges that were sure to come when they were together. He left his mind drift and wander where it pleased as the time passed almost unnoticed.

As they finally approached the shore, dark clouds began to clutter the sky and far-off thunder rumbled. They hit the sand with a jolt and dragged the boat up on the beach. It felt odd, stepping onto the soil of Regnum with such ease. Everything Edward had gone through over the past month had been solely to reach this point. And now here he was. There was no army there to meet him. No evil overlord. Nothing but a bunch of rocks and sand. He scanned the beach, beyond the dunes, the earth jutted upward, exposing jagged stone beneath patchy dead grass.

"I know we're all tired, but we should cover as much ground as possible before dark," Brooks said, sheathing his daggers. Gathering their packs, they headed out over the sand dunes and quickly found themselves climbing steadily uphill with Brooks in the lead.

After a few hours traversing the rocky terrain, Cliff stopped breathlessly and plopped down on a boulder. "How much farther are we supposed to go?"

Brooks grunted in annoyance.

"Maybe we should stop for the evening," Edward said, eyeing the storm clouds, now churning menacingly overhead.

"The peak isn't far. We'll rest there."

Cliff begrudgingly agreed, and they continued trekking. Finally, as the sun reached the horizon, they arrived at the crest of the rocky hill—which had felt more like a mountain—and laid down to eat. Hikoo, who had been his old cheerful self ever since they'd returned to solid ground, bounced around Edward's feet, scrunching up his whiskered nose at the aroma of food. Edward ripped a piece of lagora fish off from his portion and threw it to him. It rolled away into a large, dead bush, and the little creature hopped over to retrieve it, disappearing beneath its branches for a moment before darting back to Edward's side, shaking with terror.

"What is it?" Cliff said.

Edward stood up, drew his sword, and strode over to investigate. "What in the—"

The others rushed over. Behind the bush, the ground gave way to a steep cliff, and beyond that, nothing but wasteland as far as the eye could see.

"Oh, my god," Willow said, covering her mouth with her hands.

Scorched earth stretched for miles in every direction. Trees turned to ash, burnt grassland, dry and cracking riverbeds... The only things living were tiny, distant figures, ambling sluggishly around makeshift shacks. Willow pulled out her spyglass from her pack and handed it to Edward. He put it to his eye and what he saw made his stomach turn. Pale, emaciated forms were pushing trollies overflowing with some sort of stone, while others dug and hammered at the earth with shovels and picks, each of them looking on the verge of death.

"They're mining," Edward said. He had never seen such a retched sight.

"This must be where Gorlak gets the iron for his cannons and guns," Cliff mused.

Willow scoffed. "He's destroyed his own realm and turned it into a work camp."

Suddenly, an ear-splitting shriek filled the air. Edward grimaced and pressed his palms against his ears. Out of the dark clouds, a flock of massive, featherless birds shot towards them like hail in a cold wind. Their slender, pale bodies were covered in lean muscle, and they moved with incredible speed. Edward staggered sideways as the first bird swooped down at him with its beak open, revealing rows of razor-sharp teeth. He put his hands up, but the bird never reached him.

Instead, it shrieked as an arrow penetrated its belly. Its wings sagged, and it crashed into the mountaintop. Willow glanced at him. "That's another one you owe me." She loaded her bow again, taking aim at a second bird and letting her arrow fly. The arrow hit its target between the eyes, and it plummeted from the sky.

Soon the flying creatures were swarming all around them, blocking out the clouds in a blanket of pale, avian flesh. Brooks leapt off a rock and sank his daggers into the underside of a low-flying bird. Swept up by its momentum, he let go just before the beast skidded into the dirt. Edward waved his sword in an arc above his head as the beasts dove by seemingly at random.

A short distance away, Cliff cried out as he was grabbed by the talons of one bird. On his other side, Willow was being harried by another. He held his breath as she spent her last arrow, which hit the bird in the neck, causing it to fall into a spiral. He glanced back at Cliff only to find him being lifted, squirming, into the air. Edward dashed towards the bird with his sword raised, but a scream behind him made him stop short. Willow's eyes were wide as she was also plucked from the ground by one of their attackers.

"Willow!" he cried, his mind pulling him in two directions, but before he could even move, she was being carried away and was soon no more than a speck in the distance.

He sank to his knees. "Stop," he croaked, his heart in his throat.

Another shout reached his ears but barely registered in his

mind. A second bird was fighting for hold of Cliff, pulling against the other's grasp, stretching him between them in opposite directions. Through his haze, he watched Brooks slide between them and cast his dagger up through the air. It missed its target, but the second bird released Cliff and dove towards the duke, who tried to spin out of the way, but it was no use. They were like sitting ducks on the mountaintop. The bird yanked him from the dirt and leapt back into the air.

Edward hadn't even noticed himself get up, but he was on his feet now, rushing towards Cliff who was still within reach. Willow was gone, but maybe he and Cliff could get her back together. But it was too late. The creature, now free and clear with its prize, sailed away, its Teradowian capture daggling beneath it.

"Edward!"

He shot around. Brooks' bird had not been able to take off with him, struggling as fiercely as Brooks was to free himself from its grasp. Edward's heart leapt, and he charged in to help, but the bird had had enough. With a horrible squawking cry, it twisted its neck and caught Brooks in its beak, clamping down on him and shaking him like a wet rag. Too weak and battered to fight any longer, Brooks hung limply in its grip as it spread its wings and launched itself from the mountain before dropping out of sight.

"No!" Edward stretched out his arms and leapt off the cliff after it. Wind whipped past his face with incredible force. A dizzying distance below, the mountainside gave way to the blackened landscape. The bird was directly below him, its wings spread wide as it searched for an updraft. At any moment, it would pull up, and he would plummet to his death. He tucked in his arms and dove, closing the distance between them, his stomach rising in his chest, and his coat fluttering all around him as he fell. Finally, he reached out and dug his fingers into the animal's leathery back, feeling steely muscles under its hide. Instantly, the bird angled its wings and pulled out of the dive, soaring upwards.

His grip faltered, and he found himself sliding along its back, clawing at the beast's hide and finally catching the bottom of its wing just as his legs slipped over its side. He didn't dare look down as he slowly managed to shimmy his way onto its back, gasping for air. They had climbed to a significant altitude now, and his vision was beginning to go spotty, but then the bird levelled out.

Edward's vision gradually returned to normal, but the air was so clogged with soot and smoke that he closed his eyes and mouth against it and tried not to think about what had just happened.

Eventually, the giant bird began to descend. Ahead of them, another mountain range marked the end of the decaying landscape, yet there was nothing joyful about the row of black peaks they were approaching. They glided over them and dove down the other side, mere feet off the steep rock face. When they reached the bottom, the bird pulled up and finally perched atop the thick, gnarled branches of an enormous, blackened tree. All the trees here were dead and scorched. A loud thump came from below, followed by a moan.

Brooks had been dropped to the forest floor.

In an instant, Edward too was jolted from the animal's back and landed on the smouldering earth. He got up, rubbing his shoulder. With a final angry squawk, the bird flapped its wings and shot back into the sky.

He watched it disappear, then turned to Brooks. "Are you

okay?"

The duke waved away his concern and staggered to his feet, scrunching up his nose at the smell of charred wood all around them. "Where did those other birds go?"

"I don't know."

All Edward could think about was Willow being swept away and what might have happened to her and Cliff. He felt sick.

"That bird didn't kill us, so the odds are good that they're okay too," Brooks said, reading his thoughts.

Edward slumped to the ground. "It's my fault. I could have saved them, but I just... stood there and watched."

Brooks put a hand on his shoulder. "There was nothing you could have done."

Edward didn't believe that in his heart, but he nodded anyway. He was lucky to have Brooks. He wouldn't have a clue what to do next if he were alone. A part of him feared that he'd simply remain there forever, frozen in indecision. *Who was I kidding to think I could be a leader? I couldn't even protect my friends.*

From behind them came a low growl, startling them both. Spinning around, they saw a wild dog, snarling about ten yards away, its eyes darting around madly. As oddly naked as the birds, its pale skin shivered as it flashed its oversized teeth.

Edward groaned. "What is it with this place?"

The dog shot forward.

"Run!"

Edward turned and cut through the burnt trees with Brooks right behind him. Bare branches sliced his cheeks as the dog nipped at their heels. Then the trees abruptly ended, and the ground vanished beneath his feet. He rolled down a hill, slamming into one rock after another until he stopped dead at the bottom, and Brooks crashed into his back.

Writhing in agony, Edward rolled over. His back and face were badly bruised, and he was cut in several places. Brooks hoisted him to his feet.

"Look!" The duke pointed.

Edward could hear the excitement in his voice. Following the man's outstretched finger, he suddenly saw why. A fortress loomed ahead of them amongst the rocky hills, down which lava flows carved out the landscape, casting an eerie red glow over the area. From the centre of the fortress stood a massive stone tower, around which the pale birds were obsessively circling in numbers too great to count.

"I bet that's where Willow and Cliff are!" He turned to Brooks. It was time. "There's something you should know."

The duke smiled knowingly. "You found the stones."

Edward stared at him. *"You knew?"*

"I had my suspicions."

He shook his head. "So then, you know about the legend of Akmenadon?"

He nodded. "King Sento has long believed in the myth; I never did, but when you asked me back in Candosia if I'd ever encountered any strange artifacts, I began to wonder."

Edward felt his mind explode with questions. "You agree then? It doesn't make sense. Why are the stones reappearing now, after so long?"

Brooks' face was grim. "That is what I've been asking myself."

The sky churned darkly overhead. Edward couldn't even tell if it was day or night as he pressed on. "I haven't found the Teradowa stone."

Brooks looked sceptical. "I think that you have."

Edward frowned, and Brooks gestured for them to huddle behind a boulder as one of the birds passed overhead. When he continued, the duke's voice was barely above a whisper. "I think you've found it once before and may have just forgotten."

Edward furrowed his brow. "I don't understand."

"The stones form a bond with whomever controls them. After finding one, you can never truly lose it. It will always come back when called upon, and it will guide you to the rest."

"But I've *haven't* found it," he insisted.

"You must have," Brooks argued, "because you found the others! You just have to *trust* that! Close your eyes and search your memory."

Edward sighed through gritted teeth and did as he was told. "All right." He closed his eyes and saw nothing. Nothing but darkness. How was he supposed to trust that something had happened when he knew that it hadn't? He opened his eyes.

"This is pointless."

"Try again," Brooks said. "Forget where we are. Forget all the bad things and just focus. Think of somebody you love… someone who loves you…"

Edward shut his eyes again, expecting to see his parents, or perhaps even Willow, but instead, his grandfather appeared before him, his grizzled face smiling down at him. There was something sad behind his eyes though. He put something in Edward's hands, but they weren't his hands, they were the hands of a child. The image vanished then, and everything became light. A little boy was running in the forest.

Edward gasped and chased after the boy. He was young, three or four at most, but running. A small creek cut through the bush. The boy sat down on the bank and dipped his feet in the water. Edward did the same. The water was cold as ice, but the boy seemed to enjoy it and said nothing, just splashed in the creek. Yet something told Edward that the boy knew that he was there. His blue eyes kept darting over to him, though they looked right through him. The boy waded out into the creek then, singing a little song.

A beautiful, oddly hollow-sounding song.

The water was shallow, only rising to the boy's knees. He giggled as he skipped rocks along the choppy surface. Edward laughed too. Then the child pulled something different from the water...

A glowing red stone.

"Hey!"

The boy glared at him then and slipped the rock into his pocket, darting across the creek. Edward took off after him, splashing through the water, but he had no idea where he was, while the boy clearly did.

"Come back!"

But the little boy was gone. His song was silent, and the only sound was the trickling flow of the creek. Still Edward kept his eyes closed. He *did* know this place.

He waited.

The sun dipped below the horizon, the stars came out, and then the world spun around him at incredible speed, elevating everything around him, and his senses, to a new level of clarity. The sounds of the birds, the smell of the flowers... the unmistakable mark of his home. The sun returned then—though he could somehow sense the moment had hardly changed by more than an hour—and soared across the sky, returning to its late-afternoon perch. Then he heard splashing again from the creek. The boy had returned and was frowning at the stone in his small hand.

Edward approached him. "Hello."

The boy pushed a few strands of blond hair out of his eyes and squinted up at Edward, who crouched down in front of him. "Are you returning that?" The boy nodded. Edward extended his hands. But he already knew what would happen.

The boy hesitated. "Promise you'll keep it safe?"

"I promise." He uncurled his tiny fingers and dropped the stone into Edward's palm. "You'd better get home," he said then, smiling at the child. "You don't want your mom to worry." The boy stared at him for a moment before turning and trudging off. He stopped on the far side of the creek and waved to Edward. Edward waved back, smiling sadly. He wanted to go with him. He wanted to see his mother and father and tell them that he loved them. But the image and the little boy was already fading.

He opened his eyes.

A tiny weight dropped into his hands.

Brook's eyes gleamed. "Incredible."

The stone was identical to the others, red and smooth. Edward slipped it into his pocket.

"You were right."

"What did you see?"

"Not much," he lied, feeling oddly at peace.

Brooks eyed him closely, and then raised his head and peeked over the boulder. The coast was clear. "Time to rescue your friends."

Together, they broke free from their hiding place and dashed between the foothills and craters, heading steadily towards the fortress. Ashes crunched under Edward's boots as they travelled, and once, he tripped and started stumbling towards a pool of boiling lava, but a yank on the back of his waistcoat pulled him back, followed by an annoyed look from Brooks. But Edward didn't scoff at the looks any longer, they had become a part of the duke's charm.

The far-off rumble of thunder echoed across the dark grey sky. Edward was beginning to think it never stopped storming in Regnum.

They soon reached the outer wall of the complex. There was no gate, only an opening between two stone walls. He poked his head around the corner. Not a soul was in sight. The courtyard was barren, and its cobblestones were cracked and riddled with holes.

"This way," Brooks whispered. They dashed forward and raced across the yard to a series of arches at the base of the tower. "There." He pointed to a set of winding stairs. It was the only way up. Cliff and Willow were surely being held at the top. They bounded up the staircase, which spiralled so steeply that it made Edward's head spin. Through the shattered glass windows around each turn, the ground appeared farther and farther away. At the top, they emerged into a circular chamber with a wide balcony that wrapped around the outside. A polished marble floor gleamed under his feet in stark contrast to the cracked cobblestone below. Edward looked around frantically, but the room was empty.

"I don't understand."

Then a human moan, muffled by the wind and barely more than a whisper, drifted down from above. Edward craned his neck. A small, steel cage was swinging from the ceiling.

"There!" he cried. A rope fastened to the cage held it aloft, attached to a pully against the wall. Edward dashed over and cranked the lever. The old mechanism creaked in protest, but slowly, the cage dropped downward. The voice from within had sounded barely alive. Edward's whole body shook at the thought of what had become of his friends. The cage thumped to the floor, and the rusty door clanked open.

A figure was huddled in the corner, pale, emaciated, and mumbling incoherently. Then he turned his head, and Edward's heart stopped.

"Grandpa?"

Chapter 22

Tower of Darkness

The word felt dull and unfamiliar. Edward hardly recognised the man staring back at him. His grandfather's eyes, so large and pale against his sunken face, seemed completely empty. He could not even speak. His mouth moved frantically, but he was too weak, too close to death to properly articulate.

Edward stepped into the cage with him. "Grandpa, it's me," he said gently, grabbing the old man's hands. "It's Edward."

Simon's mouth kept opening and closing but producing no sounds.

"I got your letter," Edward said, carefully pulling the man's brittle frame into an embrace. "I came to rescue you."

After a moment, he pulled back and began rummaging in his pocket. He pulled out a piece of bread and offered it out to his grandfather, but the man could only frown absently, his head shaking on his thin neck.

Edward felt like dying. He had come so far… only to find that he was too late. His grandfather was already gone, and as punishment for failing to save him, he would have to watch him die.

Finally, the elder Sting gripped Edward's shirt in his bony fingers. Edward leaned in close as a single word emerged from his trembling mouth, barely louder than a breath:

"Run."

Edward frowned and looked into his eyes, but his grandfather was staring past him. Edward turned then, following his gaze. Brooks stood outside the cage, smirking. Edward got to his feet and moved towards the doorway, but metal bars suddenly materialised in the air before him, trapping him inside.

"Brooks?"

"You should have listened to your friends," the duke said with a humourless chuckle.

The cage lifted smoothly back into the air. Then a voice that seemed to come from nowhere echoed around the chamber.

"Edward Sting."

Flames erupted around the periphery of the room, and he winced at the sudden brightness.

"You've kept me waiting a long time, boy."

Edward couldn't locate the speaker but had no doubts about their identity. "I know who you are," he said, fighting to keep his voice level.

"Oh? Then what is my name?"

Edward felt the hair on the back of his neck stand up. "Lord Gorlak."

Manic laughter echoed around the room, and a torrent of wind swept through the archways, building in the centre of the chamber. Edward watched in horror as a form began to take shape in the air. First a body, then limbs, and finally a head...

The face it wore was not human. Scaley grey skin covered it, and the eyes glowed deep orange like a lizard, though the creature before him would clearly stand on two legs like a man if it weren't floating in mid-air.

Lord Gorlak sighed in deep satisfaction as the wind died away, and Edward watched in disgust as Brooks moved towards him and fell to his knees, bowing his head.

"Shanley Brooks," he said, "you have done good work. It is because of men like you that we will soon live in a more just world."

Edward glared at Brooks, but the duke had lost all interest in him. Like an old rag, he had been cast aside.

Then Gorlak looked up, turning his attention to Edward. "At last, the famous Edward Sting. It was not easy getting you here." He smirked, exposing teeth like razors. "Such a pity. After all your hard work, Edward, you're not going to see the good it will do."

"You'll have to kill me if you want the stones."

Gorlak laughed. "You shouldn't make it so easy, Edward, but we'll get to that."

Edward wished he would stop using his name. He gripped the bars of the cage so tightly that his knuckles were white. "So now what? You'll destroy the realms?"

Gorlak snorted. "Destroy them? My friend, I seek only to fix what is broken. Both the stone and this world we live in! You and I both know the realms have become vile and corrupt places, but we have the power to change that. I will reform the stone my father shattered, and with its power, reunite the realms... wiping out a thousand years of error and recreating my kingdom to rule as my father once did."

Edward grimaced at the thought, and then something he'd said suddenly registered. "Your father?"

Gorlak nodded, an amused smile on his thin lips. "That's right, Edward. You see, the King of Regnum never died as the legend would have you believe..."

Swiftly, the king pressed forward through the air without seeming to move at all, stopping only a few yards away. *"I am the King of Regnum, Edward. The one and only King of

Regnum, and I have been waiting for this moment for a thousand years!" He raised his arms out to his sides then, as if acknowledging the admiration he assumed he was due. "Immortality is hard on the body, I confess... but a sacrifice I was more than willing to make."

Edward shook his head, trying to reject what he was hearing—to keep himself from listening... from questioning. But he couldn't help himself.

"How?"

Gorlak floated down to the chamber floor. "My siblings were fools to cast away the immense power they had in their grasp. But I knew better. The peasant who came to visit my father... Where do you think he'd found such a treasure? It hadn't come from nothing, and surely, hadn't been intended for the likes of him. I knew that there had to be a place in our world that held its secrets. After it was shattered, its pieces spread far and wide, I was determined to find that place and set it right. And thanks to good men like Shanley Brooks, I did."

Moving towards Brooks, he reached down with a monstrous grey hand and patted the kneeling man gently on the head. Edward thought he saw Brooks' shoulders tense at the demeaning action, but it was just as likely to be his imagination.

Gorlak wasn't done. Crossing his arms, he looked up at his captives once more. "I spent the next thousand years carefully orchestrating my plans, inserting myself into the politics of my brothers and sisters' kingdoms and preparing for the time when I would be strong enough to restore the stone *and* the glory of Akmenadon... Then all I had to do was wait."

"Wait for what?"

Gorlak smiled. "For you, Edward. You see, nearly twenty years ago, a little boy found the Heart of Teradowa. I know this because my own stone told me so. At the time, I was tricked into believing it was your father who had found it."

With a sigh and a tilt of his head, he continued. "I have to hand it to your family, Edward. They are a clever bunch. Still, after a few years, I realised my mistake and that it must have been you. So, I waited. I knew that, given the opportunity and proper guidance, you would find the rest of the stones as well and bring them to me. That's why I lured your grandfather here. You see," his orange eyes twinkled. "It was Shanley who slipped that letter into your house."

Edward gritted his teeth so hard that he thought they might crack as he looked down on Brooks. "Cliff was right. You've been against us from the very beginning."

The duke looked up at him for a moment, his black eyes inspecting him with indifference.

"Don't feel too bad, Edward," Gorlak said. "He played his part very well. I needed someone to help you through the realms. After all, I couldn't just tell the kings to let you through lest they become suspicious. No, I still needed those dim-witted fools to play the roles I'd assigned them, just as I needed Shanley. Besides, I needed you to have plenty of opportunity to find me the stones."

Edward shook his head, unwilling to accept this. "But in Decius... in the arena... Brooks was going to let himself be killed?"

Gorlak laughed. "Don't be naïve. Who do you think placed that bet against you? I needed Shanley to offer himself up in order to gain your trust so that you could deliver us the final stone."

"So all of that was just a ruse?"

"Of course, it was. I knew your little friend would save the day. While Shanley was away *training*, I saw to it that he had plenty of time to keep an eye on her. You see, Edward, at every turn, I have ensured that you would arrive here safely with the stones. How do think Andron knew you were in his castle that night? Why did that monster not devour you out at sea? Nothing happens in this world without my hand in it."

"But why did you need me at all?"

Here Gorlak paused, and an extraordinary expression crossed his face, a look of envy and fascination and confusion all wrapped together. "Because only *you* could find the stones. They choose you. Just as the original stone chose my father, using that peasant farmer as a vehicle to deliver itself into his worthy hands. When you pulled that little gem out of the river all those years ago, I knew that I had found someone of his lineage. The ancestor of my brother, the King of Teradowa, to whom its stone was bound."

Gorlak gave him a wicked smile then. "So... you see, Edward... in a way, you and I are family."

Edward was appalled. "You're mad."

"I'm a saviour. And now, thanks to you, the time has come for me to rectify my misguided siblings' mistakes and free the world from tyranny."

Edward spat. "More like replace it with your own."

Gorlak frowned, shaking his head. "I can't understand how the stones could choose you when you clearly lack the will to use them properly."

"Well, they did. And I'd rather die than give them to you."

The King of Regnum laughed. "It's not your life that's on the line."

There was an ear-splitting shriek then, and two of the enormous birds sailed towards the tower, perching on either side of the balcony. One held Willow in its beak, and the other held

Cliff. Edward felt his legs go numb.

"No," Gorlak said. "You, I can't kill just yet... but your friends are much less important. So, we'll make this simple for you—"

"Don't give him anything, Ed!" Cliff shouted.

"Edward, don't!" Willow screamed.

He glanced at them both in turn, beaten and bloodied but still firmly on his side. After all he had put them through, they were still prepared to die for him. His heart sank. He had been an utter fool. A fool to endanger them. A fool not to listen to their concerns.

But he wouldn't be the fool who killed them.

He closed his eyes and called for the stones. He surely needed them now. All four dropped into his open palm.

Lord Gorlak licked his scaley lips, his eyes sparkling with an inhuman lust—a look Edward had seen once before, not half an hour ago, in the eyes of Shanley Brooks. Numbly, Edward tossed the stones through the bars of the cage.

Lord Gorlak stuck out his muscular arms, freezing the stones' descent in midair. "That was the right decision, Edward." Then, with his eyes gleaming, he pulled them into his grasp. "Now," he said, "if you'll excuse me, I have work to do."

With that, he strode out onto the balcony and whistled. A massive, featherless bird, twice the size of the others, swooped down and landed before him. It had a wooden carriage on its back. Gorlak ascended the carriage steps and took up the reins. Brooks followed him.

"What about them?" Edward called after him, looking at his friends. Willow and Cliff struggled desperately against their captors.

Gorlak laughed. "Like I said, they're far less important."

Edward clenched his fists in silent rage as the beast carrying Gorlak and Brooks took off and quickly disappeared into the hazy sky. He slammed against the bars until his shoulders ached. In the absence of their master, the birds holding his friends were growing anxious, shifting their weight menacingly on their perch.

"Hold on!" Edward called out to his friends. His eyes darted around the small cage. There was nothing inside it with him except his grandpa, still huddled in the corner, rocking back and forth.

He heard the shrieks first. Then the screams.

The beasts released their grip on his friends and Willow and Cliff dropped over the edge of the balcony. Edward's heart leapt out of his chest.

"No!"

He slumped to the bottom of the cell, his tears dropping silently to the floor, polishing its grimy surface. Then another shriek filled the sky, this one sounding much deeper and more powerful, and a dark shape flashed past the tower. Edward rose to his feet and gripped the bars. For a long moment, silence blasted like thunder in his ears, then the shape streaked past once more, this time shooting towards the heavens before coiling nearly around itself and diving back towards the chamber.

An arubbak landed gracefully on the balcony, and Willow and Cliff jumped off, followed by Kincaid. Edward's eyes welled up again, this time with joy and disbelief at seeing his friend from Candosia. Willow sprinted past the others and grabbed the lever, cranking it fast and bringing the cage to the ground.

Kincaid whistled then and pointed, and the arubbak carefully turned, manoeuvred its tail into the chamber, and then reached between the bars with its narrow, spiked tip. With a single muscular twist, it snapped the lock, and the door swung open.

Edward pushed his way out, rushing towards Willow. "I'm so sorry!" He wrapped his arms around her then, kissing her fiercely.

She kissed him back, then pulled back.

For a moment, everything was perfect, and it was a struggle not to just huddle there within that perfection forever. But there was work to do.

He turned to Cliff. "You were right about Brooks; I should have listened to you."

"Yes, you should have. But It's all right, Ed. Right now, I'm pretty glad just to be alive."

"Speaking of which…" He sighed and looked at Kincaid. "You sure showed up for us when we needed you."

"It was all this old girl," Kincaid said, slapping the arubbak's neck. "She appeared out of the blue one day and wouldn't stop pestering me. Eventually, I just hopped on and let her fly. I've no idea how she knew."

Willow put a hand on the beast's snout and smiled knowingly. "I do."

"Well, we're sure glad you came," Cliff said, wiping sweat from his forehead.

Kincaid eyed them. "So, what exactly have you gotten yourselves mixed up in?"

"We'll fill you in on the way," Edward said, helping his grandfather out of the rusty cage.

"On the way where?"

"Home."

*

The countryside of Candosia rolled by beneath them, so close that Edward could hear the rustle of the trees. Forests and fields stretched out to the horizon, with the occasional farmhouse or settlement peppering the landscape.

"So, this Lord Gorlak is a thousand years old?" Kincaid said.

Edward stopped pacing the small cabin. "Exactly. He is the original King of Regnum. Somehow, he has sustained himself for years using the stone."

"Just like Kip, and the rest of the crew," Cliff said, "with the Heart of Tydor."

Edward shook his head. "That's what I thought at first too. But Kip and the crew were just able to live by the power of the stone alone, as its protector somehow. Gorlak..." He shook his head. "I don't know. It's almost like he fused himself to it."

"How?"

"He mentioned a place he'd discovered that allowed him to learn the secrets of the stone, back when it was first destroyed. Maybe that's where it came from, and he was able to keep himself alive by using the secrets he'd learned..."

"Is that why we're going to Teradowa?" Kincaid asked.

Edward nodded. "He said it was because of men like Brooks that he'd found this hidden place. I think he meant men like him specifically from Teradowa... I think that's where it has to be."

"But where in Teradowa?" Cliff asked. "And how could it have stayed hidden for so long?"

"Is there any place there that nobody has ever been?" Willow said absently as she inspected her new arrows, given to her by Kincaid.

Edward stopped dead. "That's it!"

"What?"

It was so obvious he couldn't believe he had missed it before.

"Where did I find the stone when I was a baby?"

"In the Great River," Cliff said, frowning. "Or... well, one of its creeks anyway—"

"Cliff!" Edward said, cutting him off impatiently. "What's the one place back home that nobody has ever gone?"

His old friend's expression was blank for a moment. Then all the colour drained from his face as he connected the dots. "You can't mean the *Vortex!*"

"There must be something hidden underneath it!"

"Ed, are you completely mad?"

Beside them, Willow and Kincaid exchanged glances. "The Vortex is a giant whirlpool that forms every ten years in the Great River in Nodington Valley," Edward explained. "Nobody knows why it forms or *where* it leads. That's why Gorlak lured me to Regnum now! If he doesn't get there and succeed in reuniting the stones before it dissipates in the fall, he'll have to wait another ten years!"

He was certain he was right. Something in his gut told him this was the answer. Outside the front windscreen, the landscape gave way to a wide embankment at the top of which stood a massive stone wall—the border into Teradowa.

"Nobody who goes down the Vortex ever comes back, Ed."

Edward set his jaw as they soared over the wall.

"Then you'd better wish me luck."

*

Cold, white water churned ferociously below in a massive spiral that would crush anything that dared cross its path and swallow it whole.

"Okay, I'm gonna jump."

Willow crossed her arms. "Not by yourself, you're not. I'm coming with you."

He shook his head, but he could see she was not going to take no for an answer.

"Me too," Cliff said.

Edward sighed. "All right." The three of them strode out onto the deck. Edward glanced back and saw Kincaid grinning at him.

"Good luck, kid. I'll be waiting for you."

"Thanks." His grandpa was curled up in the corner of the cabin, muttering to himself. Edward forced himself to look at him for a moment before turning back and climbing up onto the railing. The whirlpool waited like the open jaws of an enormous beast far below them, its movements almost mesmerizing.

"Ready?" Edward asked. His friends nodded, and he let go of the rail. Wind whipped past his face as he dropped towards the river, filling his lungs with air right before his feet splashed down in the cool water, and then suddenly, he was submerged. Instinctively, he waited either to drown or for his inevitable return to the surface, but neither came.

Instead, a tremendous force began dragging him deeper, pulling him down in slow, shallow circles. His ears popped, and his body screamed for air. Above him, the light faded as he sank further into the depths, and then his feet landed with a thud on damp sand, and he drew in a huge breath of air.

Astonished, he looked up. The ceiling above him was formed by a pool of water, suspended by some invisible force, turning in circles and randomly casting ripples of dim blue light on the rocky walls around him. The cave he had fallen into—as that was the only word that he could think of to describe it—was enormous, filled with crooks and crevasses and areas of flatter ground like the one on which he now stood, which was carpeted with fine white sand. Patterned ripples of light from the water above danced across its surface.

"Beautiful, isn't it?"

Edward jerked his head around and saw Lord Gorlak, standing before an altar in the centre of the cave. He took a few uneasy steps forward. High above them, the bottom of the Vortex continued to spin around its axis, completely devoid of substance. Around the room, water flowed over and around the rocks in lazy streams that seemed to defy gravity in places.

"Where are we?"

"A gateway, I believe… to a place neither you nor I can understand. A place outside of time and space, Edward. It's where the original stone came from. I'm sure of it."

The five small red stones were on full display on the altar, lined up neatly in a row.

Edward felt a sudden anger building within him at the grotesque sight of Lord Gorlak looking so at home in such a special, magical place. Then another thought struck him, as he realised they were alone. He drew his sword. "What have you done with my friends?"

Lord Gorlak smirked. "Nobody but a descendant of my father may enter this place, I have made it so. To your friends… I'm afraid it simply does not exist."

Edward tried to calm himself, he could not let Lord Gorlak get in his head. For all he knew, Willow and Cliff were just fine.

Seemingly unconcerned, the King of Regnum produced a golden chalice and set it on the altar. "All the better that you are here, Edward," he said. "You deserve to witness all your hard work coming to fruition."

One by one, he took each stone in his scaly fingers and

dropped them into the chalice. Edward stepped forward then, but Lord Gorlak raised his arm dismissively, and Edward froze in place, no more able to move than if he had been carved from stone.

"You see, Edward," Gorlak said, his tone almost conversational now, "this is why you will never understand. You are just like your father. And like your grandfather. Arrogant. You think you can change the world in a few days. It took me a thousand years of planning to bring us to this point. Imagine it: No more war, manipulation, corruption... No more of the wealthy elite preying on the poorer masses... Just one kingdom. Under a single ruler. The tainted legacy of my foolish family ends today, Edward, and the realms will be better for it."

He moved then towards one of the nearby streams of water—this one cascading naturally down the rockface—and placed the chalice with the stones beneath it, filling it to the brim, then returned with it to the altar, where he set it down. Edward watched as he closed his eyes briefly and lowered his head, then grabbed the chalice and gulped down its contents. He watched in horror as Lord Gorlak rose into the air then, his grey, reptilian body twitching uncontrollably, the chalice slipping from his grasp and striking the altar with a sharp metallic tone, the stones scattering across its surface.

Edward enjoyed only an instant of relief that the stones themselves had not been consumed by the demented king before a beam of brilliant green light shot up from the centre of the room, directly through the altar itself, through Gorlak, and up into the eye of the churning storm above. Gorlak absorbed the blast, his eyes sparkling madly. Then he leapt from the beam and landed nimbly in the sand, smiling and raising his left arm.

A flash of green light exploded from his palm, striking the

wall and sending chunks of rock flying in all directions. He roared with laughter. "And now you see the true power of these stones!" Edward watched in mute terror as Gorlak stepped closer, looming over him. "I'm sorry, Edward, but I have to kill you now. I can't have you meddling any further."

Still unable to move, Edward watched with wide eyes as Gorlak raised his arm again, his palm turned directly towards him. The last thing Edward saw before he closed his eyes was that same emerald-green light, erupting from the king's palm and streaking straight towards him.

Chapter 23

Smoke in the Sky

Willow splashed in the torrential surf. The cold water gripped her whole body, making every movement laborious. A short distance away, she spotted Cliff, who was also struggling against the current. Edward was nowhere to be found. Her mind raced. If he had been right, then they all should have been sucked through the Vortex to some unseen destination. Yet here they were. Did the mean that Edward had—

No. She refused to allow herself to think like that. He was alive. Above them, Kincaid circled their position.

"Cliff!" she called out, coughing and choking in the turbulent water. Cliff splashed around to face her. He looked white as a sheet. She pointed to the arubbak. He nodded in understanding. There was nothing they could do for Edward now, splashing around in the water. She signalled Kincaid to come get them, and then swam over to Cliff. Together, they watched as the arubbak circled slowly downwards towards the water's surface, a rope ladder dangling below its powerful body. "Hold on," she said, as the end of it came within reach.

Almost in unison, the two of them grabbed the ladder.

Kincaid signalled the arubbak to bank towards the safety of the shore, but suddenly, several loud noises startled the mighty beast, and it climbed sharply into the sky, leaving Cliff and Willow clinging to the ladder as it swung wildly through the air.

Another boom erupted in the distance, billows of smoke filling the sky to the east.

"That's the village square!" Cliff said.

Willow pursed her lips angrily. "Brooks."

The arubbak dipped and dove of its own accord, anxiously trying to avoid any approaching cannonballs, though there didn't appear to be any. Whatever was going on to the east, Willow didn't think it had anything to do with them.

"Look out!"

Willow twisted her body just in time to avoid being speared by branches as they grazed the treetops along the shore. The arubbak sunk even lower as more explosions shook the area, then veered back the way it had come, dragging the pair through the river, and filling Willow's eyes and ears with water, before it shot skyward again, giving them a complete view Nodington Valley.

Willow noted that it was quite large, though not nearly the size of Dobson's Canyon, and that the attack they'd gotten caught up in seemed to be targeting a palace that stood out in stark contrast to much of the surrounding countryside, which was dotted with strange, red and gold trees that she couldn't identify. It seemed that the explosions they'd heard had been the work of improvised devices—rather than cannons—not entirely unlike the kind she herself had once dabbled with. The damage to the palace, however, appeared mostly superficial.

Finally, Kincaid tamed the nervous beast and brought them down safely in a meadow above an embankment of the river. Cliff and Willow quickly climbed on board, soaking wet and short of breath.

Kincaid inspected the two of them. "Where's Edward?"

Willow trembled.

"We don't know," Cliff said.

Kincaid frowned. Willow turned away and gazed at the river.

She didn't want them to see her cry. *He has to be alive.* She thought back on the time they had spent together since meeting in the forest. For the first time in her life, everything had felt real to her.

"Willow?" Kincaid said.

She took a deep breath, but before she could say anything, their attention was drawn across the hills. A massive beam of green light was shooting out of the centre of the Vortex and painting the sky like a canvas in brilliant green hues. They all looked at each other blankly. Then a hand fell on Willow's shoulder. She turned around. Edward's grandfather was gazing past them at the beam of light through a pair of steely blue eyes.

Chapter 24

The Legend Undone

Suddenly, Edward was soaring through the air… but gently. He landed softly on the sand and found that he could move all his limbs again. Lord Gorlak stood aghast, confusion washing across his face like a wave as Edward got to his feet and picked up his sword.

"I guess it won't be that easy after all," Edward said. Then he felt a solid weight land in his pocket and noticed that the small, scattered stones had disappeared from the altar. When he reached into his pocket to gather them though, what he pulled out was a single large red stone, shinning as bright as the sun. Lord Gorlak roared then and pounced at him. Edward thrust his sword forward and a flash of red energy exploded from its end, striking Gorlak in the chest. The ancient king flew backwards, smashing against the rock wall. He staggered to his feet and locked eyes with Edward.

Neither moved for a moment. Then Gorlak brushed himself off. "I see the stone hasn't given up on you yet… Fine, I'll just have to eliminate the competition." Slamming his palms together, a ball of green energy built up between them like static. He sent it hurtling towards Edward, who flashed his sword again, deflecting its energy into the sand and walls. A new sense of power was emerging within him. He felt unstoppable.

Gorlak leapt across the distance separating them, knocking

Edward's sword away and throwing a punch. Edward dodged it, feeling the force of the wind near his cheek, and connected with a blow of his own, striking Gorlak in the ribs and sending a shockwave through the chamber. Staggering backwards, the king clutched the altar to stay on his feet, while Edward dashed forward, slamming him back against the flat surface and swinging again.

This time, Gorlak saw it coming and sidestepped, turning and pinning Edward to the altar and glaring at him with his orange reptilian eyes as he tore into his side with his talons.

Gorlak smiled wickedly as Edward cried out in pain and leaned in even closer. "You should have let your grandpa die."

With an added twist of his talons for good measure, Gorlak pushed away from him, marched over to where the stone had fallen during their altercation, and scooped it up. Edward tried to move but found himself immobilised once again, this time by the pain. Blood was oozing from a deep gash near his ribs. He gripped his side and leaned on the altar.

Gorlak had the stone again. It shook in his hand as he tried to control it. Then a bolt of fiery red energy erupted from it, streaks of green careening through it as it shot forward, striking Edward in the midsection, incinerating his shirt and waistcoat and sending him flying through the air to crash hard against the cave wall with only torn strips of cloth left dangling from his shoulders. He crumpled to the ground as Gorlak's blurry image danced across his vision.

"Poor little Edward Sting... disowned by his kingdom. No home. No parents... Perhaps, the stones took pity on you... Perhaps, *that's* why you were chosen."

Edward crawled across the sand, trying to get away. Gorlak roared with laughter and followed with ease, lifting Edward's limp form into the air and tossing him across the chamber.

Slamming into the rock once more, Edward felt all the air leave his body; he must be close to death. A short distance away, he spotted the hilt of his sword, poking up out of a mound of sand, and his eyes fixated on it as he pushed himself back up to his feet.

Gorlak howled with laugher. "You never quit, do you, boy?"

Edward scooped up his sword and hobbled back over to the altar, leaning his hip against it to stay upright. He just needed Gorlak to come a little closer.

"You don't have to oppose me, Edward," Gorlak said, striding towards him. "We want the same thing. Even as we speak, my agents—men like your friend Shanley Brooks—are preparing for the unification of the realms."

He was only a few yards away now.

Taking a deep breath and concentrating, Edward extended his hand and silently called out for the stone... *demanded* that it come to him. And to his shock, he felt its weight suddenly drop into his outstretched hand. Edward turned to the altar then, slamming the stone down onto its hard surface, and raised his sword over his head, ready to strike. "It's over," he announced coldly, his intent clear.

Lord Gorlak stopped dead in his tracks, his face darkening. "Edward... that stone is a part of you, just as it is me. If it is destroyed, you'll die with it."

Edward shook his head. "You act like these stones are the solution, but they're the problem. They have brought nothing but misery to this world. They don't save people. They corrupt them. Turn them greedy and evil. They harm those who don't desire them and make those who do wicked and vile. Maybe they *are* a part of me... but if they are, they're a part I don't want."

Gorlak raised his hands. "Think about what you're doing, Edward. Are you really willing to give up a chance to change the world for the better?"

Edward's arms wavered above his head. He couldn't deny the truth. They did want the same thing. To change the world. He stared at the ancient king, whose twisted form was barely human any longer. In Gorlak's hands, the stones would surely be a force for evil. But what about in his own? With the power of the stones, he could eradicate the corruption that plagued the realms, oust the kings, and make things free and fair for all. He could do it now. Today...

But then what? What would he become? When the world was perfect, and there was nobody left to save...

He knew what he would become. He was looking at it.

With a deep breath, he thought of his grandpa, wishing he'd had a chance to tell him how much he loved him. He thought of Cliff, who had stood by him all these years. He thought also of Willow and all the things they hadn't yet done together... Then he thought of what she would do when she found out he was gone. Maybe she would understand that this was the only choice. The right choice. Maybe one day she could forgive him.

He brought the sword down.

"No!" Gorlak cried.

The stone shattered beneath his blade.

Millions of tiny fragments exploded across the altar, and in an instant, the world turned upside down. Light flashed around the chamber, so bright that Edward couldn't see a thing. Then he felt his feet leave the earth... He was floating through the air.

Across the rocky chamber, Lord Gorlak was also floating.

Edward watched as the creature evaporated into a shapeless ball of mist... and then everything went black.

*

Faces flashed by in his memory too quickly to make out. He felt weightless, like he was on a cloud. All around and beneath him was empty space. Then a face flashed by, its owner in possession of the stone, holding it out to him.

He reached out but whoever it was skipped away. All of a sudden, the space was shaking and crumbling around him, trapping him...

He opened his eyes.

He was lying on his back in the sand. Staring up at the Vortex from below.

"Edward?"

He hadn't noticed the hand resting on his shoulder. He sat up fast, then shook his head and blinked to get the sand out of his eyes.

"Grandpa?" he said, immediately recognizing the old, wrinkled face and kind eyes. His grandfather's colour had returned, and he looked quite revitalised as he smiled at his grandson with all the love and affection in the world. Edward embraced him.

"How did you know I was in trouble?"

His grandfather chuckled and then pulled away, winking at him. "I guess I just assumed."

Edward was about to ask how he'd gotten past the Vortex but then realised that if he really were a descendant of the King of Teradowa, then so was his grandfather.

"Grandpa... is what Lord Gorlak told me about us true?"

Simon Sting folded his hands in his lap. "Oh, well... I imagine he told you quite a bit."

"He said I was a descendant of his brother, the King of Teradowa."

Simon nodded sadly. "That is true, though I'd hoped you would never have to bear the burden of it. I was wrong... and I'm sorry."

Edward smiled, happy at having his grandfather back. "So, how come I'm not dead?"

Simon thought for a moment. "If what I suspect happened down here actually happened... when Lord Gorlak drank from the chalice, he forever linked his soul to the fate of the stones, just as his father had once done. As such, when you destroyed the stone, you also destroyed him. You, however, were *chosen* by the stones. They trusted you but were not bound to you. It's possible then that they were willing to give up their own existence for a cause you believed in."

Edward considered this. Lord Gorlak had let time and greed twist him into something evil. He considered himself lucky not to have made the same mistake.

"So, I was chosen then?"

Simon stroked his beard. "Perhaps... but perhaps not for the reason Gorlak thought. He believed it was because you were a descendant of the king, but so was he himself. So, perhaps, the stones allowed you to use them because they knew you had a noble heart. Rather than it being a case of you *being chosen*, it might simply be that Lord Gorlak was *not.*"

"But doesn't that mean that anyone could have been chosen?"

His grandfather laughed. "That is optimistic thinking. But yes, I suppose there are many out there who could have resisted temptation and corruption and gained the stone's trust." He smiled sadly. "Perhaps that is what they were trying to teach us all along."

"Is he gone forever?"

"Gorlak?" His grandfather's face grew grim. "I don't know for certain. But I do know that we're not finished yet."

Edward nodded, getting slowly to his feet. His side ached horribly where Gorlak had punctured him with his talons, and the rest of his battered body felt not much better, but he suppressed the pain.

They had a long swim ahead of them.

*

They soared low over Nodington Valley until the roofs of the city's buildings appeared sharp and clear, the cobblestone streets were in focus—cutting through the village like veins, carving a path through its body to the heart—and they could make out the fear and confusion on the faces of the men and women who stopped and gazed up at them. Edward felt his heart grow warm at last with the joy of seeing his home again, as though a lock had been broken inside him, and he had been set free.

"Where are they all going?" Kincaid asked.

Edward squinted. Everyone did appear to be going in the same direction.

"The village square," Cliff said.

Then Edward's heart leapt again, this time reminding him that his job was far from over. As they neared the square, black smoke filled the sky. King Sento had been pulled out onto the stage—the same stage, it seemed, where Edward had last seen the king, praising the gods with false sincerity.

It sure looked as though Sento should be praying now.

"Oh my…" Kincaid said.

The former tyrant was now chained to a wooden post, his beaten and bloodied face oozing like an overly ripe tomato. Standing smugly over him was Shanley Brooks, who seemed to be in the middle of a speech.

"For years, we have been lied to!" the duke shouted. "While the king and his noblest subjects grew rich and fat!" The crowd roared. "No more! A new era is dawning. Soon, we will open our gates and unite with the people of the other realms! I will show you the way."

The townspeople cheered Brooks and taunted the deposed king like a pack of wild dogs ready to tear him apart. The duke beamed down at them.

Shaking his head, Edward spun around to face the others. "We need a distraction in order to get to Brooks."

"Like what?" Cliff asked.

Kincaid smirked. "How about us?" he said, gesturing to his ride. "It certainly got the attention of the villagers we passed."

The others nodded. "All right," Kincaid said, taking the reins. "Hold on."

Edward braced himself against the rail as Kincaid yanked on the reins, and the beast unleashed a throaty growl that he could feel deep in his stomach. Spreading its wings wide, the arubbak effortlessly soared over the courtyard in plain sight, climbing high and diving low to its heart's content. Edward found it strangely satisfying to watch the terrified, confused reaction of the crowd below them, scattering like sheep, forgetting their strife and breaking for the hills. *Maybe this will finally wake them up.*

Just then, he spotted Brooks, leaping from the stage.

"There!" Edward pointed. They landed in the centre of the courtyard. "This way," he yelled, jumping quickly to the ground and breaking into a sprint. The wind rippled across his bare chest as he sidestepped the far side of the stage and started up the stone path that led to the castle. Brooks' black cloak wisped around the bend in the path up ahead, under the arch that marked the beginning of the castle grounds.

Hot on his heels, Edward rounded the corner and skidded to a stop, looking down the barrel of Brooks' gun. The two men stared at each other then, catching their breath.

Then the others arrived and stopped short as well.

"It's over, Shanley," Simon said. "Gorlak is dead."

Brooks spat at the old man's feet; his upper lip curled upward in a savage snarl. "This isn't fair, you know. I was patient. I put up with these fools," he gestured to Cliff and Edward. "I *deserve* to win!"

"You deserve a punch in the face," Cliff said.

"Shut up!" Brooks shouted, waving his gun at him. His eyes darted among them all, finally resting on Edward. "You...! You had to go and screw it all up! Didn't you? Well," he said, a mad look crossing his face as he cocked his weapon, "this'll be the last time—"

With a sudden uproar, Brooks dropped the gun. In a flash, Cliff sprang forward, swinging his fist and striking him square in the centre of his face, breaking his slim, nose. The duke crumbled to the ground.

Edward raised his eyebrows. "Thanks."

Cliff grinned. "I've been waiting a long time to do that."

A furry blue creature shimmied out from underneath the unconscious duke.

"Hikoo!" Edward couldn't believe his eyes, as the skulposis scurried over to him and leapt up into his arms. "We thought we'd lost you."

"Oh," Kincaid said, "I forgot to tell you. I picked him up on a mountaintop on my way to rescue you in Regnum. Guess he was too small for those birds to bother with. He's been sulking ever since. Not too happy to have missed all the fun I suppose."

Edward grinned as Hikoo wagged his bushy tail.

"Hikoo is always ready to help Master Sting and his friends... *when* he is with them."

The others laughed at the indignation in his voice.

"You just saved my life for the second time, you're welcome anytime, buddy."

The reunion was interrupted by a whimper from Brooks, who had started to come around, holding his bloody nose with one hand and his savaged leg with the other.

Kincaid bent down and picked up Brooks' gun from the ground where it had fallen. "I don't think you'll be needing this anymore."

Back in the courtyard, the townsfolk were beginning to emerge from their hiding places, mumbling in small groups at first, but eventually, gathering around the stage once more.

Simon chuckled. "I think it's time for us to explain ourselves."

Edward and the others followed him back down the pathway, and together, they climbed the steps onto the platform. As Edward looked out at the growing crowd, he saw frightened, confused faces staring back at him.

Willow slipped her arm around him. "The work is just beginning, isn't it?"

He had no doubt that she was right, but he realised suddenly that he didn't dread it. In fact, he felt more alive than he ever had.

"Well, what are we supposed to do now?" a man shouted from the crowd.

"Yeah," called another. "Who's to lead us then?"

Edward glanced at Simon, and the old man stepped forward and cleared his throat.

"I suppose you'll have to decide that for yourselves. But first, there's a story I think you should hear." He looked at Edward and smiled. "A story that will tell you how this world we live in really works and what it really looks like. Not the story the kings *want* us to believe. A story that—"

"Is it a story we're gonna hear anytime today?" shouted Scruff, who smiled up at his old friend from the side of the stage, where he was leaning against a building, cradling a mug of fiddleberry beer in his gnarled hands.

Nervous laughter rippled through the crowd, as Simon grinned hugely at him, then nodded in acknowledgement.

"All right then," Simon began, turning back to face the crowd. "It all started fifteen years ago, when my grandson Edward discovered a small, red stone in the woods. Little did he know of the catastrophic events he had unwittingly set in motion."

END